His voice was low and husky. "Your *heart is beating a mile a minute."*

Tess looked up into his eyes and saw mischief residing there. "How would you know?"

He grinned, and his disarming dimple deepened. "I'm the doctor, remember? I get paid to know about those things."

Funny, but his dimple didn't look like a doctor's dimple, and his silk-and-gravel voice didn't sound like a doctor's voice. This was a man. Unadorned by profession. Undiluted by civilization. A man looking deep into a woman's eyes.

She turned, uncomfortable in the shadow of Rhune's regard. She was, quite frankly, out of her element.

Dear Reader,

The skies won't be the only place to find fireworks this month. Special Edition has six wonderful, heartwarming books for your July.

Babies are fun in the summer, and this July we're highlighting "the little ones." We begin with RITA-award-winning author Cheryl Reavis, and our THAT SPECIAL WOMAN! title for the month, *Meggie's Baby*. You last saw Meg Baron in Cheryl's book, *One of Our Own*. Now Meg returns to the home she left—pregnant and seeking the man she's never been able to stop loving. In *The Bachelor and the Baby Wish*, by Kate Freiman, a handsome bachelor tries to help his best friend achieve her fondest wish—to have a child. And the always wonderful Susan Mallery gives us a man, his secret baby and the woman he's falling for in *Full-Time Father*.

And rounding out the month we've got the ever-popular JONES GANG—don't miss *No Less Than a Lifetime* from bestselling author Christine Rimmer. Also, it's time for another of those SWEET HOPE WEDDINGS from Amy Frazier in *A Good Groom Is Hard To Find*, and Sierra Rydell brings us a sizzling reunion in *The Road Back Home*.

A whole summer of love and romance has just begun from Special Edition! I hope you enjoy each and every story to come!

Sincerely,

Tara Gavin, Senior Editor

Please address questions and book requests to:
Silhouette Reader Service
U.S.: 3010 Walden Ave., P.O. Box 1325, Buffalo, NY 14269
Canadian: P.O. Box 609, Fort Erie, Ont. L2A 5X3

AMY FRAZIER

A GOOD GROOM
IS HARD TO FIND

Silhouette ®

SPECIAL ▼ EDITION ®

Published by Silhouette Books
America's Publisher of Contemporary Romance

To my editor, Melissa Jeglinski, whose skill and
encouragement have made this new career a joy.

 SILHOUETTE BOOKS

ISBN 0-373-24043-0

A GOOD GROOM IS HARD TO FIND

Copyright © 1996 by Amy Lanz

Books by Amy Frazier

Silhouette Special Edition

The Secret Baby #954
*New Bride in Town #1030
*Waiting at the Altar #1036
*A Good Groom Is Hard To Find #1043

*Sweet Hope Weddings

AMY FRAZIER

has loved to read, listen to and tell stories from the time she was a very young child. With the support of a loving family, she grew up believing she could accomplish anything she set her mind to. It was with this attitude that she tackled various careers as teacher, librarian, freelance artist, professional storyteller, wife and mother. Above all else, the stories always beckoned. It is with a contented sigh that she settles into the romance field where she can weave stories in which love conquers all.

Amy now lives with her husband, son and daughter in northwest Georgia, where the kudzu grows high as an elephant's eye. When not writing, she loves reading, music, painting, gardening, bird-watching and the Atlanta Braves.

You're Invited!

The folks of Sweet Hope, Georgia, invite you
to yet another wedding!

(But this one's hush-hush 'cause the bride and
groom don't know they're getting married—yet.)

Help us rejoice as
Dr. Rhune Sherman
(town heartbreaker)

weds

Tess McQueen
(Ms. "just passing through")

Though no official date for the nuptials has
been set, we're aiming for
Saturday, the 15th.

Hope you'll join us to celebrate another
Sweet Hope Wedding.

Chapter One

Rhune Sherman stood amid the rubble spewing out the front door of his double-wide trailer and watched a raccoon make off with his favorite tropical shirt.

This was not an auspicious beginning to the doctor's new life in Sweet Hope, Georgia.

Setting his fishing gear on the ground, he rubbed the back of his neck. The hot and humid late-June air pressed heavily upon him. What in tarnation did the animals of this hollow have against him? First the squirrels had wreaked havoc on his new home's wiring system. Then the woodpeckers in an amplified mating display had hammered holes in the aluminum siding. And now... He looked around in awe at debris hanging from the branches of surrounding trees. Everywhere limp remains of the raccoon family run amok. A macabre Spanish moss. Ghostly in the gathering evening gloom. The rascally crows would have a field day come morning.

Fortunately, the trailer had contained few possessions short of clothing. He recognized the tattered fabric of his second-favorite tropical shirt caught in a sweet gum tree, swinging listlessly in the breeze, a sorry symbol of surrender.

He loved that shirt.

With a disbelieving shake of his head, he picked up his fishing gear and headed down the long dirt driveway toward the two-lane road. He'd better call someone. Animal control, perhaps. It wasn't likely any of his neighbors had seen or heard a thing. The trashed trailer sat smack in the middle of fifteen undeveloped acres of northwest Georgia woodland. Easy prey to forest marauders who must feel as if man's encroachment into their territory was cause for guerrilla warfare. It would serve the furry vandals right if he decided to call the exterminators, though he wouldn't. The last thing Rhune Sherman wanted was harm to come to any living creature. Possessions—no matter how difficult it was to get really good tropical shirts—he could replace. Living creatures, on the other hand, came too dear.

Lucky, too, the only possessions with any meaning to him were clear of the disaster. He held his fishing gear in his hand. His sailboard was down at the lake. And his Harley was in the shop.

He stepped to the side of the narrow dirt driveway as he spotted headlights coming toward him. It would be Boone O'Malley; Rhune could tell the sound of that monster truck engine anywhere. As Boone slowed his enormous black pickup, Rhune hopped on the running board and rode back up to the clearing. The whiplash stop told him Boone had spotted the rubble around the trailer.

"What in blazes happened here?" Boone's voice was an awed growl as he swung down from the truck. "You playing with your chemistry set, Doc?"

Rhune shook his head.

A smile played at the corners of Boone's mouth. "Or is this your first attempt at cooking on your new gas stove?"

"Very funny." Rhune narrowed his eyes. "Raccoons," he muttered in terse explanation. "Can I use your truck phone to call animal control?"

"Sure thing. Tell them it's a Code Twelve, and they'll send someone out pronto."

"Code Twelve?"

"Yeah." Boone chuckled. "It's actually the town code for Something-Just-Happened-That's-Worth-A-Laugh-And-A-Morning-Of-Gossip-At-The-Back-Of-The-Drugstore."

"As if anyone in Sweet Hope needs more fodder for speculation where I'm concerned."

Boone clapped Rhune on the back. "That's the initiation fee you pay for acceptance in a small town."

Rhune climbed into the cab of the truck and picked up the cellular phone. "Know the number?"

"Dial 911. In Sweet Hope, marauding raccoons count as an emergency. But tell them you won't be here when they arrive."

"Why not?"

"You have a patient waiting in your office. Looks urgent."

A patient waiting in his office? Couldn't be. His practice wasn't set to open officially till next week. After the Fourth of July weekend. Rhune tried to keep his mind on the information he was giving the dispatcher.

"Someone passing through town," Boone continued. "Keeled over in the Hole-in-the-Wall Café."

Rhune hung up the truck phone. "Did they eat Esther's chili?"

"No." Boone grinned, swinging himself behind the wheel, then starting the engine. "She hadn't even ordered yet."

"*She?*"

"Yeah. Some businesswoman. Fancy briefcase. Expensive suit. Big BMW with out-of-state tags. Good-looking."

"The BMW?"

"No, Doc, the woman. Pay attention. And close your door." Boone carefully maneuvered a turn, then headed down the dirt driveway.

"Sorry." Rhune nodded over his shoulder in the direction of the wreckage. "I'm a little distracted. It's not every day my home is trashed by forest creatures."

"It's not the spot I would have picked to plunk a trailer. Wild animals can be a real pest. Just wait till deer season." Boone turned the truck onto the two-lane and headed to town. "You have fifteen acres. You really should have let me build you a house on the open knoll where the old Patterson homestead stood."

"No...." Rhune slit his eyes. No, the double-wide had been about as much of a commitment to permanence as he'd been willing to make. "I can move into the apartment over my office. Temporarily. Until animal control and I work out some kind of solution."

"Look, Doc, I know it's none of my business—except that you're my brother-in-law—but you've made a commitment to a permanent medical practice here in Sweet Hope. You could at least commit to a permanent residence."

Boone's words echoed Rhune's thoughts. You'd think it would be easy. He'd bought the fifteen acres. The least he could do was build a house. The nomad in him shivered. Easy for some. He threw his arm over the truck seat back and lifted the lid of Boone's toolbox. "You wouldn't have a spare shirt in here, would you?" Whether his practice was officially open or not, it didn't seem appropriate to show up in front of his first patient in day-old fishing clothes.

"Sorry."

"Could we swing by your house and pick something up?"

"I really don't think there's time. This woman looked real shaky." Boone cast Rhune an appraising glance. "But if I were you, I'd scrub hard and throw on a lab coat. Patsy's with her. At least there will be one professional-looking representative of Sweet Hope in that examination room."

"Patsy?" Patsy Sinclair was Rhune's newly hired receptionist.

"She was having supper in the Hole-in-the-Wall when the woman collapsed. She had your office keys on her key ring and saw no reason she shouldn't open up."

Small towns.

Rhune shook his head and smiled ruefully, letting the warm evening air from the open truck window wash over him. "You know, I'd kind of envisioned private practice starting out differently. This is shades of my D.C. residency—being rousted from the few moments of free time to tend to emergencies."

"You had more of the country gentleman doctor in mind?" Boone chuckled. "If so, I think those raccoons did your practice a favor."

"Oh, thanks. What do you mean by that?"

Boone grinned as he pulled on to Main Street. "I'm assuming that's the last of those tropical shirts you're wearing. No successful country gentleman doctor 'round here ever sported shirts quite that wild."

Before Boone had come to a complete stop in front of his office, Rhune opened the door to the truck and swung to the ground. Over his shoulder he said, "Okay, okay, I'll see if I can find a lab coat."

The minute he opened the door to his office and smelled that antiseptic smell, Rhune became a different man. The lazy cobwebs of a vacation day of fishing disappeared. The concern over his now topsy-turvy living quarters evaporated. His resolve stiffened. The adrenaline began to pump. No matter the form it took, this was what he lived for. The practice of medicine.

"Patsy?" He hurried through the waiting room where several of Sweet Hope's residents waited, care obvious on their faces. Most likely they were the ones who'd formed the emergency cortege. "Patsy, where are you?"

"In exam room number one," came the receptionist's reply.

"I'll be right there. I have to wash up." Rhune ducked into the next exam room, hastily scrubbed, then threw on a clean lab coat. Glancing in the mirror, he grimaced at his day-old beard and tousled hair. There was nothing quick he could do about the beard, but he ran his fingers through his hair as he smoothed the lab coat over his one remaining tropical shirt. No point in scaring the woman half to death. He grabbed a stethoscope from the counter and headed for exam room number one.

Pushing the door open, he stopped abruptly as he saw the patient lying on the exam table, her eyes closed, her hand in Patsy's hand. He'd seen beautiful women in his day, so it was not the beauty of the stranger that stopped him dead in his tracks. It was the extraordinary feeling that she didn't belong here. Neither on this examination table nor in Sweet Hope. It was as if she'd dropped from the sky, a beautifully exotic creature. Someone truly just passing through. Not of this world.

Dressed in an expensive black suit, she lay unusually still, her face and her hands in alabaster contrast to her dark clothing and midnight dark hair. Long, straight and glossy hair that fanned out around her on the table. Her eyebrows and lashes, too, were the color of night. Lashes thick and rich, resting lightly on cheeks that could have been carved from the palest marble. A cool, compelling beauty that drew Rhune's attention and held it.

Despite the woman's closed eyes and the intense look of worry on Patsy's face, the room hummed with energy.

Humming energy, indeed. Rhune shrugged. He'd watched too many late-night sci-fi movies. Either that or the desecration of his trailer had him rattled to the core. He forced himself forward. Forced himself to pick up the blank chart that lay on the counter.

"I'm sorry," Patsy whispered. "I didn't even take her blood pressure. I didn't think it would be right, me being your receptionist and all. I've just tried to offer what comfort I could while waiting for Boone to bring you back."

Rhune smiled at her. "You did the right thing. Now, let's start with that blood pressure." As he reached for the cuff, he saw the patient's eyelids flutter.

When he turned fully toward her, he found himself snared by a pair of clear, startlingly violet eyes.

Tess McQueen stared at the man before her. Surely *he* wasn't the doctor.

Surely *he* wasn't the man she'd come all these miles to wreak revenge upon.

Her sister had described Dr. Rhune Sherman as a sophisticated playboy. A rogue and a rake. A smooth operator. A seducer of innocent women. Cool. Urbane. Irresistibly charming and utterly heartless.

This man... this man who now strapped a blood pressure cuff around her arm was... was... quite frankly, not within Tess's definition of urbane. Nor smooth. This man was most certainly rough around the edges and... well... extraordinarily *different.* A surfer dressed up to impersonate a doctor. Unshaven, tanned face. Sun-streaked hair. A wild tropical shirt peeking out from under the pristine lab coat. And deep dark brown eyes that weren't heartless at all. From where she lay, she could see only concern in this man's eyes.

His unexpected appearance so unnerved her that, for the first time in her life, Tess found herself speechless and unable to wrest control of the situation.

And control had been what had driven her life to this point.

"I'm Rhune Sherman, Sweet Hope's newest and only family physician," the man said, smiling and unwrapping the cuff from her arm. "And you are?"

"T-Tess," she stuttered. "Tess McQueen of Washington, D.C." She felt like a fool. Rather woozy. Helpless in her supine position. And, surprisingly, rather foolish in her helplessness.

"Well, Ms. McQueen, for starters, your blood pressure's elevated." He popped a thermometer in her mouth, then began to examine closely the skin on her hands and face. "And my guess would be that you've gotten yourself dangerously close to dehydrated. When was the last time you drank anything?"

Maneuvering the thermometer with her tongue, she mumbled awkwardly, "I had coffee..."

"Not coffee. Water. Juice. A sports drink, even."

Tess wrinkled her nose. "I only drink coffee." Coffee positively fueled her hectic schedule. She tried to rise.

Scowling, the doctor gently pressed her shoulders back on the examining table before he flashed a light in her eyes. "How many cups a day?" His voice rumbled disconcertingly in her ear.

In exasperation, she removed the impeding thermometer. "I lose track after ten o'clock in the morning."

"What have you eaten today, Ms. McQueen?"

"I was about to eat something in your café, but I suddenly felt very strange. Too warm. Dizzy. Weak."

"What had you eaten before that?"

The cool professionalism of his questioning was, inexplicably, beginning to grate on her. "On the road, when I put gas in the car, I grabbed a bag of tortilla chips."

"Ah, yes," he said, helping her to sit up. "Caffeine and sodium. The two basic food groups."

She felt additional irritation rise at the truth. "I'm a very busy woman, Dr. Sherman. I often don't have time to eat right. But I'm young and basically healthy." She jutted her chin stubbornly. "This is the first time anything like this has happened to me."

The doctor flashed an unexpected smile of dazzling white teeth against bronzed skin. In a fleeting, all too disturbing moment, Tess saw the man and not the physician. Recognized the raw male charm. The allure. The ability to seduce. She shivered.

"Then this time is a warning," he said, his smile disappearing, his voice impeccably professional. "Your job is to learn how not to let it happen again." He turned to the woman who had kept Tess company. "Patsy, would you please get Ms. McQueen a large glass of water, for starters?"

"What will you prescribe?" Tess steeled herself for the anticipated regimen of pills.

Dr. Sherman turned to her and leveled a gaze of such arresting brown that Tess found it impossible to look away. "Do you have a stressful job?" he asked.

"Challenging," Tess corrected. "I'm an efficiency expert."

His eyes widened as if this were an alien occupation. "Efficiency expert," he repeated, turning the words over carefully. "How long can you stay in Sweet Hope?"

His unexpected question flustered her. "Well, actually...I have business this week in Sweet Hope."

Cocking one eyebrow, Dr. Sherman looked for all the world as if he didn't believe her. However, he replied evenly, "One week should be enough."

"Enough for what?" One week was certainly enough for her agenda, but what was he talking about?

"Ms. McQueen, I intend to contact your physician in D.C. first thing tomorrow morning. I'm sure he or she will agree with my recommendations."

"I've kept all my regular checkups, and I'm not allergic to any medications, if that's what concerns you." Tess accepted the large glass of water Patsy now offered. Drinking thirstily, she emptied the glass and handed it back to the doctor's assistant.

"I'm not prescribing any medications." Dr. Sherman narrowed his eyes. "I'm prescribing a week in Sweet Hope. I'm prescribing a week of good food, plentiful fluids, light exercise and small-town relaxation. There's no reason a woman of your age shouldn't be able to lower her blood pressure naturally." He crossed his arms over his chest and skewered her with a serious look.

He couldn't be serious.

"I'm as serious as a heart attack," he said, as if reading her mind.

Adjusting the cuffs of her deliberately elegant power suit, she sat ramrod straight on the end of the examining table and sent him one of her board-room glares. "Dr. Sherman...." *Doctor.* She had doubts that this rakishly disheveled man even was a legitimate doctor. "My time is valuable.

I have no intention of spending my week in Sweet Hope relaxing. I'm here on business.'' Here to deal with your disastrous monkey business, she added mentally. ''Aren't there
pills for my condition?''

''Do you want pills or do you want good health?''

''I want,'' she said evenly, feeling her jaw muscles tense,
''the most efficient procedure possible.''

He moved to put his arm around her shoulder. She
flinched at his touch. ''I'm sorry to startle you,'' he said, his
voice deep and surprisingly reassuring. ''We need to get
some food into you. Patsy, would you get on the other side
of Ms. McQueen? I think, with our help, she can get over to
Mel and Ida's.''

''I'm sure I can make it on my own.'' Tess's feet hit the
floor, and her knees buckled. Apparently, to her dismay, she
did need assistance.

Dr. Sherman caught her. ''You're woozy. Too much time
on the road. Too little food and fluids. We'll get you into
Mel and Ida's bed-and-breakfast. They'll coddle you. It'll
be just what the doctor ordered. If you're not right as rain
in a couple days, we'll run some tests.''

This was ridiculous. No doctor in his right mind prescribed a week of inactivity in a bed-and-breakfast in a town
that barely had its own dot on the map. This was a scenario
that screenwriters thought up for screwball romantic com-
edies.

Except that, at the moment, Tess definitely was not
laughing.

''Dr. Sherman, please,'' she protested. ''I'm not at all
certain this is the right prescription for me.''

As Patsy opened the door, the doctor with the soulful
brown eyes tightened his hold on her. ''Would you rather we
call an ambulance to take you to Atlanta tonight?''

''No!'' Tess shook her head. The man was a provocation. ''Is there no sensible, in-between solution?''

''What's more sensible than giving you a decent supper,
putting you to bed and checking on you in the morning?''

He had her there. There was nothing of the B movie when he put it that way. "All right," she agreed. "But in the morning we reevaluate."

"Of course," he replied with exasperating patience, helping her through the exam room doorway, then down the hall to the waiting room.

As they turned the corner they were met by a half dozen of the townspeople who had been in the Hole-in-the-Wall Café and who had helped get her to the doctor's office. Spotting Dr. Sherman and Tess, they broke into a round of applause. Stunned, Tess turned to the doctor, question scrunching her brow. These people had waited to see how she was? She couldn't imagine a group of strangers in D.C. caring enough to do the same.

Dr. Sherman grinned and spoke low. "Get used to it. Sweet Hope's a little like Brigadoon."

"You need some help, Doc?" someone called out.

"Just clear a path. We need to get Ms. McQueen to Mel and Ida's for a good night's rest."

"I'll run ahead," a different voice offered, "and make sure they have the room ready."

"Really, Dr. Sherman . . ." The fuss made Tess feel terribly conspicuous and uncomfortable. "This isn't necessary." She was beginning to find his closeness very unnecessary. Overpowering in its maleness. And far too disconcerting.

He held her firmly on her feet, imparting a sense of infinite strength, infinite patience. And something else . . . a vibrant warmth and energy. Whenever he spoke, his voice slithered over her senses and left her feeling disoriented.

Keep it together, Tess, she chided herself mentally. As soon as you're in top form again, if this man truly is Dr. Rhune Sherman, you have your work cut out for you. For your sister's sake.

"Would you please let me decide what's necessary, Ms. McQueen?" Rhune held the elegant, slender woman firmly at his side. With her eyes open she'd not turned out to be the ice princess he'd observed when he'd first entered the exam room. No, this woman was filled with spark and sizzle. Trouble was, all that energy seemed to be directed at countermanding any and all of his recommendations.

Her wide violet eyes took in the activity in the waiting room. "This is really too much," she whispered, as if to herself.

Rhune chuckled. That's what he'd thought, too, on his first encounter with Sweet Hope and its residents. "You get used to it. But at first, small-town involvement tends to overwhelm you." Feeling her sag just the slightest against him, he tightened his grip around her. "Come on. Let's get you across the street."

As Patsy opened doors and directed traffic, Rhune managed to get a shaky Tess McQueen across Main Street and up the steps of the rambling Victorian house that had been Mel and Ida Drake's birthplace. Never-married sisters of indeterminate age, the Drakes had turned their home into a bed-and-breakfast that consistently lured even the most discriminating city folks for weekend getaways. Rhune figured that if the stiff Ms. McQueen would just loosen up this would be the perfect place for her to relax and recuperate. Inside, glancing around the ornate foyer, Rhune suppressed the thought that, but for the fact that he'd sworn off romantic entanglements, this would be the perfect setting for . . . well . . . a romantic entanglement.

He had no time for further speculation, for Ida Drake, the more formidable of the two sisters, bore down upon him like a locomotive under full steam. "Dr. Sherman! We've just heard that you're in need of our services."

Tess McQueen pulled away from him and, with great dignity and obvious effort, stood on her own and extended her hand. "I'm Tess McQueen," she said gravely, "and I need a room for a week."

Taking her hand, Ida replied, "I'm very pleased to meet you, Ms. McQueen, but what finds you under our doctor's care?"

Rhune began to speak for her, but Tess cut him off. "I overdid it today. Too much work, too little thought to creature comforts. A good meal in your dining room—"

"Not in the dining room." It was Rhune's turn to interrupt. "Ida, would it be possible for Ms. McQueen to have her supper in her room? Preferably in bed?"

"That's ridiculous. And totally unnecessary," Tess sputtered.

"That's perfectly all right." Ida put her arm around Tess and slowly directed her to the grand curving staircase. "Dear heart, you listen to Dr. Sherman. He'll put you fit as a fiddle. Why, the first time he visited Sweet Hope, he suggested the most wonderful natural remedy for my dry skin...."

"Wait!" Tess, obviously flustered, turned and looked at Rhune. "I have no overnight bag, and my car's in front of the café."

Rhune held out his hand. "Give me your keys. While Ida and Mel settle you in, I'll play valet."

"But that's not necessary," Tess exclaimed.

Rhune grinned and kept his hand extended. "You efficiency experts sure do use the words *necessary* and *unnecessary* a lot." He wiggled his fingers. "Give me the keys, Ms. McQueen. Necessary or not, you'll find that Sweet Hope is a full-service town."

Tess McQueen gave a frustrated little sigh, but did, finally, hand over her keys.

Rhune flipped the keys into his pocket. "I'll be back to check on you once you're settled in."

"That won't be—"

"Necessary. I know. But I'll be back just the same." He turned, then added over his shoulder, "And, Ida, supper *in bed* would be best."

He stepped out of the foyer and onto the veranda to the rhythm of Ida's solicitous clucking. Patsy, her face all concern, stood outside at the head of a small group of residents. "Well, Doc?" she asked.

Rhune smiled. "Ms. McQueen will be fine, thanks to y'all. Right now she needs rest and quiet. You can express your concern later. She'll be here the week."

"She said she was an efficiency expert here on business." Patsy looked puzzled. "Now, who in all of Sweet Hope would call for an efficiency expert?"

"Beats me." Rhune shook his head and ushered the small group down the veranda steps. Sweet Hope was seductively inefficient. Slow. Mellow. And brimful of quirkiness. He sure hoped no one would be so traitorous as to call in an efficiency expert to change a thing.

He said his thanks again and his goodbyes to Patsy and the ad hoc emergency crew of residents, then, jingling the keys in his pocket, headed leisurely across the town green toward the Hole-in-the-Wall Café and Tess McQueen's car. Better keep it slow so that Mel and Ida would have a chance to settle their guest in and serve her supper.

He found the car easily. Not being the usual practical Sweet Hope vehicle, the expensive European model stood out. Unlocking it, he slid behind the wheel and into the embrace of leather and luxury and high technology. His gaze moved over a phone, a fax, a pocket electronic personal manager, a laptop computer and an open briefcase full to overflowing with paperwork. Ms. McQueen certainly was a busy bee.

But more than the hardware, an exotic woody fragrance that must be Tess McQueen's perfume caught Rhune's attention. The faint but distinctive sensuality of the scent jolted him. Until now, he hadn't seen this newcomer as particularly sensuous. Beautiful, yes. Cool. Capable. Feisty in an imperious way. Yes. But this intriguing perfume hinted at another side of the elegant Ms. McQueen. A side that smoldered.

And this side of her intrigued the daylights out of him.

"Get real, Doc," he muttered, turning the key in the ignition. As the powerful engine sprang to life, Rhune Sherman mentally upbraided himself for letting his imagination wander.

He'd relocated to Sweet Hope to turn his life around. He'd come to practice medicine in an environment where he could make a noticeable, positive difference. And he'd come to rein in and redirect his personal life. The wild man he'd become in Washington, D.C., had in the end startled even himself. The horrors of his job were no excuse. He needed to find his center. He needed to let fishing in his pond be the most exciting thing in his life for the moment.

He did not need to fall under the spell of a lovely stranger's wide violet eyes or her exotic perfume. With this admonition firmly in mind, he drove the short distance from the café to the Drakes' bed-and-breakfast.

Why, then, if he understood himself so well, did his pulse pick up as he parked the car in front of the rambling Victorian, then climbed the stairs to check on his new patient?

Mel Drake stood on the top step of the veranda, apparently waiting for him. Shyly, without speaking, she beckoned for him to follow her inside, then upstairs and through the enormous old house. Finally she stopped before a closed door and knocked.

"Come in." Ida's voice rang out from within.

Rhune pushed the door open and stepped into the large bedroom softly illuminated with antique lamps. Ida was just removing a tray from the canopied bed where, propped up against snow-white pillows, Tess McQueen sat. Regal. Still. And exceptionally beautiful. Her midnight dark hair spilled luxuriantly over shoulders encased in a flowered silk wrapper. Her pale, slender hands lay folded in front of her on the lace coverlet. Imperiously, she focused her arresting violet gaze directly upon him, causing him to catch his breath.

He'd come to check on his patient. Why, then, did he get the distinct impression that he had been granted, upon sufferance, an audience with Her Highness?

Ida Drake bustled by him. "You did bring Ms. McQueen's luggage?"

"I'm sorry. It's still in the car," Rhune replied sheepishly, feeling too warm and far too uncomfortable with his lapse in attention to details. Had he been that eager to check on this particular patient?

"I'll just see to it, then," Ida clucked.

"That won't be necessary," Rhune and Tess exclaimed simultaneously. Obviously, Ms. McQueen didn't wish to be left alone with him any more than he wished to be left alone with her.

"Of course it's necessary. You need a little privacy and quiet, Dr. Sherman, to check on your patient." Ida nodded to Tess. "You just ring, dear, if you need anything. Anything at all." She left the room, smoothly pulling the door closed behind her.

Rhune inhaled sharply. Had he missed this lecture in med school? "How to deal with an unsettling and queenly patient during a house call in a lavender-and-lace bed-and-breakfast—101." He stepped toward the bed. Quite frankly, he'd never had a comparable experience in the gritty and bloodstained inner-city emergency room that had shaped his residency. And he'd certainly never envisioned country doctoring beginning this way.

He moved to the bedside and reached for Tess's wrist to check her pulse. He noted that, after her supper, her skin tone had regained a healthier hue. Not quite peaches-and-cream. Ms. McQueen didn't seem the peaches and cream sort. More roses and alabaster. Elegant roses and cool, immovable alabaster.

Rhune tried to concentrate on the steady pulse under his fingertips.

"Are you really a doctor?" The low, husky voice at his side made him start.

She'd jolted him.

And pricked his ego.

He laid her wrist gently but firmly on the coverlet. "I received my degree from Harvard Med. I did my internship and residency at St. Michael's ER in D.C. It's not fancy, but you know your stuff when you get out."

She cocked an eyebrow. "You don't have to tell me. I know St. Michael's. It's capable of taking the best, chewing them up and spitting them out. The staff, that is, not the patients.''

The quirk of her mouth asked in no uncertain terms if that's what had happened to him.

''If you're asking if I'm a reject, I'm not.'' The good Dr. Sherman glowered at her. My, my, she'd hit a nerve. Good. Perhaps she could find a way to use that knowledge to her advantage. Later. When she'd had a decent night's sleep. When she'd regained the top of her form.

Tess was not about to let the ministrations of Sweet Hope's kind folk sway her from her original purpose. She hadn't intended to get sick on her arrival. She'd intended to arrive in town strong and in command. She'd intended to confront Dr. Rhune Sherman immediately. With the precision and cool determination that had earned her a powerful reputation. And, with any luck, she'd intended to have matters settled—*efficiently*—and be back in D.C., at her job, within a few days.

She had not anticipated first meeting the man flat on her back. This second encounter proved no less satisfying. Here she sat in a lacy bower, wrapped in a borrowed silk kimono, less than eye-to-eye with a man she found exasperating. Exasperating because he was not what she'd been led to expect. Exasperating because, in the short time she'd been in his company, he'd shattered the stereotype. Exasperating because she couldn't figure him out.

Tess prided herself on being able to figure people out. Their strengths. Their weaknesses. Their characters and their character flaws.

If she could believe her sister, Dr. Rhune Sherman was riddled with flaws. A detestable lowlife. A bastard. But in the past hour she'd seen only kindness and professionalism in the man. Except for now. When she'd questioned that professionalism, she'd seen irritation. And pride in his work.

If she knew nothing, she knew that this man took his career seriously. As she did her own. She'd always admired like-minded people of singular purpose.

She softened despite herself. "I didn't mean to question your credentials. I'm sorry. I'm not at my best right now."

His face relaxed. "Not now, perhaps, but you will be after a week in Sweet Hope. As I said before, it's a little like Brigadoon. You've fallen into it. Shortly, it will take hold of you. Then, unexpectedly, you won't want to leave."

She raised one eyebrow in surprise. "I assure you, Dr. Sherman, I *will* be leaving in a week . . . or less."

He smiled. "Depending, I suppose, on how efficiently you can wrap up your business."

"Precisely." If only he knew that *he* was her business.

Softly he patted the bed. "Get some rest. I'll be by tomorrow morning with the dreaded blood pressure cuff. If I were you, I wouldn't bother getting out of your robe tomorrow. Let Mel and Ida wait on you hand and foot. They'll love it."

He winked. A comforting wink. Not a leer. Definitely nothing suggestive. Not at all a move her sister had led her to believe would be his stock-in-trade.

Heading toward the door, he added, "And order the fruit compote for breakfast. It's Mel's specialty. If you haven't eaten by the time I get here, I might join you and order one myself."

At the door he shrugged out of his lab coat, revealing the wildest tropical shirt Tess had ever seen. The shirt provided only half the shock. The other half came from the sight of his long, well-muscled, bronzed arms, dusted with sun-bleached hair. She inhaled sharply. Those arms had been firmly around her not an hour ago. The thought made her flush.

At her too obvious agitation, he cocked an eyebrow and grinned. It seemed the good doctor had shed his professionalism with his lab coat, for his grin was pure mischief. Dazzling. Full of vitality. And very definitely, very dangerously attractive.

He nodded slowly. "Tess McQueen, I'll see you tomorrow," he said, his voice lazy and low, as he left the room.

And Tess in a swither.

Now, *that man* she could believe capable of a playboy reputation.

She turned and pummeled the pillows behind her. What had her sister gotten her into? And how was she to deal with this Dr. Rhune Sherman, who, with his credentials, could be practicing in any high-rent district in the country but instead seemed perfectly at ease in his role as a sleepy town's physician?

At ease? Who really knew if he was at ease? The man had as many expressions as a chameleon had colors. He could behave with the utmost care and civility while wearing a most unprofessional tropical shirt. And that beard. A rogue's beard. It wasn't even neatly trimmed. It was more like a leftover from a night of carousing. No, he didn't look like any doctor Tess had ever seen, but he'd certainly acted like a doctor. Kind. Concerned. Cautious. Even his holistic prescription for her recovery was, she had to admit, cautious.

Yes, he'd behaved like a doctor, except for that smile. It seemed to slip out from under his medical persona. That dazzling smile that made color rise to her cheeks and her toes curl. That smile. Sudden. Unexpected. Devastating. Pulling from her heart a flash of attraction.

Tess flounced back on the pillows, disgusted with herself. The last thing she needed was a flash of attraction for her sister's seducer.

Chapter Two

Why wouldn't she have stayed put?

Standing the next morning on Mel and Ida's bed-and-breakfast veranda, Rhune ran his fingers through his hair in exasperation. Ms. Tess McQueen was neither sleeping in her bedroom, nor eating in the dining room, nor sitting in a porch rocker on the veranda, nor strolling in the Drakes' extensive flower gardens. And those were the only activities Rhune thought fit for the recuperating Ms. McQueen. At least until he'd checked her blood pressure.

Obviously, the lady had her own agenda.

And with it, she hadn't seen fit to confide in either Mel or Ida. They had appeared as surprised and as troubled by their guest's disappearance as had Rhune. The only thing that kept him standing and waiting was the fact that Tess's luggage remained in her room and her BMW remained at the curb. It seemed, at least, that she hadn't left town.

He really didn't have time for this nonsense.

In the first place, he had the aftermath of the raccoon rampage to deal with. In the second place, he had less than a week of vacation left—less than a week to make up for ten years of nose-to-the-grindstone work . . . and the fish were biting. The fish were biting, and his Harley was out of the shop.

In the third place, Ms. Tess really did need to abide by his medical recommendations. For her own good. His irritation grew as he waited. He'd dealt with life and death in D.C. He didn't need to baby-sit some high-strung, corporate brat who refused to take proper care of herself. He had half a mind to let the McQueen woman mismanage her health; the other half of his mind—the professional half—couldn't leave a job unfinished.

Tess McQueen. Some job.

He scanned Main Street and shook his head. Efficiency expert. Hmmph. In his opinion she needed to exert a little more efficient care on her well-being. Coffee and tortilla chips, indeed. He glanced at his watch. Nine-thirty. He just bet the woman had gone out this morning without first having breakfast.

As if the thought alone conjured her, Tess came out of a storefront a block down Main on the other side of the street. Unless Rhune missed his guess, that was Wally Buckminster's office. Wally was a young, hotshot lawyer. Just like him to call in an efficiency expert.

Crossing his arms on his chest, Rhune waited as Tess made her way back toward the bed-and-breakfast. In a town where the women wore pale, flowery sundresses in the middle of summer, Ms. McQueen stood out. She wore black slacks of a lightweight material that flowed seductively against her long legs as she walked, and a deep violet blouse so silky looking Rhune's fingers itched to stroke it. On anyone else the effect would have been too dark. Somber. But on Tess McQueen, with her alabaster complexion and her thick fall of midnight dark hair, the effect was exotic. Exotic and breathtaking. The sound of her dress-shoe heels clicking on the pavement in the early-morning quiet echoed Rhune's pulse.

My, but she was a stunner.

It took every ounce of professionalism Rhune could muster to quell thoughts of the possibilities were she not his patient.

But she was.

And he'd sworn off romantic entanglements.

Finally climbing the bed-and-breakfast steps, she extended her hand to him. "Dr. Sherman, I didn't properly thank you yesterday."

Rhune took her hand in his and looked squarely into those wide violet eyes. "And so you thought you'd start today by ignoring my recommendations." Irritation rose in him, not so much because she had ignored his instructions, but because he now stood like a flustered schoolboy in her presence. At a loss. Rhune Sherman, by his own admission, had many shortcomings, but being at a loss with women had never been one of them.

She smiled, and that put him off-balance even more. Her smile was slow and unexpectedly sensuous and involved her entire beautiful face. Not an efficiency expert's smile, by any means. No, this smile wasted major wattage.

"Why, Dr. Sherman," she drawled dramatically, "I've done nothing but follow your instructions this morning. I rose at eight o'clock—three hours past my normal rising. I put on casual clothing as if I were indeed on vacation. And, as you can see, I've been for a walk." Regally she withdrew her hand from his. "Now, would you care to join me for breakfast? Mel and Ida told me they've planned something highly nutritious. You can check my blood pressure afterward."

Rhune swallowed hard, not exactly confident of his own blood pressure at the moment. "Sure," he heard himself say.

The fishing could wait.

Without another word he followed her into the Drakes' sunny dining room. Silently he watched Mel and Ida cluck over Tess as if she were visiting royalty. The sisters finally seated them at a table for two in a bay window overlooking the gardens. Remaining mute, he gazed out at the garden.

Not that he'd know a petunia from a peony, but he needed time to pull himself together. This *sort-of* patient of his was far too compelling to deal with on an empty stomach.

"So, Dr. Sherman, do I get to live dangerously and have a cup of coffee?"

He swung his gaze across the table. At first he thought she was teasing. But her raised eyebrow and imperious posture told him that Tess McQueen seldom teased. He'd bet she was now, as always, efficiently serious.

"Rhune," he said finally. "Or Doc. That's what everyone in town calls me." He nodded in assent as Ida poured two cups of coffee. "And let's just say I won't make you go cold turkey on the coffee. You can start cutting down on that today. But it is cold turkey for the tortilla chips."

She began to smile, then stopped. "I do feel better this morning. It's amazing what a decent night's sleep will do for you."

"Do you make a habit of neglecting your health?"

Tess flashed him a warning look. "If you weren't my doctor of the moment, I'd think you impertinent."

"Well, how's this for impertinence? What were you doing conducting business before you'd even eaten a mouthful of breakfast?"

She looked startled.

"Wally Buckminster is your business in Sweet Hope, is he not?"

Tess's eyes widened. "I do have business with Mr. Buckminster... yes." Her tone of voice bespoke a wariness.

"Do yourself a favor. Please. Take care of yourself first, business second."

"And after I've slept late and eaten Mel and Ida's good meals, what do you recommend I do in this town, short of business?"

"Ms. McQueen, what do you usually do for fun?"

The bemused expression she favored him with told me she seldom gave much thought to this question. "Fun?"

"Fun. It's not a difficult concept."

She inhaled deeply and folded her hands in her lap. "Why, I read...although, come to think of it, I haven't had time for a book in months. And sometimes I reorganize my closets."

Rhune choked on his coffee. "Now, *that's* my idea of fun."

Tess's violet eyes clouded with indignation. "Oh, yes, I presume *your* idea of fun is to let the woodland creatures party in your residence, then leave the mess for animal control to clean up."

That bigmouth Wally.

"I left the animal control crew—to *investigate* and to come up with some possible preventive measures—because you needed attention, Ms. McQueen. I assure you that seeing my few possessions in the treetops was not my idea of fun." He shook his head in resignation. "Although the wags in town will get a lot of mileage from that one."

Tess cocked an eyebrow, looking for all the world like an empress interrogating a recalcitrant subject. "You've been involved in other disasters?"

"Not disasters. Well...not literal disasters." He didn't want to talk about his first visit to Sweet Hope and Missy Able. "I haven't been in town long enough to generate too much gossip." A slight understatement.

For a moment interest sparked in Tess's eyes. "Just how long have you lived in Sweet Hope?"

"A month. But I've visited on and off for over a year now."

Tess wrinkled her nose. Something about this time frame didn't compute. She would have to speak with her sister.

"My sister lives here," Rhune continued. "Arabella O'Malley. She runs the Belle, Book and Candle."

"Ah, yes, that odd little shop on Main Street."

"Yes, *odd.*" Rhune smiled ruefully. "The world tends to say that of the Shermans."

Tess stiffened. "And that's supposed to make me feel comfortable, accepting your professional advice?"

He leaned across the table and spoke deliberately. "That's one thing you need never feel uncomfortable about accepting from me. My professional advice."

Let no one—*no one*—underestimate him professionally.

Ida saved the awkward impasse by placing plates of steaming whole wheat banana pancakes and fruit compote before them.

Rhune looked across the table at Tess but couldn't fathom the look in her eyes. She seemed to be studying him with an intensity ill suited to either a patient for her doctor or a woman who had just made a new casual acquaintance. Her gaze pierced and probed and made Rhune feel, for an uncomfortable, fleeting moment, as if this beautiful newcomer harbored some hidden agenda.

An agenda that seemed to include—inexplicably—himself.

Picking up her fork, Tess cast her gaze downward before Rhune Sherman began to think her insufferably rude. Quite frankly, it was difficult not to stare. For one thing, the doctor's physical transformation this morning was incredible. Gone was the lab coat hiding a wild tropical shirt. In their place were a crisp, new-looking shirt and trousers. Gone, too, was the several days' growth of beard, and, shaved, his face was arrestingly handsome—tanned, smooth planes and angles, with a killer dimple near one corner of his mouth.

Dimples, quite frankly, undid her.

Lordy, she needed to remind herself why she was in Sweet Hope. If her sister could be believed, Dr. Rhune Sherman was a thoroughly irresponsible playboy who didn't give two hoots about any woman's feelings.

Tess chewed a piece of pancake without tasting it, then swallowed hard.

Today it was easier to see the handsome playboy in the man. And more difficult. It was his obvious pride in and devotion to his work that contributed toward the difficulty. With a shiver that felt like disloyalty toward her sister, Tess tried to suppress a gut reaction that this man was not totally a heartless scoundrel.

Perhaps not. But she'd made a promise to her sister, and she would follow through.

She'd lost the element of surprise yesterday when, in a diminished capacity, she'd first met Rhune Sherman. Now, today, here she sat as if the man were an old family friend rather than a rake who'd run out on her sister and his responsibilities. Why, she should be reading him the riot act.

But, ever sensible and cautious, Tess wanted more than anything to get down to the truth of the matter. And experience had taught her that hysteria accomplished nothing. Calm, rational behavior and a keen, observant eye on her part would more effectively bring about the downfall of Dr. Sherman.

If indeed his downfall was required.

Patience, Tess, she mentally chided herself. She resolved to find out everything she could about the man sitting across the table from her before she took action. And she resolved that no matter how charming he might turn out to be, *she* wouldn't fall under his spell.

"Shall we try again, Ms. McQueen?" Rhune's warm, rich voice rumbled over her senses, jolting her out of her disconcerting reverie.

Tess looked into the expectant face of a man who obviously refused to bend, bow or be discouraged by anyone. Anyone. She'd always found confidence tremendously attractive. She felt a little corner of her revenge resolve crumble. "Please...call me Tess." She rationalized that animosity would gain her no valuable information.

He smiled. A slow, lazy smile that deepened the dimple and put another ding in her resolve. "Tess."

The way he said her name—firmly, with a sense of satisfaction—made her pulse skitter. "I'm sorry...." She toyed with the food on her plate. "Where were we?"

His eyes sparkled. "We were trying to think of something fun for a visiting efficiency expert to do in Sweet Hope."

Heat rose to her cheeks as she tried to devote her attention to her breakfast. "During my walk this morning I noticed a movie house and a library," she volunteered. If he wanted to participate in small talk, so be it. She'd certainly find out nothing about him if she ate her breakfast in hostile silence.

"Come, now." His voice was a low tease. "I'm sure you can go to the movies in D.C. I had in mind some characteristically small-town fun. Like the Sweet Hope Fourth of July celebration. Only a few days away. Arabella says it's a day right out of a Norman Rockwell painting."

Suddenly, despite her original purpose for being in Sweet Hope, the idea of a small-town holiday greatly appealed to Tess. A little bit of Americana. Something she'd been too busy to participate in for the past ten years as she'd risen in her profession and been a surrogate mother to her sister. She didn't bother to mute her interest. "Fourth of July celebration?"

"Yes, ma'am. With all the trimmings, I hear tell. A parade. A picnic. Fireworks."

"Fireworks." Tess sighed. She hadn't indulged in such simple pleasures since...since she was very young. Her parents' deaths had made her grow up quickly. Too quickly. In taking on the responsibilities of raising a child then nine years old, she'd literally lost her twenties.

The idea of this Sweet Hope celebration was tempting. Very tempting. There was nothing saying she couldn't enjoy the town and its inhabitants while she investigated their doctor. Perhaps, by blending in with the Fourth of July events, she could recapture some of the element of surprise.

Surprise. More like an ambush. She shivered. An ambush was closer to the heart of the matter.

"Are you feeling well?" Rhune reached across the table and soothingly touched her arm. The concern in his voice and his feather-light touch seared her senses.

"I'm fine." She pasted her most cordial expression on her face. "I've been following doctor's orders, haven't I?"

"Continue to follow them and I'll sign the permission slip letting you go to the festivities," he said, his voice brimming with high spirits, his dimple deepening.

"That would be nice," she agreed simply. It was downright ludicrous how the idea of a small-town celebration appealed to her. As if it really would be a vacation, of sorts, even taking into consideration her obligation to her sister.

Rhune Sherman grinned. A heart-stopping grin. "Then eat up those pancakes, and drink that orange juice. I'll take your blood pressure after breakfast to see if you're allowed out of your room today."

She bristled at his gentle orders. "Do you hover over all your patients this way, Dr. Sherman?"

"I know...very inefficient." His grin seemed to get brighter, if that was possible. "But at the moment you happen to be *all of my patients.*"

She knitted her brow, not understanding him at first. Then realization dawned. "You said you'd only been in town a month. Do you mean to say your practice isn't officially up and running?"

"That's what I mean to say." With gusto he finished the last of his pancakes. "Although, don't worry. I'm fully licensed to practice."

"I'm sure you are," Tess murmured as she placed her silverware on her plate to indicate she'd finished her meal.

Rhune nodded at her half-empty plate. "You do understand you have two more of those coming."

She scowled slightly in question.

"Meals, Tess. They're called meals." He chuckled. "I expect you to recognize them and take advantage of them. Regularly."

Feeling suddenly flustered under his warm brown gaze, she disstractedly played with a button on her blouse. "You'll turn me into a regular roly-poly," she said without thinking, then flushed at the hint of vanity.

"Not if you eat sensibly and exercise."

"I've never been one for the gym."

"I'm not suggesting a gym. I'm suggesting evening walks about town when the heat of the day has lessened." He stood. "I'll be by after supper to walk with you. Now, I left my bag in the parlor. Let's take your blood pressure in there." He eyed her expectantly and waited for her to rise also.

What did he mean, he would be by after supper to walk with her? Normally, she wouldn't hesitate to ask; but now she found her tongue stuck to the roof of her mouth. In mute wonderment she rose from the breakfast table, then followed him into the parlor.

Did he have this mesmerizing effect on all his patients?

In the sun-dappled quiet of the Victorian sitting room, Tess rolled up the sleeve of her blouse and offered her arm for the blood pressure cuff. An air of unreality settled over her. This man who, with the utmost professionalism, took her arm was her sister's seducer.

Tess must not forget it.

Must not, although she was inexplicably drawn to the man.

Drawn to his obvious pride in his work. Drawn to his genuine concern for the welfare of others. Drawn to his reverence for the concept of fun. Fun had been a luxury in Tess's life. Pressed by responsibility, she'd learned to find fulfillment in work. Never fun.

"Your reading's better today. One hundred thirty-nine over eighty-eight." Rhune removed the cuff. "Although it's still a little high for a woman so young." Looking directly at her, he smiled. "A good diet will be the key. And exercise. Before I pick you up tonight, I suggest you walk across the street to Plato's Emporium and buy yourself a pair of sports shoes."

"Dr. Sherman...Rhune...you don't need to baby-sit me," she said a little too sharply.

Replacing the blood pressure cuff in his black bag, he cocked one eyebrow. "Who says I'm baby-sitting you? We're both new in town. We might as well enjoy the evening ritual together."

"The evening ritual?"

He winked. "You'll see. And I'll see you around eight."

He left Tess bewildered and not a little irritated with herself for her uncharacteristically compliant state. Even worse, she could not explain how she'd flunked miserably so far as an avenging angel. Just as she'd worked herself into a state of marvelous ire, this perplexing man had upset her with kindness. Or warmth. Or his insistence on a little innocent fun.

Stepping to the window, she parted the lace curtains and looked out on Main Street just in time to see Dr. Rhune Sherman straddle the biggest, blackest motorcycle Tess had ever seen in her life.

Oh, my. Her fingers fluttered to her throat.

Now, *that* looked like fun.

"Ms. McQueen?"

Feeling caught at the beginning of an improbable fantasy, Tess whirled at the sound of Ida Drake's voice. "Yes?"

"You had a call, dear, while you were out earlier. A Chelsey Wellington. She'd like you to call her back. Says you have her number."

Chelsey Wellington. Her sister.

Tess thanked Ida, then climbed the stairs to her room. She didn't want to talk to her sister right now. Not with vaguely traitorous thoughts pounding in her head. Thoughts of Rhune Sherman and the possibility that her sister—impetuous and demanding—*might not* have painted an entirely accurate picture of the man for Tess.

Once in her room, she stood by the phone for several minutes without dialing. Then, shrugging to dispel her worrisome thoughts, she punched in her own and Chelsey's number.

Chelsey. She would never get used to calling her sister *Chelsey*. Born Dixie Fae McQueen, her sister had recently decided on a career in acting. The first thing she'd done was change her name. Two acts of blatant rebellion.

The phone rang twice before Chelsey picked it up. "This better be my big sister!"

Tess winced. "And what if I'd been the casting director for a big Broadway play?"

"So my phone manners need work." Chelsey giggled. That bright, familiar, girlish giggle. "Well, what have you discovered, Dick Tracy?"

Rubbing the palm of her hand across her brow, Tess thought for a tiny disloyal moment that she'd discovered that Chelsey was too old to have her big sister still fighting her battles. Aloud she said, "I've found Rhune Sherman."

"Good. Now we need to plot his just desserts."

"Chelsey..." Tess didn't like the glee with which her sister anticipated revenge rather than justice. "He may be flawed, but he's human."

"Oh, God, sis, don't tell me you've fallen under his spell."

"I haven't *fallen under his spell*." Tess bristled. "I've been in town less than twenty-four hours. Have been in the man's company only briefly."

"That's why you don't know what he's capable of. I, on the other hand, do." Chelsey's voice took on the petulant tone that drove Tess up the wall. A tone that had, on occasion in the past, driven her to promise anything so long as the whining stopped. "The man seduced me and left me. Left me with emotional scars I'll carry with me the rest of my life."

"Chelsey, stop it. Don't play the victim. You're stronger than that."

"Sure I'm strong...but, in case you've forgotten, I'm also pregnant. And Rhune Sherman, the father, ran out on me."

Tess pinched the bridge of her nose. "I agree Dr. Sherman needs to face up to his responsibilities, but the situation requires perfect timing. Now, I've just seen a lawyer in town. Through him I've hired a private investigator who'll soon enough tell us exactly with whom we're dealing. If we end up going to court, we'll need to be thorough."

"My sis," Chelsey replied, her voice faintly mocking. "If she errs at all, it's on the side of thoroughness."

Tess decided to chalk her sister's dig up to hormones, and ignored it. "We should know something by day after tomorrow."

"So what'll you do in the meantime?"

"I'll do a little investigating of my own." The idea had just come to her that Rhune's concern, his checking up on her, his presence would provide a good cover for her to do a little up-close digging while she waited for the official report.

Chelsey had accused her of the heinous crime of thoroughness; Tess always erred, as well, on the side of fairness.

"Just be careful," Chelsey warned. "The man could charm a snake at the state fair, but that doesn't mean he's worth the price of admission."

"I'll be careful, li'l sis." Tess softened. This often challenging nineteen-year-old and the child she bore were the only family Tess had in the world. She owed them both. "You be careful, too. In the big city."

"I will. Call me. Let me know how the drama unfolds."

Tess rolled her eyes at her sister's theatrical tone of voice. "I will. Bye." Hanging up, she felt more conflicted than ever. On the one hand, if Rhune Sherman had played the cad with her sister, he needed to be made aware that two women, at least, didn't plan to take it without an uproar.

On the other hand, in the short space of time she'd been in town, she hadn't found a cad. She'd found an out-of-the-ordinary doctor with a warm smile. A smile and an outlook on life that made her think of the adage, "All work and no play..."

Dr. Rhune Sherman had reminded her that it had been a very long time since she'd taken any time out of the rat race. Too bad her hiatus was to cause the man's comeuppance.

Rhune guided his motorcycle along the hot asphalt. The midday heat made the pavement shimmer. After breakfast with Tess, he'd stopped at the town hall to see if the animal control workers had come up with any solutions to keeping man and beast apart. They hadn't. But already, in the retelling, the story among residents was taking on folkloric proportions.

Even with sunglasses, he squinted into the bright sunshine. Midday wasn't the optimum time for fishing, but it was better than nothing. He headed toward his property, his pond, and peace and quiet.

Wavery in the heat, the figure up ahead on the side of the road seemed like a mirage. Unreal.

Rhune slowed his bike. There could be no mistaking, however, that very real, very big black BMW and that tall, exotic beauty beside it.

Tess McQueen.

What the hell was she doing out here?

Pulling over beside her car, he cut the Harley's engine and swung himself to the ground. "What part of *stay put* don't you understand, Ms. McQueen?" he asked, not bothering to hide his irritation.

Tess pushed a damp lock of hair off her forehead. "I was feeling fine. And restless. I just thought I'd...explore the area."

"But now you're standing here in all this heat, to what end?" It had to be ninety-five degrees in the shade.

She spread her arms wide in a helpless gesture. "I had a flat."

"I'm surprised an efficiency expert doesn't know how to change a flat."

Bristling, Tess put her hands on her hips and skewered Rhune with a look of impatience. "I do know how to change a flat. The problem is that my sister borrowed my car, had a flat, then failed to have the tire repaired. It's in the trunk. Flat, too. I didn't realize I was riding on a bald spare."

"Sounds like your sister's mighty irresponsible."

Tess grimaced.

"How long have you been out here?"

"Oh, I don't know. A half hour. Forty-five minutes."

"And what have you had to drink?"

She looked down the narrow two-lane, then around at the countryside empty of habitation. Cocking one ebony eyebrow, she asked, "Do you see a drink machine?"

"One piece of advice," Rhune replied sharply, reaching into a saddlebag on his motorcycle. "If you're going to roam around the unfamiliar Georgia countryside in summer, you carry something to drink." He'd told her yesterday that she needed to drink plenty of fluids under normal circumstances. High noon in midsummer didn't constitute normal circumstances. He produced a water canteen and handed it to Tess.

Annoyance pricked his every fiber. As an ER doctor, he was used to patching up patients who weren't critical and cutting them loose, assuming they'd be sensible enough to follow his instructions. Sometimes they'd thanked him. Sometimes, if he'd had to stitch them up, they'd cursed him. But never, that he knew of, had he had a patient totally disregard him.

Not until Tess McQueen.

He glowered at her as she accepted the canteen readily. As she tilted back her head and began to drink, Rhune found himself unable to look away. With her chin raised, she exposed her lovely white column of a neck to the harsh midday sunlight, the muscles undulating sensuously as she drank. How could someone so exasperating be so...lovely? So attractive. A little trickle of water escaped the corner of her mouth and, glinting like a diamond, slid down her jaw, then down the pale, smooth skin of her neck.

Without thinking, Rhune reached out and wiped away the moisture with his fingers.

Tess froze, her violet eyes wide.

"Let's get you out of the sun," he said brusquely, remembering his professional relationship with her. "You're starting to burn." He took back the canteen and concentrated on tightening the top. He tried not to think of the texture of her skin under his fingertips.

"But my car..."

"I'll give you a ride back to town. To Homer Martin's garage." Returning the canteen to the saddlebag, he unhooked the spare helmet from the back of the bike's saddle. "He'll send someone out to fix your flat and bring your car back to Mel and Ida's." He scowled at her. "Where you'll be resting in the shade of the veranda."

She scowled right back at him. "You're trying to make an invalid out of me."

"I'm trying to get you to slow down for twenty-four hours. Enough so that I can get a normal blood pressure reading." And send you on your way, he added mentally, clamping the spare helmet on her head. "Hold still."

Her eyes flashed. "I don't like being bullied."

Buckling the helmet under her chin, he retorted, "I don't like being ignored." He didn't. No, sirree, he didn't. Impatiently he mounted the motorcycle.

Tess stood immobile by the side of the road as Rhune turned on the engine and gunned it for good measure.

"Well?" Lord, how she provoked him. "Are you going to stand there till the kudzu grows over you, or are you getting on?"

Tess squinted and looked up and down the road.

He *almost* had to admire her backbone. "Believe me," he assured her, softening his words, "you're not going to get a better offer this afternoon. Not on this deserted stretch of road." Shaking his head, he grinned despite his earlier vexation. "Come on, Tess. It might even be fun."

He liked the startled look that crept across her face. He hadn't meant to bully her earlier, but he certainly didn't mind startling her. Not if it produced that charming look of surprised self-awareness. *Fun* seemed to be a buzzword of sorts with the efficient Ms. McQueen.

Slowly, gracefully as a dancer, she mounted the motorcycle behind him, careful not to touch him.

Turning to look at her over his shoulder, he said, "You're going to have to hold on. To me." Before he turned back to concentrate on driving, he saw the clouds gather in those violet eyes. He smiled. She wasn't ignoring him now.

As he carefully pulled out onto the two-lane, he felt her hands slide tentatively to the sides of his waist. Her touch, feather light, made his pulse quicken. Try as he might, it was difficult to see this woman as just another patient. But, he reminded himself sternly, she was, if only temporarily, under his care. His professional care. He would not mix business and pleasure.

Gazing down the long, deserted road, he smiled to himself and thought, There's nothing in the medical code of ethics, however, that says I have to take the short way back.

Tess had never in her life experienced anything like it.

At first she'd vowed not to hang on to Rhune. This was just a lift back to town. This was not a joyride. She'd placed her hands discreetly on either side of his waist and had sat erect, apart from him. At least as apart as the saddle of the motorcycle would allow.

But then they'd picked up speed, and the sight of the landscape whizzing by and the enormous rumble of the bike beneath them had sent a delicious shiver through her. A shiver that was half thrill, half terror—feelings that sent her arms securely around Rhune's middle. As her arms encircled him, her body slid forward on the saddle...and pressed against him. Pressed against his unyielding bulk. On this vehicle with absolutely no protection, it was amazing how much protection Rhune Sherman's big, strong body afforded.

She tried to peek over his shoulder at the road before them, but the wind stung her cheeks and flattened her eyelashes and tickled her so unmercifully that she ducked down behind Rhune's broad back. Ducked down and pressed her face into his solidness and tried not to think of how good he felt. How warm. How hard. And how unmistakably male.

"Are you okay?" His words floated back to her, distant and surreal, then were instantly gone. Sucked away in the motorcycle's backdraft.

She could only nod her head in assent, although okay didn't half cover how she felt at the moment.

Squeezing her eyes shut, she couldn't help but think that big bikes such as this one should be illegal—or at least rated R. Even with her eyes closed, she could vividly sense her changing environment. A slow grin crept over her face. It was kind of like making love in the dark. Where sight left off, the other senses kicked in. Big time.

Sunlight caressed her back as she pressed her front against Rhune's warmth. Under her eyelids she saw the rapid, strobelike passage of sunshine and shadow. It made her more than a little giddy. Made her slide her arms farther around Rhune. She felt him settle into her embrace. Felt his muscles ripple. Felt his strength and his vitality beneath the light fabric of his shirt. She inhaled sharply and could smell almost to the point of tasting his clean masculine scent mixed with the heady fragrance of summer air, heat and wildflowers.

The motorcycle soared over a hump in the road. Her stomach somersaulted. They crossed a bridge, and the washboard sensation tickled her clear to her tonsils, made the hairs on the back of her neck stand straight up. They rounded a bend, and her body moved in sync with Rhune's to counterbalance the turn. She held on a little more tightly. Man, woman and machine, forged into a unit, hurtled through space. Soaring. Free. On an unmistakably sexy joyride.

This was crazy.

Consummately cautious, Tess had read the motorcycle insurance statistics. This machine was dangerous. It was impractical. It was...it was...

Dear Lord, it was *fun!*

She felt laughter bubble up in her throat. She opened her eyes, pressed her body even closer to Rhune, then peered over his shoulder. Oh, my. Add sight to her already overloaded senses, and the ride was pure exhilaration. The sight of his strong hands gripping the handlebars and guiding the powerful machine. The sight of sun-streaked wisps of hair escaping from underneath his helmet at the back of his neck. The sight of his neck and shoulder muscles cording as he shifted position to maintain their precarious balance. The sight of this rock-solid man so in control and so at ease.

Such sights made it difficult to concentrate on her original purpose in Sweet Hope.

Suddenly, surprisingly, she felt a surge of disappointment as she noted the houses and the commercial buildings and the signs along the road that heralded the outskirts of town. This ride—this wonderful, liberating ride of initial expediency—was coming to an end. Her senses once more became earthbound.

How frustrating. Just when her spirit was learning to fly, if only temporarily.

Slowing the motorcycle, Rhune pulled off the road into a gravel yard before a rambling building, the words Martin's Garage once painted and now fading above the four open bays. Without the roar of the wind in her ears, the crunch of tires on gravel came to her abnormally magnified. And even after Rhune stopped the bike and cut the engine, she couldn't stop the intoxicating sensation of movement.

He gently loosed her arms from around him, swung his leg over the front of the motorcycle, then stood facing her. Without warning, he lifted her easily from the bike and put her on her feet.

Oh, my. The earth moved. Her legs buckled. And he caught her. Hard up against him.

Talk about inappropriate thoughts—pressed to his broad chest, Tess began to giggle as the thought of her favorite old movie, *That Touch of Mink,* crossed her mind. Like Doris Day's character, she, Tess, was an eminently sensible woman who was behaving in a highly irrational manner.

This was dangerous indeed.

Chapter Three

Tess stood in the aisle at Plato's Emporium and wiggled her toes in a pair of sports shoes. It was truly amazing how comfortable they felt. Her last pair of recreational shoes had been...? She squinched up her face in thought. Canvas sneakers. That was it. Back when she was a preadolescent. From the time she'd become a teenager until now, she'd known what she wanted to be in life: successful. And she'd always dressed the part. Sports shoes and recreation had taken very little space on her list of priorities.

But now she needed some footwear that could stand up to future legwork. If she was to find out more about the puzzling Dr. Sherman—and she certainly had to find out everything about him if true justice was to be done—she was going to have to keep company with him. Keep her ears and her eyes open. She was going to have to graciously accept his friendly concern. If he suggested a walk around the village green in the evening, who was she to buck doctor's orders? He'd prescribed walking and sports shoes. Sports shoes it was.

Her compliance with his orders had nothing—*absolutely nothing*—to do with that rather surprising motorcycle ride earlier. She shivered pleasurably at the thought, then rolled her shoulders to tamp down the unwanted sensation of pleasure. She thought of her sister and her mission. This purchase was, plain and simple, a means to an end.

She wiggled her toes again. It was amazing how comfortable the road to justice felt already.

"How do those feel?"

Tess looked up into the store owner's stone-washed blue eyes. She sighed and smiled in answer.

Plato shook his head with a look of concern. "You need thick socks. If'n you don't, you'll be raising a crop of blisters the gov'mint will be payin' you to plow under." Smiling, he turned slowly. "Follow me, sweetheart. Socks is on aisle three."

If any man other than this kindly giant had called her *sweetheart,* she would have cut him down to size. But not Plato. She'd been in the store less than five minutes when she had a real feel for the man's gentle temperament. Five more minutes and she'd heard his remarkable Renaissance outlook on life. It seemed that in Sweet Hope there were no strangers. And no stereotypes. Now, without a word of protest, she followed the shopkeeper through the narrow aisles stuffed to the rafters with every imaginable *thing,* and thought that perhaps she had indeed, if not slipped into Brigadoon, fallen down an enchanted rabbit hole.

His real name wasn't Plato, nor was his establishment officially Plato's Emporium, although that's what everyone called it. The sign above the storefront read Dooner Thurston's Variety. The townsfolk called Dooner Plato because of his deep and abiding love of the classics. Dressed in bib overalls, he didn't look the classics scholar, but Tess was quickly learning that, in this surprising little town, anything was possible.

"Here you go." Plato had stopped and had pulled a packet of white athletic socks from the shelf. "These'll do you." He raised white bushy eyebrows in question. "You plannin' to walk the green tonight?"

"Doesn't everyone?" Tess could guess the answer to that.

"Yup."

"Then I suppose I am, too. Doctor's orders."

Plato rubbed his chin and narrowed his eyes. "Ah, yes. Doc."

"Is something wrong?" Tess peered into the man's face. "Something I should know about?" There was an oddness about the way he'd said "Doc." Sort of sad and faraway.

"Noooo...." Plato continued his squinty-eyed contemplation. "It's just that Doc's had a far journey. Needs a little nudge now on the homestretch. Maybe, just maybe, you're the one can help him." He looked at her, and his faded blue eyes seemed to assess her capabilities.

"Mr....Plato, whatever do you mean?" Tess asked, perplexed. Rhune Sherman seemed most capable. In little need of any help from anyone. Least of all from her.

Plato reached out and laid a long-fingered hand lightly on her arm. His skin felt cool and papery smooth. "Ever hear the story of Aeneas?"

"Aeneas? Virgil's Aeneas? The classic?" He had said he loved the classics.

"That's the one." Plato removed his hand from Tess's arm and rubbed his jaw. "Well, our Doc is a mite like that Aeneas fellow."

Tess's eyes widened involuntarily. "How so?" This was not the conversation she'd expected.

"I reckon his stint in that hospital in Washington, D.C., was somewhat like the Trojan War. And I also reckon that along with his heroics, our Doc did some things that he wasn't too proud of. Just like Aeneas. You know...the flawed hero."

The hair on the back of Tess's neck stood on end. "Do you know this for a fact?"

"You mean has Doc come up and confessed to me?" Plato narrowed his eyes and looked hard at her. He shook his head. "Naw. But I can read people just as good as I can read a book. And Dr. Rhune Sherman is easy to read."

Tess scowled. "I was thinking just the opposite."

"Well, now, perhaps you're tryin' too hard." Plato chuckled softly. "Or ain't tryin' hard enough. Let me get you started...." He waggled the athletic socks in her face, then began the slow, tortuous route to the cash register. Over his shoulder he spoke to Tess in hushed dramatic tones as if he were telling an epic tale. "Doc's already completed his odyssey home. Although I'm not sure he himself realizes it. There've been some false starts, some dead ends, some detours. All of them elucidatin'." He reached the counter and an antique cash register and began to ring up her purchase.

Feeling more and more lost in some strange forgotten world, Tess waited impatiently for him to continue Rhune's mythical history. Quite frankly this was not the type of gossip she'd expected. She'd envisioned Rhune Sherman as many things, but never a classical hero.

"Battle scarred and journey weary, Doc's home at last," Plato said gently, looking up at Tess. "Now...he just needs a reason to stay home."

"Begging your pardon, sir," Tess replied, "but Dr. Sherman does not seem the beaten-down warrior you describe. He seems downright hale and hearty to me." He did. Tanned and healthy. Strong and able. Not to mention handsome. Too damned handsome.

Tess swallowed hard.

Leaning across the counter, Plato handed her the sales receipt. "Look in his eyes, sweetheart. Look in his eyes. Then you'll know what ole Plato's talkin' 'bout." He glanced down at her feet. "You gonna wear them puppies outa here?"

Her new shoes. She'd forgotten about the new shoes as she'd listened to this unexpected appraisal of Rhune Sherman. "Y-yes," she managed to stammer.

"Then put on a pair of these socks. Wouldn't want it to be said I caused a pretty lady discomfort."

Unable to think of a rejoinder to continue *any* thread of this conversation, Tess wordlessly picked up the athletic socks, then found her way back to where she'd left her dress shoes. She sat on the stool in the aisle in order to add the socks.

Discomfort. Unless she missed her guess, the sage Plato had indeed meant to emotionally discomfort her. With his story of Rhune. But why?

What had he meant when he'd compared Rhune to the flawed but heroic Aeneas? Why had he made such a point of it? And to her, of all people? The only fact of which she was certain was that, to discover the answers to her questions, she was *not* going to be gazing deeply into Dr. Rhune Sherman's eyes, as Plato had suggested. Already she'd glanced into those dark brown eyes once too often. A woman could get lost there.

Her sister had.

But Tess wasn't about to.

Having put on socks, she retied her sports shoes, tucked her dress shoes and the remaining socks under her arm and made her way carefully toward the front of the store.

Behind the counter, Plato, inscrutable, watched her. Suddenly his face broke into an elfin grin. *"Die dulci fruere."*

"I beg your pardon?"

He winked. "Have a nice day. It's Latin."

"Of course," she murmured, pushing through the doorway onto the sidewalk. Nothing—absolutely nothing—in this town was going to surprise her from this point on.

Rhune took the bed-and-breakfast veranda steps two at a time. He paused, however, before opening the front door, to remind himself that he was here merely to help a patient fill a prescription. A healthy evening walk around the village green. That was all. He'd be damned if he'd let that sexy little motorcycle ride this afternoon change the way he viewed Tess McQueen.

That completely understood, he opened the front door and stepped into the Drakes' foyer.

"Dr. Sherman!" Ida Drake bore down upon him before he could even close the door. "What is this I hear about you blowing up your home?"

Rhune shook his head. "Miss Ida. I did not blow up my home. Squirrels, woodpeckers and raccoons conspired to trash my home." He sighed heavily. "This town is determined to give me a far more explosive personality than I deserve."

"One might say his reputation precedes him," Tess McQueen offered from her position descending the grand staircase.

Rhune smiled. "I think it's more a case of my reputation exceeding me."

Ida Drake clapped her hands together in delight. "Sweet Hope does love a rascal. You should hear what they're saying about you at Whitlock Pharmacy." Quickly becoming serious, she leaned forward and gave Rhune's arm a motherly pat. "Dear boy, where will you stay now? Do you need a room here?"

Rhune noted the flicker of uneasiness that passed over Tess's face. "No," he replied. "While I clean up and secure the trailer, I'm living temporarily in the apartment above my office. It's comfortable, if empty. Suits the nomad in me."

Tess's uneasy expression turned to one of concern. "Surely you're not thinking of moving on, having promised your services to this town."

"Give me some credit, Ms. McQueen. I'm committed to my practice in Sweet Hope. It's my spirit that forever wanders."

She looked at him, wide-eyed, and he felt a little wide-eyed himself, having just candidly confessed something small but very private. He'd never been a particularly introspective man. He'd always been a doer who felt no need to explain his actions. Now, however, he wasn't sure why this near stranger's opinion of him counted, but, for some inexplicable reason, it did. And because it did, he'd exposed himself in part. Uncharacteristically.

Ida Drake reached out and again patted him gently on the arm. "You need a kindred spirit to wander with you...or perhaps a complementary spirit to ground you." She glanced at Tess and smiled sweetly. "Have a lovely walk, you two. I need to plan tomorrow's breakfast with the cook." She turned and swooped down the hallway, leaving only a lavender scent behind.

Rhune turned to Tess and found her watching him, one midnight dark eyebrow arched speculatively. Rhune started. He'd seen that dramatic pose before. On a younger woman. A woman the thought of whom triggered memories he'd just as soon bury.

Ghosts.

Ghosts he'd hoped to outrun.

Tess seemed suddenly to relax, and the disconcerting resemblance to that other woman disappeared.

He exhaled in relief.

"Shall we go?" she asked. "As you can see, I took your advice and visited Plato." She extended one leg.

Rhune's gaze slid down her body. Since the motorcycle ride this afternoon, she'd changed clothes. Merely a variation on a theme, however. Wearing a pristine white silky blouse with plum-colored slacks, she looked elegant and professional...except for her feet clad in athletic socks and a pair of brand-new sports shoes.

"Well?" She waggled her foot.

For a fleeting moment Rhune heard in her voice not the queenly woman but an eager girl. He wondered if, slipping on the new shoes, she'd slipped out of character as he had, briefly, earlier.

"I take it you've decided to be a good patient," he said, his voice sounding gruff. He cleared his throat. It was difficult concentrating with her so close.

"Let's just say I know when to fight and when to give." With a decidedly determined glint in her eyes, she squared her shoulders and moved past him toward the door.

Following, he caught just a whiff of that exotic woody fragrance he'd inhaled last night in her car. The scent disrupted his mental equilibrium even further. It was difficult to think of this woman as merely a patient.

Difficult but not impossible.

As he closed the door to the bed-and-breakfast behind them, he tried to concentrate on the possible. The possible and the necessary.

He caught up to her on the sidewalk and tried to let the quaint after-supper ritual relax him. There was no prettier town than Sweet Hope, Georgia, in the evening. And, as if it were a point of pride, most of the residents turned out in the evening to stroll Main Street and the village green. To greet their neighbors. To breathe deeply of the sweet honeysuckle and the dusky crape myrtle. To meander under the spreading oaks and the flowering mimosa and to relax.

Tess, however, had set an energetic, no-nonsense pace. He smiled to himself. Give her a week and he'd bet she'd slow that city gait to a country stroll with the best of them. Despite signs to the contrary, he suspected she could get the hang of relaxation.

"Hold on, there," he said, chuckling. "This isn't a marathon."

"You said *exercise,* Dr. Sherman." She increased her pace as if to deliberately challenge him.

"I meant exercise as in recreation. Not work."

They were walking so briskly that there was little time to stop when Homer Martin stepped out of the ice-cream parlor directly into their path. It was a wonder all three didn't end up wearing mint chocolate chip.

"Miz McQueen!" the older man exclaimed with a laugh. "If you drive as recklessly as you walk, no wonder you had a flat!"

The roses flared in Tess's cheeks. "I'm so sorry, Mr. Martin!"

"I'm just teasin' you, darlin'. Just teasin'. Wouldn't want to elevate your blood pressure, now, would we?" He looked contrite. "How are you feelin' this evening?"

"Fine, thank you." Tess's dignity quickly returned. "I'll feel much better, however, when I get my car back."

"What's the hurry?" Rhune put in. "You're under doctor's orders to stay put." He rolled his eyes at Homer, hoping the cagey mechanic would catch on.

Bristling, Tess glared at Rhune. "I think I can be trusted to decide if I need to use my car or not." She smiled stiffly at Homer. "Mr. Martin, will my car be ready tomorrow?"

Homer rubbed the back of his neck and looked properly remorseful. "'Fraid not."

"But it's only a flat!"

"Even so..." Homer shrugged his shoulders and slid Rhune a sly glance. "I'm shorthanded this week and backed up. I'm sure if you need anything outside walking distance, someone will give you a lift. Like Doc here."

Tess looked exasperated. "Why, tell me, would I wish to impose on Dr. Sherman?"

"You could catch up on some mighty entertaining tales." Homer winked broadly at Rhune. "Have you told her yet how you got those fifteen acres of yours?"

"Homer, you're not about to pull that old chestnut out of the fire, now, are you?"

Suddenly Tess looked interested. "How did you get your fifteen acres?"

Homer Martin cackled in glee. "Some would say how a very grateful older woman left him a heap of money in her will, so smitten was she with our Doc, here."

"Homer!" It was Rhune's turn to be exasperated. There was nothing the old man liked better than a grain of truth that could be Martinized—hybridized, planted and propagated. The man was more farmer than mechanic, and his best crop was myth.

Rhune looked at Tess, and her eyes were truly saucer wide. She couldn't possibly believe that tale. "Tess," he said, in case she did, "Arabella and I inherited, yes." He glowered at a smirking Homer. "But from an elderly *aunt*, who loved us both very much. As only a relative could."

"If you say so." Shaking his head, Homer turned. "But my version's a lot more interesting." He tipped an imaginary hat at Tess. "Evening, Miz McQueen. If he won't tell you the real story behind the fifteen acres, ask him to tell you about the time he met Missy Able." With a lick of his ice-cream cone, he headed across Main Street, his step jaunty and his eyes atwinkle.

Rhune turned to see Tess's reaction. "I'm the new kid on the block, so to speak." He rolled his eyes to make light of the whole conversation. "I get to be honorary grist for the town mill."

Tess narrowed her gaze and stared hard at him. "There's not a bit of truth to what he says?"

"Well, perhaps a bit." He held up his hands, not wanting to discuss Missy Able. "The less colorful parts, believe me." Now, that depended on who was doing the coloring.

It didn't look as if she did believe him, but she didn't pursue it further. Instead, she said, "If I'm not to have my car at my disposal anytime soon, maybe you could do me a favor."

"Name it." He was grateful to be off the inspection hook.

"I left my briefcase in my car. Perhaps this evening you'd drive over to Mr. Martin's garage and get it for me so that I could continue a project I was working on."

"I would prefer you got some rest after your walk tonight."

Her eyes clouded and the muscles in her jaw tensed. "Are you trying to run my life, Dr. Sherman?" She reached out her hand as if to steady herself, and rested the tips of her fingers on the flower box under the ice-cream parlor's plate-glass window. "Let me assure you I've always taken care of myself."

He was sure she had. She had spit and fire enough to take care of herself and anyone else who wandered into her path. And he certainly didn't want to run anyone's life other than his own. He was used to patching up and moving on. He didn't envision himself laying out long-term care, especially the emotional kind, for anyone.

So why was he now pressing one Tess McQueen? She was right. He was meddling beyond what was professional. But for the life of him he couldn't figure why... and couldn't seem to stop himself.

"Let me give you an opinion," he offered evenly. "Purely professional, of course. You seem to me an intensely focused woman. A workaholic, perhaps. And I think that's what landed you under my care in the first place. You need to lighten up. Take better care of yourself."

"What I think I need to do," Tess replied, cutting her words off crisply, "is find myself another doctor."

Rhune grinned. "I'm the only one in town. Now, you could travel down the road a piece to Sterling and the clinic there. Or you could head into Atlanta and hire yourself a fancy specialist...."

"Without a car? Highly unlikely."

Why did she bristle so at a little bit of banter? She certainly was far too intense for her own good. "You're set on making a mountain out of a molehill," he said wryly. "Your business in Sweet Hope is with Wally Buckminster. You can walk across the street to meet with him."

As he mentioned Wally's name, she flinched.

And as she flinched the strangest thing happened. From out of the flower box, against which Tess tapped her fingers impatiently, sprang a little anole, one of those bold and tenacious North American chameleons that Southern children so love to chase. No longer than three or four inches from head to tail, the tiny reptile sprang lightly from the purple, pink and white flowers onto the white sleeve of Tess's blouse. He sat, lime green except for his bubble-gum-pink chin pouch, and stared at Tess as she stared intently at Rhune.

He just bet the very dignified woman before him would not find this development amusing.

Rhune ticked off the options open to him. He could say casually, *Excuse me, but there's a small lizard on your arm,* and hope she wasn't the skittish city-slicker type. Or he could reach out and offhandedly brush at her arm and hope the regal Ms. McQueen didn't think he was making a pass at her. Or . . . he could try to distract her with idle conversation and hope the anole became bored with the chitchat and left of his own accord.

Rhune chose the last option. "Well . . . and how do you come to know old Wally? Family? School?"

Tess looked puzzled, then vaguely suspicious. "Why would I have to know him from before?"

"It just seems a little odd that Wally would import an efficiency expert—a stranger—all the way from Washington, D.C., when he could get a perfectly good stranger from closer. In Atlanta. Surely closer would cut down on expenses."

For a moment Tess actually seemed at a loss for words. She cleared her throat. She pursed her lips. She knit her brow.

And Rhune couldn't suppress the thought that she looked unduly beautiful in her intensity. He grinned. Beautiful, especially, with a nearly neon anole perched, now, on her shoulder in contrast.

Tess responded to his grin with irritation. "What is so amusing?"

"Tess . . . did you like bugs and snakes and crawly things as a child?"

Poised, the anole turned its head as if to hear her answer.

"Did anyone ever tell you, Rhune Sherman, that it's near impossible to carry on a sensible conversation with you?" She swept her hand up to brush back her hair. He knew the minute her peripheral vision picked up the little green lizard.

She turned her face toward her shoulder. Her violet eyes widened and darkened. Her mouth opened. As if mimicking her, the anole opened his mouth, then inflated his bubble-gum-pink chin pouch for good measure.

No sound came out of the anole's mouth, but Tess screamed.

Dear Lord, this was Friday fright night at the movies, and they were being invaded by little green creatures.

She reached out to steady herself as her knees buckled, and felt strong hands grasp her.

Her heart thumped wildly as she sank against Rhune's hard chest. The strangest feeling came over her that she was smack in the middle of a "Twilight Zone" episode. Doctors who looked like surfers. Merchants who spouted Latin. And little green...*things*...that dropped out of the sky into the middle of already bizarre conversations. This was the most inefficient, most impractical, most improbable town she'd ever come across.

It was not that she was ordinarily a swooning weakling. It was simply that she was a tried-and-true realist. But her experience so far with Sweet Hope and its doctor had been surreal at best.

"Good God, what was *that?*" she uttered finally, finding her tongue.

She felt the rumble of laughter deep inside the man who held her. "*That* was a harmless anole," he said, chuckling softly. "Kissing cousin to a chameleon."

She felt strong arms envelop her, hold her upright. "Harmless?"

His laughter increased. "Harmless to you. But the scare you gave him turned him pink and blue with purple polka dots, last I saw."

She struggled against his embrace. She was no shrinking violet. Not normally spooked by mice or spiders or the sight of blood. It's just that this *thing*—as with everything in this town—was so unexpected. She placed her hands flat against Rhune's chest and pushed hard. "I'm fine," she said briskly. "I don't need to be rescued."

He let her go, in part, but still held lightly to her upper arms. "But your heart is beating a mile a minute." His voice was low and husky.

She looked up into his eyes and saw mischief residing there. "How would you know?"

He grinned, and that disarming dimple deepened. "I'm the doctor, remember? I get paid to know about those things."

Funny, but his dimple didn't look like a doctor's dimple, and his silk-and-gravel voice didn't sound like a doctor's voice. This was a man. Unadorned by profession. Undiluted by civilization. A man looking deep into a woman's eyes.

She turned, uncomfortable in the shadow of his regard. She didn't need—didn't want—anyone's chivalrous protection. Especially not this man's. And she was no good at easy, flirtatious banter. She was, quite frankly, out of her element. This man—this Dr. Rhune Sherman—was as startling as the anole. And as quickly changeable. From one minute to the next she had no idea what to expect from him. Or how to deal with him.

She struggled mentally to get back to a world she recognized. "Our walk," she murmured, grasping at straws. "We seem to have forgotten our walk."

Silently he fell into stride beside her. She didn't dare look at him for fear she'd see amusement on his face. Or worse...satisfaction. If her sister could be believed, Rhune Sherman was no stranger to the practice of discomfiting women.

She walked and tried to ignore him, hoping he'd remember something he needed to do. Elsewhere. But he showed no signs of leaving her side. Nor did he give off any hint of being nonplussed at her silence. He called out to the residents who passed them, and they called back to him as if they welcomed the very sight of him. His tone of voice with all was open and friendly, without a trace of condescension, flirtation or disrespect. He seemed to like being in this tiny town, and seemed liked in return. At this moment he seemed no more a rascal than the boy next door.

Certainly not the utter scoundrel her sister had described.

She had to believe Chelsey, however. As challenging a child as she'd been to raise, she was family. More than that, the only family left to Tess. She wanted to avenge the wrong done her sister. Wanted to hold Rhune Sherman accountable for his actions. But...

Tess McQueen prided herself on being fair.

What had she seen of Rhune since she'd been in town? Perhaps a slightly unorthodox physician. A man who, with grace and good humor, let wild rumor slide easily off his back. A man who thought fun should be part of daily life. There were discrepancies here between the heartless playboy Chelsey insisted he was and the gentle, caring man she herself had observed. Eminently fair, Tess would wait and watch further before she determined her course of action.

"Come on." Rhune pointed across Main Street at the village green. "I want you to meet my sister and her family." Pride and genuine affection seeped into his words.

Tess's confusion increased. Had this man truly hurt her own sister?

She had no time to think further on it, for Rhune grasped her elbow firmly and guided her across the street toward a crew erecting scaffolding and red, white and blue bunting. Children as well as adults worked on the project, which had the air more of party than of labor. For an instant Tess envied the residents their easy connection. Their sense of belonging. Suddenly the idea of sending down roots enticed her.

"Doc!" a chorus of voices called out, and Rhune waved in return.

"Over here," he said to Tess. He didn't remove his hand from her arm, and his touch seared her skin even through the fabric of her blouse.

They stopped before a ladder upon which a diminutive woman dressed in an unusual, gauzy outfit stood, stapling bunting to a finished area of scaffolding. Catching sight of Rhune, she smiled from ear to ear. "Well, if it isn't the prodigal brother." When the woman spoke, Tess could have sworn she heard the tinkle of bells.

Gallantly, Rhune offered his hand so that his sister could dismount. "Belle, I'd like you to meet Tess McQueen. She's working with Wally Buckminster this week. Tess, my sister, Arabella O'Malley."

The two women exchanged pleasantries and handshakes.

"And I'm Boone O'Malley." An enormous blond bear of a man stepped to Belle's side, then reached out to give Rhune a playful punch. "This scoundrel's brother-in-law."

A breathtakingly beautiful little girl ducked underneath Boone's legs and popped up jubilantly before Rhune, extending her cupped and closed hands. "And I'm Margaret. Uncle Rhune, guess what I caught?"

Rhune bent down and tried to peer between her fingers. "What, girlfriend?"

"A 'nole," she whispered, wide-eyed. "Mama says I can take him home and keep him in my terrarium."

Rhune chuckled. "*If* you can hold on to him till you get home."

Margaret looked up at Tess. "They're *fast*."

At the girl's solemn declaration, Tess had to smile. "I know," she agreed. "I just had a close encounter with one myself."

"Did you catch him?"

Rhune winked and ruffled Margaret's chestnut curls. "No. I caught Miss Tess."

Genuine concern spread across the child's face. "Did you faint, ma'am? I've seen ladies faint on cartoons."

Tess cut Rhune a quick warning glance. "No, I didn't faint. The anole just startled me and I...jumped. And bumped into your uncle."

"Sure felt like I caught you," Rhune persisted, his eyes twinkling.

Boone shook his head. "If I had to believe one or the other of you, I'd have to believe Tess. Ole Doc here's famous for chasing the girls, but he's too cagey to ever really catch one."

Tess arched one eyebrow. "Really?"

"Fiddle-dee-dee, Boone O'Malley!" Belle laid a reassuring hand on Tess's arm. "It's merely my brother's runaway reputation." With her other hand she reached out and gently pinched Rhune's cheek. "Tess McQueen, you're in good hands with this man."

Tess flushed. "I wouldn't say I was in his hands," she protested. "I'm only in town temporarily. And I think I'm beyond needing Rhune's services as a doctor."

"Good." Belle flashed a dazzling smile. "I wouldn't want to suggest anything improper."

"I beg your pardon?" Tess had suddenly lost the thread of this conversation.

"I'm glad you're no longer doctor and patient. If you were, I couldn't invite the two of you to dinner socially, now, could I?"

Tess felt the heat of the flush extend from her cheeks to her ears. "I'm afraid I won't be in town long enough to accept social engagements...of any kind. But I thank you." She felt at a loss.

Boone put his arm around Belle and drew her to him. "Now I'm the one to have to tell you to pay no never mind to my spouse. The O'Malley women are incorrigible matchmakers."

Belle gave her husband a playful swat.

"And you haven't even met my mother, Alice Rose, or my daughter, Cathryn," Boone added.

"Oh, no!" wailed Margaret suddenly. "My 'nole got away!"

"Then, by all means, let's find it," Tess offered, bending quickly to look at the ground. Anything, even searching for a scampy lizard, was better than having herself matched with Rhune Sherman.

"Sorry, folks, but we're out of here." Rhune slipped his arm around Tess's shoulders, pulled her to him, then turned her toward the sidewalk. "I'd better get her out of here, folks." He winked. "Anoles are drawn to her fancy city clothes."

Tess barely had time to utter goodbye before she and Rhune were again walking at a brisk clip, she more a hostage than a willing participant. "Now, you just wait a minute, Rhune Sherman!" she exclaimed, stopping abruptly and shrugging out of his grasp.

"What?" He stopped, too, and turned a dimpled grin on her.

She jammed her hands on her hips and glared at him. "Not only did you imply back there that I was a simpering lass prone to fainting at the sight of a little ole lizard, but you've manipulated the pace of this evening from the get-go."

His grin intensified. "What's your point, Tess?"

Her point, she suddenly thought, and one that she couldn't very well admit to him, was that whenever she was in his presence she became . . . well, swept away in his wake. Both physically and emotionally. As with the motorcycle ride earlier. As with this forced walk now. And because of that, her anger was as much directed at herself as at the man who stood before her, smiling and apparently enjoying himself.

"Ooh . . ." She shook her head in disbelief. "You are . . . something else!"

He cocked his head to one side. "Because I wanted to accompany you on your first walk? Because I wanted you to meet some of the good folk of Sweet Hope? Because—"

"*Because,*" she flared, interrupting him, "like all men, you have to be in control."

His dark brown eyes widened. He paused before speaking and simply looked at her, one corner of his mouth quirked in a half grin. "Tess McQueen." He said her name so softly, so sensuously, drawing out the s and the n sounds so much—too much—like a caress, that she paused in her anger. "Do you know what I wish for you?"

That pesky swept-away feeling washed over her. "What?" The word came out barely a whisper. A surprised whisper. Tess couldn't quite believe Rhune Sherman could defuse her ire so effortlessly. Could make her go absolutely still. Awaiting the next development in this all-too-strange scenario.

He reached out and slowly brushed a strand of hair away from her face. "I wish that you would lose a little of that efficient self-control of yours. That you would fall under the spell of Sweet Hope. And of Belle. And Boone. And Margaret. And the dozens of other flat-out wonderful people here.''

His deep brown gaze kept her immobilized. Unable to look away, she saw a new expression in the shadows of his eyes. A flicker of longing. Before it passed, it flamed, and she wondered if the searching intensity she'd just seen was the hidden Rhune Sherman of whom the merchant Plato had spoken. If so, that hidden Rhune was a man of passion, yes, but a man in desperate need of something.

Or someone.

She shuddered. That someone could not possibly be her.

''I wish,'' Rhune said, his voice rumbling hypnotically, ''that you would forget for a moment about control. About who leads and who follows. And just enjoy the moment. I wish...'' His fingertips brushed her cheek. ''I wish...''

Good Lord, it looked for all the world as if he were going to kiss her.

Chapter Four

Rhune had never wanted to kiss a woman as much as he now wanted to kiss Tess McQueen. And that realization alone made him stop dead in his tracks.

As much as her lush, slightly parted lips tempted him, he couldn't. Shouldn't. Wouldn't. This was Sweet Hope, Georgia, not Washington, D.C. This was his new leaf. Tess McQueen was leaving in a week or less, and he was finished with short-term affairs.

Her thick, dark lashes fluttered, and for a moment Rhune thought he could see deep in her eyes just a hint of uncertainty. Of vulnerability. She might insist that she could take care of herself, but there was a part of her that lay unprotected. He'd be damned if he'd be the one to take advantage.

He realized with a start that his fingertips still rested against her cheek. That she'd made no attempt to brush them away. He pulled them away now and felt them tingle as they left her soft, smooth skin.

She let out a little puff of breath, and the spell was broken.

Being chivalrous was not all it was cracked up to be.

"I'm sorry if I seemed controlling," he said by way of lassoing reality. "I guess I just wanted you to sample a little of all this town has to offer. I didn't mean to control you, but I plead guilty to hurrying you."

"Apology accepted," she said hesitantly, smoothing her hair back away from her face. As she did so, he could have sworn her fingers lingered for a moment on her cheek where he had touched her.

From experience he could read the signs. There was no doubt that he could have kissed her earlier, and that she would have kissed him back. The moment had been that right. The realization infused his whole body with warmth.

"You were right, too, earlier," she admitted with obvious reluctance. "I generally operate in a business mode, keeping track of who's leading and who's following. I rarely slow down enough to savor the moment. I've learned to be wary."

Not wary enough, lady, he thought. You nearly let a stranger kiss you.

"Sometimes the wariness comes out as edginess," she added. "I'm sorry. Too."

"Shall we start all over?" he asked evenly to cover up the uncomfortable lingering feeling that he still wanted to kiss her.

"How's that?"

"The evening's still young. You haven't had much of a walk. How about once around the green? And I won't stop you or take a detour unless you want it." He took a step backward and raised his hands in a sign of noninterference. And peacemaking. "Later I'll swing by Homer's garage to get your briefcase out of your car."

She smiled, and her whole face came to life. A beautiful, tempting animation that wouldn't let him forget the *almost* kiss. He stuffed his hands into his pants pockets to quell his desire to reach out and touch her.

"I'd like that," she said, her voice husky, as if more in answer to his thought of touching her than to his verbal offer of a walk. "The walk and the briefcase," she added.

Something had changed between them, and he wasn't sure what it was. He was only certain that their established edginess had gone for a moment, replaced by a softness of heart-wrenching proportions.

She turned slowly with a tiny smile on her face, then chose the pathway that cut diagonally across the village green. He followed, feeling like a smitten schoolboy. This had to stop. This feeling that he would like to lose himself in this woman's kiss. In her embrace. That he would like to know what it felt like to thread his fingers in her thick, dark hair. That he would like to hear the sounds she would make when she was happily aroused.

He pulled his fantasies up short. The rush to instant gratification in the past had never led to satisfaction. It had, in fact, sometimes led to pain.

He scowled now as he thought of one instance in particular. A case where his consenting-adults philosophy of life had backfired—with unpleasant consequences.

No, he wasn't about to rush headlong into anything either un-thought-out or transitory. And kissing Tess McQueen would be both.

"I liked your sister." Tess's voice startled him. "She seems to think the world of you."

"Yeah, she does," he grumbled, suddenly feeling out of sorts. "Sometimes to a fault."

Tess cocked her head abruptly. "Whatever do you mean?" There was an unusual flash of recognition in her eyes.

"I mean that there have been times I haven't been exactly worthy of her unconditional love." It was too true. "But she's Belle. And she's my older sister. And that makes her blind to my faults."

He shifted uncomfortably as he walked. What was it about Tess that pulled these miniconfessions out of him? That kicked his conscience into high gear? Whatever it was, he wasn't used to it, and it made him feel brusque and ill at ease.

A thoughtful expression came over Tess's face. "I have a younger sister... and I guess you could say I'm sometimes blind to her faults."

"Like leaving you stranded with a bald spare tire?"

"That and..." The small frown on her face made it appear as if she were about to confess something uncomfortable, too. But suddenly she shook her head and laughed, the sound of which didn't ring quite true. "Oh, the usual sibling stuff. Borrowing my clothes. Meddling in my private life. I'm sure she'll grow out of it. She's only nineteen."

Tess made her sound so young. Nineteen. Rhune felt a jolt of regret course through him. He'd known a nineteen-year-old who'd been going on a sophisticated twenty-nine. And his experience with her had almost cost him his career. He tried to push those troubling thoughts from his mind.

"So, as the younger sibling," Tess asked briskly, "what do you recommend we older siblings do to make this a better relationship?"

"Honestly?"

She cast him a prolonged, probing glance. "Yes. Honestly. I'd like to know."

"Keep the unconditional love. But add a little realism. A little tough love, if you will."

Tess looked surprised. "You actually wanted your sister to be tougher on you?"

"Not at the time, I didn't." He shook his head ruefully. "Not at nineteen, certainly. But now...."

"From the perspective of the ripe old age of...?" The corner of her mouth tipped up. Pert. Challenging.

"Thirty-two." He grinned. "*Now,* as a thirty-two-year-old geezer, I realize I would have been better off if she hadn't fought so many of my battles for me. If she hadn't made so many excuses for me."

"Perhaps she wanted to protect you. Because she loved you so much."

"Sure she did. But her good intentions often backfired. I came to dismiss thoughts of the consequences of my actions in everything but my studies." He rolled his eyes for emphasis. "Hey, why worry? Belle would bail me out." He stiffened. "Of course, that was when I was a kid."

Now he faced the consequences of his actions alone. Like a man. Or did he?

"Of course." Narrowing her eyes, Tess gazed off into the distance. When she spoke, it was almost as if to herself. "But what if you had legitimately needed bailing out? What if you had really needed help against someone unscrupulous?"

"Call me a cynic, but in my experience there are always two sides to a story. If a person grows up thinking he or she is always in the right—totally—and that someone else will clean up his or her messes, why should he or she bother to make the effort to ever think about the other guy in any interaction—business, political or personal?"

"You're saying that when older members of a family constantly help the younger members, the younger don't learn to stand on their own two feet?"

"That, and they grow into self-centered people." He scowled. "Not a very attractive trait."

Suddenly she stopped and turned to confront him. "Do you consider yourself such a person? Self-centered?"

"Not in my work, no. Definitely not in my work."

"But in your personal life?" Her look was strangely gentle, as if she wanted him, for some unknown reason, to be all right. All right and upright.

"I'm working on it," he said, his words unusually curt. He didn't mean to be rough with her, but here she was again, wresting confessions from him. The woman would have made a terrific grand inquisitor.

She sighed. "I'd like to see signs that my sister is at least working on it. But maybe nineteen's too young." She turned a look of appeal upon him. "Do you think?"

"You really worry about her, don't you?"

"Yes," she answered wistfully. "We're all each other has."

"Your parents?"

"They died in a plane crash when I was twenty-two and my sister was nine. I've raised her." There was absolutely no note of self-pity in her voice. Only cool, clear fact.

"And, as a single parent, made your way through the business world?" The thought of being an instant new parent at twenty-two—of a nine-year-old, no less—made his head spin. The thought of scraping out a high-pressured career on top of that boggled the mind. This elegant woman who stood before him was turning out to be one tough cookie. He had to admire her grit.

"Work and family." She smiled. "They've been my life."

"What about something just for you?" He couldn't quite imagine such single-minded devotion to duty. Yes, he'd given his all to his medical studies and practice. That's why his few free hours had been so explosive. He couldn't picture getting by without an escape valve. A release.

Her smile stiffened. She looked down at her hands, then back up into his eyes. A faint blush of roses colored her cheeks. "Do you mean did I have a love life?"

"Well, no, it didn't have to mean that...but, yes, that could be part of it." His tongue refused to work properly. "I didn't mean to pry. I just thought that work and family sounded pretty intense."

"It's okay." She seemed to be letting him off the hook. "I dated. But I was careful to break things off before anything got serious. Not too many men are interested in a ready-made family."

"I don't know if that's a fair assessment."

"Maybe not. Maybe a fairer assessment would be that I was afraid to share my sister with anyone. She's all I have of real family."

The look of unguarded honesty in her eyes made him start.

"I guess that could make anyone pretty intense," he offered, not knowing what else to say.

She didn't answer, but began to walk again, this time more slowly. A stroll rather than a hike.

"Older sisters," he said to break the silence. "Can't live with 'em . . ."

"Can't shoot 'em?" she asked softly.

"Hey . . ." He reached out and touched her arm to stop her. "Don't be so hard on yourself. I bet you've been one hell of an older sister."

She looked up at him and smiled tentatively. "Thanks," she said. "I mean it."

"No problem."

As she gazed up at him, a genuine look of gratitude on her face, a dangerous thought crossed his mind. Tess McQueen needed a stronger prescription than evening walks around the village green. If his diagnosis was correct, she needed at least a week's dose of fun. The motorcycle riding, fishing, windsurfing kind of fun that always unjangled his over-worked mind and body.

And being the doctor, he was in the right position to administer her rehabilitation.

Without a thought to the consequences, he asked, "Would you like to go to the lake with me tomorrow?"

Her eyes widened, but almost without hesitation she breathed, "Yes!"

In her room at the bed-and-breakfast, Tess, with a great deal of irritation, pulled on the shorts and T-shirt she'd just purchased at Plato's Emporium. She was getting to be quite the regular at that establishment. And not quite a voluntary regular. The cheerful morning sun pouring like honey through the bedroom window only darkened her mood.

She was supposed to be investigating Dr. Rhune Sherman. Conversations. Possibly a business lunch or two. An occasional impersonal walk around the village green. She was *not* supposed to be preparing for a morning at the lake *alone* with him.

How had she let him talk her into this?

She didn't have to look far for the answer. She had one vulnerability, and only one—her sister and her own desire to do right by Chelsey.

Chelsey had always been a handful.

Sometimes Tess hesitated and wondered if indeed she'd done a good job raising her younger sibling. Last night she'd let that hesitation show. And then, in an unguarded moment, she'd let Rhune reassure her. And in a second weak moment, this of gratitude, she'd agreed to an outing. What an extraordinarily dangerous chain of events. With an outcome she could ill afford.

She would have to be much more wary in the future.

In the meantime, she looked in the mirror and was startled by the unfamiliar woman who stared back at her. This woman was not the usual pearls-and-silk efficiency expert who greeted her in the glass every morning. This woman, in sports clothes, with her hair pulled back in a ponytail—a *ponytail,* for goodness sakes—looked as if she were about to go for a run in the park. Enjoy some recreation. Play. Have fun.

Where in heaven's name had this total stranger come from in less than forty-eight hours?

Tess shook her head, fascinated by her unfamiliar reflection. Sweet Hope, Georgia, certainly did make a body do some strange things.

The phone rang, and she picked it up absently.

"Sis? Chelsey!" Her sister didn't even give Tess a chance to speak. "Anything new?"

"Good morning, Chelsey. I'm fine, thank you," Tess replied deliberately. Once, just once, she'd like her sister to think before she dashed headlong into anything. A conversation, even. "And, no, there's nothing new. Just an old, recurring, problematic thought."

"Which is?"

"I'm not sure we've located the right man."

"Get serious!" Chelsey hooted. "What would make you say that?"

Tess felt a twinge of disloyalty, but the truth as she'd seen it was the truth. She couldn't remain silent. "This man is nothing like you described, Chelsey. He's obviously proud of his career as a doctor. He has a genuine concern for people. The entire town seems to have a soft spot in its collective heart for the man they call Doc. And aside from a healthy belief in fun, he hasn't done anything that strikes me as heartless or underhanded." There, she'd said it.

Chelsey's voice went icy. "Are you saying I lied?"

"Maybe this is an altogether different man." Tess knew her response sounded weak.

"With a moniker like Rhune Sherman, how many could there be?" It sounded as if Chelsey was drumming her fingernails impatiently on the receiver. "Not likely, sis. Either you haven't followed the guy's trail well enough, or he's got you bamboozled."

An ugly thought crossed Tess's mind. "Chelsey, you did confront him with news of your pregnancy, didn't you?"

"Would I be so upset if he didn't know?"

Tess could spot an evasive answer when she heard one. It suddenly struck her that she'd been placed in a patently unfair position. "Perhaps you should come down here to look out for your own interests," she replied tartly, her patience wearing thin. "Or at least be with me when I confront him."

"Come on, Tess," her sister coaxed. "We agreed the element of surprise would be most effective. Plus, you have all that vacation time, while I'm just now carving out my career. It would be professional suicide for me to take days off now."

Tess sighed. Some vacation. "Perhaps we'll know more with the investigator's report," she admitted. "He promised me something—anything—tomorrow."

"I'll call you then. And sis?" Chelsey's voice held that unmistakable poised-on-the-brink-of-asking-a-favor tone.

"Yes?"

"Do you think you could stick close to your room and wait for my call?"

Typical. Tess held her tongue. "I'll call you. Promise. Take care."

"You're a doll. Bye!" Chelsey hung up before Tess had a chance to answer.

An unnerving thought flitted through her consciousness. This was a child about to have a child.

Placing the receiver back on the phone, Tess suddenly felt weary. She was not trying to thwart her sister's quest for justice if she had indeed been wronged. It was just that, as she'd said earlier, she hadn't seen the man Chelsey described. She picked up the new bathing suit that lay on the bed and headed for the door. Perhaps, alone with her at the lake today, the real Rhune Sherman would reveal himself.

A part of Tess wished, however, that Chelsey's urban playboy would remain hidden beneath the country Doc she herself had observed since arriving in Sweet Hope.

Descending the grand staircase, she saw Rhune waiting below in the foyer, dressed in shorts and a T-shirt that read I Fish, Therefore I Am, grinning up at her in a way that made her pulse quicken. Her previous wariness began to ease, leaving her with a delicious expectancy. A sudden thought of riding that big Harley made her look forward to this morning after all.

That nagging feeling of disloyalty to Chelsey slithered around her conscience. Pricked her unmercifully.

"Why, Ms. McQueen," Rhune drawled, "you do have legs!"

Tess grinned to make light of the blush she felt creep into her cheeks. "I surprised old Plato, too," she replied, coming to a standstill before Rhune.

"*Old* Plato?" Rhune's eyebrows shot up in exaggerated surprise. "You work fast, girl. He only lets a select few call him old Plato."

"We're best buddies." She chuckled softly, recalling the eagerness with which the merchant had wanted to discuss the new doctor in terms of heroic struggle. "He's spinning an epic tale for me. In installments. Yesterday the listening fee was a pair of sports shoes. Today play clothes. Tomorrow... who knows? He's making a new woman out of me, this Plato. I'll be made over and with a classics education, to boot."

His clear, observant eyes held a hint of mischief. "I told you Sweet Hope would get hold of you, then change you."

"Is that what happened to you?" Suddenly, feeling too at ease in his presence, she turned the conversation in a direction that might produce some information. That might provide a rationale for her keeping company with the disconcerting doctor. Was his decision to leave D.C. choice, plain and simple? In answer to the call of small-town living. Or—a dark suspicion crossed her mind—had he been driven here?

She saw no flicker in his eyes that might constitute a guilty conscience. "I came here," he said candidly, "to turn my life around."

"And has it worked?"

He grinned, and his dimple deepened. "Let's just say I'm a work in progress." He indicated the door. "Ready?" Obviously, he'd just put a roadblock on her avenue of questioning.

Tess moved toward the door—but was she really ready to be alone with this puzzling man? Stepping onto the veranda, she had to admit that she'd never done anything quite as impulsive as placing herself—alone—in his company.

She halted when she didn't see the big black motorcycle.

"Come on." He took her arm and guided her down the steps. "There are more people I want you to meet."

"More people?" Why did nothing in this town turn out as expected?

They stopped in front of the open door of a large church bus parked at the curb. The painted script on the side proclaimed it from Grace Everlasting. The laughter and merriment inside confirmed that today it was being used as a youth bus.

"After you," Rhune said, bowing gallantly and indicating the bus door.

She couldn't disguise the look of utter surprise that crossed her face.

Rhune chuckled. "Why, Ms. McQueen, you didn't think I was going to take you out to the lake today *unchaper-oned,* did you, now?" His eyes twinkled merrily. "We've barely been introduced."

Tess didn't quite know what she'd expected. But it certainly hadn't been a church bus load of kids. "Wh...?" she began, then faltered, unable even to formulate a question.

"Doc's Club," he said simply, as if that answered everything. "Come on. I'll introduce you to the gang."

With trepidation Tess entered the bus. Immediately the chatter and laughter subsided, and she felt a dozen pairs of eyes staring at her. Suddenly what looked like an assortment of dirty rags lumbered up the aisle and threw itself upon her.

"Dog!" the entire bus load of children shouted.

"Down!" Rhune commanded, and the pile of rags collapsed at Tess's feet. "This is Dog, my sister's charity project," he explained. "He's our mascot."

"I see," Tess squeaked, feeling suddenly overwhelmed. "How nice." Her voice trailed off in disbelief.

"Not quite the adjective I'd use to describe this bag of bones." Rhune bent around Tess to scratch the happily panting creature. "He'll be your slave by the end of the day. Now, to introduce you to my superstars..."

Tess heard his introductions through a muted haze. She had definitely slid too far down the rabbit hole. This was beyond Wonderland.

Rhune sat high in a tree and grinned as he watched Tess, on the dock, helping a young girl bait a hook. He had to admit he'd thrown the elegant efficiency expert a curve, but after her initial surprise she'd stepped to the plate and homered.

The kids loved her.

The children were part of a big brother-type group that Rhune and the local pastor, Jacob Matthews, had formed.

Rhune was officially the big brother. More often than not, he felt like one of the kids.

Lord, with her hair pulled back in a ponytail and dressed in shorts and T-shirt, Tess looked like a kid too. Who would have believed the change in her appearance? Who would have believed she could have survived the swirl and chaos of twelve preteen kids and one flea-bitten mutt? But she had. With aplomb.

He turned to the job at hand—securing a thick rope to the largest branch of a hundred-year-old oak that sat on a rise on the edge of his pond. It was going to make one heck of a Tarzan swing. He wiped the perspiration from his brow. Even perched in the leafy shade, he felt the July morning heat begin to wilt him. A devilish thought crossed his mind. Maybe, under the pretense of testing the swing, he could be first in line. He could use a refreshing dip.

If only to cool off the thoughts he'd been having about one lovely, long-legged, extremely adaptable Ms. Tess McQueen.

It had floored him how he couldn't dismiss her from his thoughts. It wasn't as if she'd encouraged his attentions in other than a professional capacity. Hell, she'd even resisted his professional attention. And when she'd finally accepted his company in small doses, he had the feeling that her guard was up. There was a distinct edginess to even the best of their moments together. So it wasn't a matter of attraction in the traditional sense. But in the short space of time she'd been in town, she'd drawn him out as no other person had done before. Not even his sister, Belle. With Tess he'd articulated little but deep and usually hidden aspects of his personality. Why, he'd slipped into introspection more in the past couple of days than he had before in his entire life.

That was enough to overheat any man.

There. He thumped the rope, wrapped and knotted securely now around the tree limb. That should be able to hold an elephant. First checking his pockets to make sure he'd left the keys to the bus *in* the bus, he swung himself from the branch to the rope, then slithered down the rope and dropped into the pond's spring-fed, chilling embrace. He surfaced and easily cut through the water toward the dock where Tess and a half dozen kids waited.

He knew how to get Tess alone. "Rope swing's ready!" he shouted, then chuckled at the sight of the mad scramble that ensued.

Tess stood on the now-empty dock, and waved him away. "Don't come any closer, Rhune Sherman, or we'll spend the rest of the day untangling you from these fishing lines."

"Then you come in. Use the boat landing."

"There's no place to change into my bathing suit."

"Swim as you are."

"In my clothes?" She wrinkled her nose.

She was obviously the-right-tool-for-the-right-job kind of person. The-right-article-of-clothing-for-the-right-activity kind of woman. In short, practical. Loaded with common sense. Rhune could just bet she was the type of person who had a very specific utensil in her kitchen for each cooking task. He bet she'd never flipped her eggs with one of those nice thick inserts from the Sunday paper.

"They'll dry," he called out, grinning. Hell, she'd made him, with his miniconfessions, step out of his normal modus operandi; it'd be fun to see her step out of hers. "Come on. We'll swim to the float and watch the kids on the swing."

"Come on, Miss Tess," shouted a boy from the bluff. He held the Tarzan rope in his hands. "You and Doc can rate us, like in the Olympics." With a whoop he grasped the rope and swung far out over the pond. Letting go, he did a cannonball that sent spray almost to the dock.

"Come on, Miss Tess," coaxed Rhune, rolling her name sensuously on his tongue. He turned his back on her and started swimming to the float.

Not having heard her enter the pond, he was surprised to suddenly find her abreast of him, her strokes, long, strong and clean, cutting the water. She was a powerful swimmer. And why should that surprise him? He'd begun to suspect that anything Tess McQueen attempted, she did well. He added an extra effort to his kick, and the two of them reached the float at the same time.

Pulling herself easily onto the free-floating dock, Tess leaned back on her elbows in the sunshine, smiling, fully clothed, sleek and glistening.

And too damned attractive for her own good.

Rhune looked away. She would have been less sexy in a bathing suit.

"I thought you didn't frequent gyms," he said, his voice raspy in an attempt to cover up his overworked imagination.

"I don't. But I've always loved to swim. I guess it's like riding a bicycle—you never forget."

Her voice beside him was honey rich and low and very disconcerting. Rhune began to think this getting her alone idea had been a mistake. He tried to concentrate on the laughter of the kids and his responsibilities as a lifeguard.

She chuckled. "You never did tell me how we ended up here with a church bus of twelve kids."

This question required a straight answer. He could handle that. "The bus belongs to Grace Everlasting. The pastor and his wife, Jacob and Cathryn Matthews, are friends of mine. I was looking to form a club of sorts. Big brother and a few rug rats. Jacob suggested I take on some of the middle schoolers in Grace Everlasting."

"Why specifically this age group?"

"He said they were the toughest. The church runs a lot of programs. They can scare up tons of volunteers for the little kids and then the high schoolers. But people tend to shy away from this age group. Their newly emerging hormones make them mini Jekyll-and-Hydes." He shrugged. "I guess I can identify with that."

"Are your hormones raging, Dr. Sherman?"

Surprised, he turned to look at her and saw a mischievous grin on her face. Surely she wasn't teasing....

Andy Parsons saved the day by popping up out of the water at the edge of the float. "Come on!" he yelped. "You just gotta try that swing!"

Rhune looked back at Tess. "If you gotta, you gotta...."

Her violet eyes flashed an unmistakable challenge. "I'll race you to the shore."

What in blazes had gotten into the regal Ms. McQueen?

What had gotten into her?

Even raising Chelsey, Tess hadn't let herself get so involved in play. With Chelsey, she'd always acted the mature parent. Guiding. Instructing. Encouraging. Especially because Chelsey had been such a rambunctious, ever-testing child, the process of raising her hadn't left Tess much room for letting go.

She pulled herself out of the water and scampered up the bank to where a girl held out the rope swing for her. She shook the excess water off her as she'd seen Dog do earlier, then laughed aloud. What would the members of The Reserve think if they could see her now? The Reserve was the staid country club outside Washington to which Tess belonged but seldom had time to retreat. She knew for a fact that one wasn't allowed to swim there in one's clothing. Nor shake oneself at the pool's edge like a dog.

"Take a running start," the girl insisted, shivering certainly not from cold but from undiluted eagerness. "It's some ride, Miss Tess! Some ride!"

Tess grasped the thick rope in her hands and shivered slightly herself. This was craziness. She was supposed to be checking up on Rhune Sherman, not swinging like Jane through the jungle.

"Go on," a deep, rumbling voice behind her fairly purred. "I dare you."

She turned and looked directly into Tarzan's eyes.

The running start she took was as much to escape Rhune's smoldering gaze as it was to enjoy the simple pleasures of a rope swing. Abruptly, her feet left the ground and she swung out over the sparkling water. She clung to the rope with every ounce of strength in her. For a woman who prided herself in being firmly grounded in her everyday life, the sensation of flying intoxicated her. As it had on the motorcycle the other day. She saw the entire world from a different perspective. Tensions diminished, as did Rhune and the children on the bank.

She swooped in a long, low arc out over the water and felt the breeze slither over her wet skin.

"Jump!" came the encouragement from the shore.

But she didn't want to jump. She wanted to fly.

She hung on and felt the rope reach its zenith, then twist and begin to descend on its return to the shore. Her stomach flip-flopped. Her spirits soared. She tilted back her head and watched the puffy clouds whirl dizzyingly above her. She laughed aloud and pitied the members of The Reserve who had nothing but a stiff diving board and an unyielding concrete rectangle of aqua to entertain them. She saw the children on the bank scatter, shrieking with delight, as she swept down upon them.

Then suddenly she felt strong arms around her, felt the heat of Rhune's hard body up against her, heard him growl in her ear, "That's called hogging the swing."

She giggled, then opened her eyes wide at the strangeness of that sound in her own throat.

He let her feet touch the ground—barely—as he still held her tight. To the kids he said, "Well? Shall we kick her to the end of the line?"

"No! No!" a creative lad shouted, dancing around the adults. "Ride with her this time, and *make* her jump! Tickle her if she won't let go!"

"Yes!" came the chorus.

"Doubles it is!" Rhune declared in a swashbuckling tone that Tess could have sworn she'd recently heard in an old late-night movie.

"What are you planning to do?" she squeaked, breathless from his proximity and the hot hold he had on her.

His eyes sparked devilishly. "I'm planning to give you the ride of your life. Hang on."

She barely had time to wrap her arms and legs securely around the thick rope before he pulled her back as if she were nothing. With an earsplitting whoop, he took a running start and propelled her toward the pond. Just as the ground disappeared from under her feet, she felt him grasp the rope above her head, felt him wrap his legs around her middle.

"That's to insure you'll jump at the right time," he shouted, laughing.

There was no escaping him. No escaping his pure physical strength. No escaping his zest for life. No escaping the attraction she felt for this mad doctor.

But as she was flung into space and felt the freedom of flight, escape was the last thought on her mind.

To the cheers of the children on the bank, they swung out over the water, and this time Tess shrieked with glee. He'd promised her the ride of her life, and he hadn't been far short of the mark.

"Get ready!" Rhune called out. "Now! Let go, Tess! Let go!"

She did, as the rope was at its farthest point out over the pond.

He did, too, and they fell together into the pond with a splash that brought raucous shouts of approval from the shore.

As the cold and wet enveloped them, Tess felt Rhune's hands slide down her body and away, leaving a searing trail that defied the chilly water. She opened her eyes under water and felt that same liberating sensation as on the back of the motorcycle and high up on the rope swing. The sun cut through the clear green depths in shafts, giving everything an enchanted cast. She felt something brush her leg, whirled and saw a grinning Rhune slicing the water like a playful otter. He winked and slid by her, sending bubbles racing to the surface. She kicked and followed him. As she broke the surface right next to him, she gasped and filled her lungs with the hot, sweet summer air.

Exhilaration drenched her.

Never before had she felt so alive.

He reached for her and, laughing, pulled her close up against him. Tight. "Was that the ride of your life, Tess McQueen?"

The blood thrumming wildly in her veins, she found no words to answer. Only felt the heat of his body and the chill of the water. Conflicting sensations that mirrored the conflict in her heart.

"Out of the way!" a girl on the rise shouted. "Coming through."

Wordlessly, with a roguish grin, Rhune released her and began to swim toward the float. Her heart thumping rapidly in her chest, Tess followed.

Pulling herself up on the float, she flopped on her back on the sun-warmed boards, her eyes closed, exhausted and energized at the same time.

She felt a shadow cross her upper body. Opening her eyes, she saw Rhune's face directly above her own. Diamond drops of water fell from his hair. His eyes danced with merriment.

His closeness shut out the world.

"You're some sport, Tess McQueen," he said huskily.

She could find no words to answer as the full import of the situation hit her: up on the rope, he'd commanded her to let go.

Let go.

She had. In more ways than one.

Oh, Tess, what have you done?

Chapter Five

Tess let the supper-crowd noises at the Hole-in-the-Wall Café sink into the background as she gazed out the window from her booth overlooking the village green. She'd ordered a meal and now had time for her thoughts.

What an unanticipated day. Kids. A mangy mutt. A rustic swimming hole. A Tarzan swing. Flying lessons. And Dr. Rhune Sherman.

Rhune.

The very thought of him made her pulse pick up, and no amount of interior admonitions could stop it.

Upon reflection, she realized she'd learned more about him today than she ever would have over a staid luncheon. Or on a civilized stroll in the evening. She'd learned that kids at a difficult age and stray dogs loved him. She'd learned that he could catch her off guard and make her do things that were outside the realm of her straitlaced, everyday existence. She'd learned, much to her surprise, that she enjoyed being with him.

Because, still, Chelsey's playboy hadn't emerged.

And even more distressing, the doctor's obvious love of children belied Chelsey's insistence that he'd turned down the chance to raise one of his own flesh and blood. Despite her sister's insistence, that tiny fact didn't compute in Tess's logical mind. She would have to question Rhune directly on his desire—or lack of it—for children.

"Mind if I join you?"

Startled, Tess looked up at lawyer Wally Buckminster standing next to her table. "Not at all." Motioning to the seat across from her, she smiled uneasily as Wally's presence reminded her how she'd contracted to have Rhune investigated.

"Any word from Caldwell?" Wally asked. Caldwell was the private investigator.

"He said he'd have something for me tomorrow."

Wally lowered his voice. "You don't have to worry. He's good. If anybody can find out the real story on Sherman, Caldwell can. Then, if we need to use it in court, we'll be prepared."

Why did that not comfort Tess? Without replying, she looked down at her hands folded on the table before her.

Dramatically, Wally stretched, then asked, his voice hearty, "Where's Doc tonight? I thought he was your shadow."

"I don't know." She didn't. When Rhune had dropped her off late this afternoon, he'd said he'd be by tomorrow morning to read her blood pressure. And then he'd driven off, leaving her feeling extremely confused after one of the most pleasurable afternoons of her life.

"You looking for Doc?" an old man at the next booth asked. "You remember, he's organizing that bachelor party bash for Manuel Navarro."

"Oh, *that.*" Wally rolled his eyes, and Tess couldn't tell if he didn't approve of bachelor parties in general, or if he'd been excluded from this one.

The man at the next booth and his companion, another elderly man, began to chortle. "If Doc's plannin' it, you can be sure it'll be a whoop-de-do," said the first.

Tess's interest perked up. "Why do you say that?" Leaning to look around Wally, she spoke to the inhabitants of the next booth.

"Oh," the second man replied, turning in his seat toward Tess and smiling gleefully, "'cause Doc can stir up a good time sure as a dowser can stir up water."

"Surer," the first man added. "Why, you remember when he blew into town to visit his sister, not knowin' we were cleanin' up from those tornadoes?"

"Yup."

"What happened?" Tess asked, enticed by the mischievous grins on the elderly men. This was mythmaking at its source.

"Why, ole Doc hove to with the best of 'em for the relief effort, but at night he found the only beer joint in the county that had a live band and its own generator. You see, the rest of us—'cept for Grace Everlastin' Church—had not a lick of power. And by the end of the day we were too pooped to pop if'n we had."

The second man cackled. "Leave it to Doc. In a strange town less'n twenty-four hours, and he can *smell* a good time. Not only that, he's got the stamina to enjoy it. Stamina. That's it. That boy's got *stamina*."

Wally harrumphed.

"I take it you're not impressed by Doc's stamina," Tess said, unable to fully suppress a smile.

The two friends in the next booth began to chuckle. The first slapped the table. "Wally's beholden by blood ties to disapprove of Doc."

Tess looked at Wally, who remained tight-lipped and silent. Obviously, he wasn't pleased with this turn in the conversation.

The man at the next booth seemed to take Wally's reserve as a cue that he should act as translator. "You see, Miss Tess, Wally is second cousin, once removed, to Missy Able. And Missy Able and ole Doc had a *thing* when Doc blew into town."

Wally came to life. "It was not a *thing*. At least, not a mutual thing. Rhune Sherman seduced Missy, plain and simple."

Tess could feel her eyebrows arch toward her hairline. "He seduced your cousin?" Chelsey's playboy had just made his first appearance.

"Don't you believe a word of it." The second man at the booth cut in. "How could it be seduction when Missy made off with him in her car? If'n you ask me, *she* seduced him."

The first man seemed nearly convulsed with silent merriment. "But do y'all remember when she'd finished with him?" He hiccuped with laughter. "That woman always could wring the juice out of a man and throw him away like a used-up grapefruit rind."

Wally's ears were turning red. "I prefer to interpret it that she came to her senses," he retorted prissily.

"*What* happened?" Tess didn't bother to hide her fascination. How much of this was truth and how much Sweet Hope legend? How much could back up Chelsey's accusation?

The man at the next booth was now thoroughly warmed up, obviously enjoying his own storytelling, evidently pleased as punch with an audience. "Well...twenty-four hours after they take off together, little Miss Missy pulls her sporty red convertible up in a cloud of dust before Grace Everlastin' and dumps ole Doc on his keister on the church steps. In front of God and the entire congregation. Then without so much as a bye-the-bye she peals out of the parking lot, hell-bent for Tennessee. Haven't seen her since, now, have we?"

"My cousin," Wally drawled, narrowing his eyes, "has obviously learned a valuable lesson."

"*What* happened?" Tess still didn't know.

Edna, the Hole-in-the-Wall waitress, approached the table. "Doesn't matter." She rolled her eyes and flicked her head at the two old gentlemen in the next booth. "The truth's been lost in storytelling by now." She plunked the vegetable plate before Tess but stared at Wally. "But if you ask me, Wally Buckminster, Doc doesn't need to do anything underhanded to get a woman. *Any* woman. Why, he can park his shoes—''

Tess cleared her throat loudly. She didn't need an endorsement from Edna. "Could I have some ketchup, please?''

Out of one deep apron pocket Edna produced a ketchup bottle. "You ordering again, Wally?''

"No, I've paid my bill. Why?''

Edna flicked her head toward the door. "I need to talk to Tess, here. Girl talk.''

Wally rose slowly. "You know where to find me, Tess.'' He glowered first at Edna, then at the two grinning men in the next booth, but did finally make his way to the exit.

Edna slipped into the booth in his place. "He bothering you, honey?''

"Bothering me?''

"Making a move on you.''

Tess found that idea startling and particularly unappealing. "No.'' She smiled uneasily. "We're doing a little business together this week.''

Slipping her pencil into her considerably teased hair, Edna appeared to think that over. "Don't be influenced by what Wally thinks of Doc. Those two were never meant to be friends. But Doc's okay.''

"What about the stories?''

Edna sighed contentedly. "Probably true, to some extent. That Doc's a caution. A rascal and a caution.''

"And that doesn't bother you?''

"Honey, are you dead?'' Edna hooted. "Did you ever look into those brown eyes of his? Oh, my. If I were twenty years younger...''

Tess chuckled in spite of herself. "Edna, is this the girl talk you wanted to have?''

"Lordy, no!'' Reaching into another pocket of her apron, she withdrew several small figurines, then stood them on the table before Tess. They were tiny grooms for the top of a wedding cake. Just three grooms. No brides.

Tess looked at Edna in confusion.

"It's a long story," Edna said.

Tess smiled. Everything in Sweet Hope seemed to be.

"Esther, our cook, does special-order cakes on the side." Edna indicated the large woman at the grill behind the counter. "Maria—she's marrying Manuel Navarro, the one having the bachelor bash—asked Esther to do her wedding cake."

"And?"

"Right away, Esther found the prettiest bride for the top of the cake. Looks like Maria's twin. But the groom...well, the groom's another story."

Tess squinted at the miniature men before her. They were a pitiful puny lot. Not a heartthrob among them. "And?"

"Well, we're asking all the women that come in here their opinions on the choices. And, so far, these are the choices."

"My opinion?" Tess didn't even know Maria and Manuel, but she smiled at the warm feeling that washed over her at the thought of being included in the Sweet Hope opinion poll.

"Personally," Edna said, shrugging, "I think these guys are tacky. Like their little plastic hearts aren't into going to their own wedding. Besides, not one of them looks remotely like Manuel."

Tess didn't know Manuel, but she had to agree with the tacky part. These wee fellows had all been to Budget Rent-a-Tux. "Tell Esther to keep looking," she replied seriously. "Maria deserves a groom with a little muscle and a custom tux." She grinned. "That's my opinion."

It surprised her that suddenly she cared that everything at this wedding should be just right for the newlyweds whom she'd never met. Right down to the little figurines on the top of their wedding cake.

This town. It drew you under its sweet spell before you were totally aware of the bewitching process.

"Edna!" Esther the cook bellowed. "Pick up!"

Edna scooped the little men up and, dunking them into her apron, winked at Tess. "I always did say a good groom is hard to find."

Tess smiled warmly back at the waitress. "I know. I've been looking."

Bending, then looking over her shoulder conspiratorially, Edna whispered, "Honey, as per the topic of conversation much earlier...whoever convinces *that man* to approach the altar wins major bonus points." She rubbed her arms and shivered in obvious pleasure. "It'd be worth the tales a body would have to live down. Yes, indeedy." Chuckling heartily, she returned to work, leaving Tess to ponder her words.

Tess could picture Dr. Rhune Sherman as many kinds of people rolled into one. If Chelsey and the gossips tonight were to be believed, he was a rogue. An irresponsible playboy. But neither she nor the children today had seen that side of him. This afternoon they'd seen a caring man—full of rascally fun, to be sure, but generous and unselfish. A man who loved children.

At least two kinds of man.

But no matter how much Tess thought on it, there was one kind of man she definitely couldn't see in Rhune, despite Edna's suggestion. The marrying kind. She could picture him engineering Manuel's bachelor party, yes. From her brief acquaintance with the doctor and her brush with his runaway reputation, she could picture him ever the party-giving best man.

Never the groom.

She tucked in to her vegetable plate. It was preposterous even to give that line of thinking space in her mind. She had other more pertinent thoughts to concern her. The way she was beginning to see it, Rhune Sherman *might be* the bad boy with a heart of gold, his love-'em-and-leave-'em trail more the result of restlessness and playfulness than of malice.

Tess winced. The disastrous results, however, were the same.

And the man still needed to be made to face the consequences of his actions.

Unwrapping the blood pressure cuff from Tess's arm, Rhune wondered at her aloofness this morning. He could have sworn they'd reached a new plateau yesterday after the fun with the kids at the swimming hole. Could have sworn she and he had gone beyond that cool doctor-patient relationship. That edgy distance of two near strangers. When he'd dropped her off here at Mel and Ida's yesterday afternoon, she'd seemed so happy. Almost carefree.

Now she seemed just the opposite. Unapproachable. Wary. And for some inexplicable reason, the reversal sorely disappointed Rhune.

"Your blood pressure is excellent this morning," he said evenly to cover that disappointment. "Sweet Hope seems to agree with you."

She looked directly at the bandage over his left eye. "I can't say the same for you." She narrowed her eyes and skewered him with a penetrating violet regard.

When he shrugged and pointed to his brow, she shifted her gaze to the larger bandage covering the knuckles of his right hand. "The party turned...playful," he said, unable to impart the full scope of last night's adventure.

She arched one eyebrow imperiously. "Have you been brawling, Dr. Sherman?"

He grinned. "Ms. McQueen, I'm a lover, not a fighter." At her grimace of distaste, he altered his tack. "Two of the party goers had a little too much to drink and chose the occasion to settle an old family boundary dispute. I merely helped separate them."

She seemed appalled. "Do you find yourself in the thick of things often?"

"You don't?" He'd always thought you were either in the center of activity or you were dead.

"Rarely."

"Then I can rectify that. Today." At her look of confusion, he explained, "Belle and Cathryn—that's Belle's stepdaughter and Pastor Jacob Matthews's wife—suggested you help gather magnolia boughs for the garland they plan to make for the village green gazebo. For the Fourth celebration.''

''All that red, white and blue bunting isn't sufficient?''

''The garland is town tradition. The Southern touch.'' And a ready excuse to throw you and me together, Rhune thought wryly, picturing the incurable matchmaking duo of Belle and Cathryn.

Tess lifted her hands in protest. ''I wouldn't know a magnolia bough from a pine.''

''Normally I wouldn't, either, except that my property has a beautiful grove where a former owner once had his house. The house is now just a pile of ruins, but the stand of magnolias is magnificent.''

''Did the house blow up, burn down or get destroyed by animals?''

''I beg your pardon?''

''The house in the magnolia grove. Did it meet with a disastrous fate?''

''No, it was abandoned. Why?''

''I just wondered—with your trailer and all—if you might have purchased a cursed parcel of land.''

He could detect the faintest hint of mischief in the depths of her eyes. ''Belief in curses doesn't seem very efficient,'' he grumbled. The limbo that was the present state of his trailer still pained him. Especially since the animal control people seemed to be dragging their heels. Seemed more interested in contributing to local legend than in seeking permanent solutions.

He scowled. If they didn't come up with any helpful hints soon, he'd take steps himself. People, not animals, were his usual area of expertise, but he was certain he could figure out something. Just as soon as he needn't fill his thoughts any longer with Tess McQueen.

Reaching out to lay a hand on his arm, Tess smiled, and Rhune felt an answering response clear down to his toes. ''I'm sorry,'' she said. ''That was thoughtless. I don't know what came over me." She squeezed his arm gently. "Truce?"

He wouldn't tell her that if she continued to smile, he could forgive her just about anything.

Instead he asked, "Will you come with me to get the magnolia boughs?"

She withdrew her hand quickly. "With you? I thought I'd be going with Belle."

He chuckled. "Belle and Cathryn and the O'Malley matriarch, Alice Rose, are the movers and shakers behind this celebration. They issue the orders. The underlings—you and I—carry them out. We're going to have to live in Sweet Hope longer than a week, or even a month, to move up the duty roster."

"You're joking."

"Only partly." He shrugged. "Small-town hierarchies. So... are you coming? I've promised Belle buckets of boughs. I could use the help."

"How are we going to bring back *buckets of boughs* on your motorcycle?" Her question seemed far too evasive.

"Belle loaned me her vintage VW convertible."

"Oh." Tess now sounded faintly disappointed.

Quite frankly, he'd prefer her clinging to him on the back of his Harley. He quickly tamped down that particular thought. "What could a little community service hurt?"

She looked down at her obviously new snug jeans and loose Oxford shirt. "I suppose it couldn't hurt," she said, her tone vaguely distracted. "But I have to be back by midafternoon. I have a... business appointment."

"Never let it be said I stood between a woman and her business. I'll have you back in time."

Squaring her shoulders, she seemed to come to a decision much deeper than that of picking magnolia boughs. Although she looked him directly in the eye, her expression was unreadable. "What are we waiting for?" she asked briskly.

Those were practically the only words he got out of her from the time they left the bed-and-breakfast to the moment he pulled in to the back dirt road to his fifteen acres.

He seldom came this way across his property, and he'd feel foolish trying to explain to anyone why. To him, the ruined house amid the stand of magnolias was a sad testimony to a family's dreams gone awry. In one sense, sacred ground. In another, a warning that sometimes commitment can be far more painful than emotional detachment. He needed to heed the warning. Needed to live clean from now on. Emotionally detached.

So why had he threatened his newfound equilibrium by bringing one all-too-attractive Tess McQueen to this paradoxical spot? For the life of him, he couldn't find an honest answer. Not even for himself.

As he unloaded the buckets from the back of the VW, Tess looked around. The expression of preoccupation on her face had turned to one of genuine interest in her surroundings. "You're a very lucky man," she said softly. "Did you know that?"

Yes, he had been a very lucky man. In many more ways than one. And he didn't care to push that luck. Not by having Tess poke around in his psyche. Heading for the grove of magnolias, he treated her question as if it had been deliberately rhetorical, and didn't answer it. "Grab those two sets of shears, would you?" he asked instead, his words far more brusque than he'd intended.

She didn't seem to mind his brusqueness. Having gathered up the shears, she fell into step beside him, her own mood seeming to lighten as his darkened. Odd how the two of them always seesawed in opposing rhythms. Just one more indication that a passing acquaintance was all there was meant to be between them.

His irritation grew as they silently cut magnolia boughs and placed them in the buckets of water he'd drawn from the still-sweet homestead well. This had been a mistake, bringing Tess here. A mistake for the plain and simple reason that, despite all logic to the contrary, he was attracted to her. He was attracted to her strength and her dignity. He was attracted to her ability to remain silent when there was nothing to be said. And he was attracted to the flashes of the other woman in her—the woman who could let loose on a Tarzan swing at a swimming hole full of preteens.

He was attracted to her, he liked being with her and, against all reason, he was beginning to take her presence in Sweet Hope as a given.

"Not smart, Sherman," he grumbled, half to himself, half out loud.

"I beg your pardon?" Tess, brushing up against him as she reached for the perfect bough, froze, wide-eyed.

He tried to ignore the awareness the fleeting pressure of her body against his gave him. "Sorry," he muttered. "I seem to be distracted."

Looking down at the bough she held in her hand, she traced one large, shiny leaf with her finger. "It must be difficult for you to be here... amid this family's ruins... what with the recent trashing of your own home. I heard that, once you got back in to survey the damage, it was much worse than you'd first thought."

Rhune took a deep breath. "It wasn't much of a home to begin with. Just a shell that kept the rain off a few articles of clothing."

Her gaze lifted abruptly and caught him off guard. "Why?"

Not wanting to discuss his nomadic tendencies, he turned the question around. "Do you have a home?"

"Yes." Her smile was faintly sad. "We've never had more than an apartment or a condo, but, yes, we've always managed to turn it into a home."

"Then you must have a knack." Abruptly he turned, intending to put the now full buckets of magnolia boughs into the back of the car. "I don't."

He didn't want to tell her that a home, to him, involved at least two people to share it. He'd never found that other person, and so his wandering spirit needed no more than a roof over his head. It had never mattered what form the walls had taken.

"I would have put your trailer right here," she said, buoyancy filling her voice. "Amid the magnolias. Someone, at some time, must have started out with homing instincts. They built the original house. The high hopes and dreams of that first family would have filled your trailer. Would have begun to make it feel like a real home."

He stopped dead in his tracks. "What did you say?" No one had ever articulated his feeling that this place still generated an enormous energy.

"I'm saying that I think you should place your trailer or build a new home right here over the original."

He turned slowly to see her standing, radiantly satisfied with her suggestion. An unnerving thought flashed unbidden across his mind: Tess McQueen *fit*. Right here. And if he'd only allow himself to admit it, he fit here, also.

So where did that leave the two of them?

Nowhere. That's where.

For if he ever were to let himself become serious about a woman, he would have to let her know the whole Rhune Sherman. Not that he was an advocate of spilling one's history. No, some tales remained better left untold. But honor dictated that he not misrepresent himself. If he were ever to allow himself to get serious enough about a woman to discuss home sites—which he most definitely wasn't ready to do—he would have to make certain she saw the real man and not some infatuation-induced model of romantic perfection.

And knowing Tess McQueen's uncanny ability for pulling confessions from him, he needed to steer clear of any path that might lead to further intimacy with the lovely efficiency expert. She was leaving in less than a week, and, as he'd reminded himself time and time again, he was finished with brief affairs.

"Would you like to have a family someday?" Her question jolted him. "I mean, you seem so good with kids."

Uh-oh. Confession time.

"I love kids, yes," he replied cautiously. "But the right woman and the opportunity for a family have as yet to present themselves."

She cocked her head and shot him the most curious glance.

"I think we have enough magnolia boughs to satisfy the movers and shakers." He changed the subject abruptly and tried to keep his voice even. "Ready to roll?"

"Not quite yet." The wistfulness in her voice floated out to him, wrapped around his senses and ensnared his heart-strings. "It's such a beautiful day. Would you give me a tour?"

The last thing he needed was to spend one more minute in this too-powerful-already place with a woman who scrambled all rational thought.

"Sure," he muttered, and immediately wondered who had uttered that traitorous word.

Whoever had, he was going to live to regret it.

Tess turned in a complete circle and let the dappled sunshine and shadow wash over her. No matter how determined to be wary she'd been at the outset, Rhune and his remarkable piece of property had—twice now—enchanted her. Filed away the rough edges of her objections and suspicions. Left her in a state of relaxation and well-being. Despite her most ardent mental chiding, when she was with Rhune she wanted the moments to stretch infinitely.

Clearly recognizing the danger of such feelings, she nonetheless disregarded them.

"Come on!" Impulsively she reached for the buckets in his hands. Taking them from him and setting them on the ground, she reached for his hand, threaded her fingers through his and tugged. "This way. I want to see what's over that rise."

Scowling for a moment as if he thought a tour a bad idea despite his agreement, he resisted. But only for a moment. Suddenly he withdrew his hand from hers but began to walk in the direction she'd indicated. "So you have it in your head you'd like some land?" He looked sideways at her, his gaze hooded. "Planning to raise a big family?"

"Not necessarily." She needed to quell that fantasy. "But nothing says I can't enjoy an acquaintance's plunge into squiredom."

Rhune snorted. "Something tells me the town of Sweet Hope wouldn't tolerate a motorcycle-riding doctor with pretensions to squiredom."

Tess swept her hand along the tops of the thigh-high grasses as they made their way across the field. "The residents seem to tolerate you now—even embrace you." She grinned. "Despite your proclivity for creating legends."

"There's something you should know about small towns," he replied, pulling a stalk of grass out of its shaft and chewing on the tender, newly exposed end. "At the same time small towns can be a haven of conformity, they can and do tolerate—even embrace—out-of-the-ordinary individuals. The price the individual pays, however, is that his or her life becomes a public property of sorts. A communal interest and entertainment."

"And that doesn't bother you?" It would certainly bother her. She considered herself an old-fashioned person who believed in privacy.

"Not really. I haven't seen any signs of disrespect." His words were flat, as if he were holding back, trying hard not to infuse his speech with any emotion. Almost as if it pained him to open up to her.

They bridged the rise, and Tess saw that they were on the lip of a ravine, perhaps twenty yards or so deep, with a narrow stream running along the bottom. Quite spectacular, but with a hint of danger. She took a cautious step backward. To either side as they stood, a rocky path skirted the steep, irregular embankment.

Rhune scowled. "You can't explore the ravine in only a few minutes. We probably should head back." His words were riddled more with command than with suggestion.

Tess glanced at her watch. "Just a few more minutes, please. I hate to leave." She did. It was so peaceful. And it

felt so good to have Rhune beside her even if he was more
taciturn than usual. She pointed to a boulder under an
overhanging tree several yards down the path. "Can we sit
there in the shade for a minute before going back?"

"Let me go first. And watch your step," he ordered.

"Any particular reason why?" Very odd, but she was beginning to find his protectiveness charming. She shook her
head. Must be the heat.

"Snakes." The word hung in the air as he headed toward
the boulder. "They love to sun themselves on a day like today."

This new prospect simmering in her mind, she didn't follow him immediately. "Maybe we should turn back," she
murmured, gazing warily at the ground. Anoles were one
thing; snakes were something else altogether.

Perhaps it was a disturbed pebble on the path that made
the faint noise behind Tess. Or the skitter of a field mouse.
Or her imagination. In any case, she whirled around, wanting to make absolutely certain it wasn't a snake Rhune had
conjured with the very word. In so doing, she skidded on a
loose stone underfoot and lost her balance.

With a little yip of surprise she stumbled toward the steep
embankment. At that open point on the path, there was
nothing to grasp except the long fronds of taunting field
grasses, which proffered deceptive support.

Don't lose your head, Tess McQueen. Don't lose your
head, she warned herself as she began what seemed a dizzying, slow-motion tumble. Better a bruised bottom than
broken limbs. Deliberately she sat.

The tough fabric of her jeans protected her, but provided
a smooth surface that facilitated her slide across the hard-
packed and pebble-strewn footpath. As she twisted onto one
thigh and slithered over the edge of the beaten track down
a steep brambled slope, she looked up to see Rhune's hor-
rified face and his hands stretching out fruitlessly to grasp
her.

A crazy prayer whizzed through her mind. Dear Lord, if it *was* a snake that started all this, scare it uphill, not down alongside me and all this falling mess.

Digging her heels into the embankment, she tried to break her slide. It did no good, for the steep hill harbored only tufts of grass lodged in loamy chunks that broke away at a touch. She reached out, grabbing frantically at any available outcropping, but sticker vines whipped her hands, leaving them cut and stinging but ultimately empty.

She looked down to see the stream and its rocky shore rushing up, it seemed, to meet her with sickening speed. She looked up and saw the blue of the sky and a gray hail of stones. She squinched her eyes shut, covered her head with her arms and gave in to the fall.

The fall and the fear seemed limitless.

Finally, with a deafening crunch and a wrenching pain in her right shoulder, she landed on the level but extremely sharp shingle of the stream's edge. Biting the inside of her mouth, she tasted blood. Her nostrils filled with the scent of dirt and crushed vegetation. She opened her eyes to see clay and stones and clumps of sodded grass bouncing around her. Fearing she had started a minilandslide, she twisted about to look up the embankment, only to see Rhune hurtling down the slope toward her, alarm etched sharply upon his features.

He came to a clattering halt beside her in a cloud of pebbles, dust and colorful expletives. He looked for all the world like an earth giant, just now untimely awakened and rising in wrath to confront the perpetrator. "What the hell!" he roared as he scrambled to her side.

She flinched, convinced for an irrational moment that he truly was about to eat her alive. Instinctively leaning back, she felt hot pain shoot through her shoulder, felt her arm weaken and crumple under her. Then felt powerful arms scoop her up and hold her. With strength, yes, but also with gentleness. No fearsome earth giant this. No, he who held her was protection itself.

This was not the Rhune of a few moments earlier. Gone was the brusqueness, the chill. This man was warmth and caring personified. He held her gently, but so firmly and so close that she could feel his breathing feather her face. The look on his own face was not the dispassionate look of a physician for his patient. His expression was one of blatant concern that came only from emotional involvement.

The fear that she had held at bay transformed itself into relief of the kind that knows full well the awful danger that has passed. Her body began to tremble without restraint. She realized to her dismay that the rat-a-tat sound in her ears was the chattering of her own teeth. How had she come to lose control?

"Take it easy." Rhune's soothing words rumbled around her like a blessing. "Be still. Then I'll take a look at you." He cradled her tenderly against his own strong, reassuring bulk. She felt the rapid in-and-out of his breathing that belied the calm of his words. "For someone who claims she's rarely at the center of things, you're a quick study, Tess McQueen." She heard him rapidly expel breath in a relieved chuckle of sorts.

She really should collect herself and say something to reassure him that, but for the pain in her right shoulder, she was indeed all right. She opened her mouth to speak, but no words came. With her left hand she pressed weakly against his chest and found herself sidetracked by the thought that, despite the accident, it was lovely to be held this way. Held by a man who vibrated energy, whose very presence reassured her that he could handle anything....

Something within her clicked in warning. Never, ever, had she let anyone else handle any aspect of her life.

Never.

If she didn't pull herself together right this minute, she was in peril of losing more than her power of speech.

She pushed more insistently against his chest until he loosened his embrace. "I'm—I'm...afraid...it's the... company...I've been...keeping...lately," she managed to stammer, still painfully short of breath.

She looked up and found herself trapped by more than his arms.

His gaze, deep brown and filled with worry, enveloped her. Those eyes. They were the eyes Plato had told her to study. They were the eyes Edna had said made her wish she was twenty years younger. They were the eyes Tess had warned herself to avoid at all cost.

Beautiful eyes. Sensuous. Beckoning. And tinged with a longing that could pull and involve a woman against her better judgment.

Tess blinked hard, trying to break the hold they had on her. Instead she caused him to smile and activate the dimple that was her undoing.

"Thank God," he murmured, his voice husky with emotion. "Don't scare me like that again. I thought I'd lost you." He closed his eyes and ever so gently brought his forehead to rest against hers.

His sigh came straight from the heart.

Chapter Six

As soon as Rhune saw the fight in her eyes, he knew Tess was going to be fine.

His alarm now had nothing to do with her well-being. He'd faced worse than this in the ER and had pulled his patients through with flying colors. No, Tess would be all right; he'd see to that.

It was his own heart he feared for.

Just moments ago, up on the lip of the embankment as she'd dropped out of sight, he'd experienced an unnerving flash—in a very few days he'd come to care for this woman. To care so intensely that he wanted nothing—*nothing*—to harm her. And he was prepared to offer his protection. Permanently.

That thought alone was enough to make a strong man hyperventilate.

But for Rhune, a man whose philosophy in life outside his practice of medicine came dangerously close to cliché—*live and let live, love 'em and leave 'em*—this new and unwanted intensity of caring was cause for considerable personal panic.

He lifted his forehead from hers. Cautiously he released her from his embrace, and marveled that his body had come to this intemperate pass while his mind had been hissing the need to remain cool and professional. No matter the danger, he'd never held a patient as he now held Tess. Had never felt for a patient the personal and unsettling pull he now felt for this woman whose questioning violet regard washed over him.

"Can you sit?" His voice sounded gravelly and unsympathetic to his own ears.

"Yes. I'm . . . fine." She suddenly didn't look fine. As if she felt as unsettled as he. "My shoulder's a little banged up."

"Let me take a look." At last. Something *to do*. Action to quell those disturbing thoughts. Those little cherry bombs of mental revelation.

He turned his attention to the shoulder she indicated. Her shirt was torn and dirty, her shoulder badly scraped. Gently he began to palpate the area, but stopped when she winced. "We need to have the clinic in Sterling take some X rays—"

"No!" The vehemence of her response startled him. "It's just bruised."

"Tess, you need to find that out for certain. It could be a lot more than just a bruise."

"No!" She began to struggle to her feet.

He rose and slipped his arm around her waist to help her. The very fact that she accepted his assistance without objection reinforced his belief that she hurt more than she was admitting. "The clinic's not far from here. It won't take but—"

"No!" She appeared adamant. "I have an appointment at four. A very important appointment."

"Damn it, woman! What business appointment could be more important than your personal well-being?"

She winced and clung to him, averting her gaze. "This one," she muttered through clenched teeth.

In exasperation, he glanced at his watch. "It's only twelve-fifteen. I can take you to Sterling and have you back by four."

"What part of *no* don't you understand, Doc?" She began to hobble toward the embankment. "We need to get out of here, and, from my perspective, that alone will prove no small feat. Then I need to get home and into a bath." She swung her gaze to his, and he was caught by the sheer stubborn will reflected therein. "I *will not* miss this appointment."

"I won't prescribe painkillers to get you through it."

"I never asked for them."

"You're going to need them."

"You seem awfully aware of my body's needs."

No. At the moment he was painfully aware of his own body's needs.

"Tess..." He softened his voice. Obviously, he was not about to win a war of wills. "*As a friend* I would recommend no less than that you get this shoulder checked out."

She sighed. "Are you willing to compromise?" The steely stubbornness in her eyes seemed to diminish. Somewhat. "If you help me get back to Mel and Ida's today, I promise to have X rays at the clinic...tomorrow."

Lord, he was glad he didn't have to deal with this hardheaded woman in a personal relationship. She'd tax his patience beyond endurance. "I suppose I can't convince you otherwise," he growled.

"No, you can't." She actually had the audacity to grin. A lopsided grin that turned to a wince, but a grin nonetheless. Challenging and thoroughly aggravating. "Now, let's see how we're going to tackle the climb up. The trip down was a snap."

He clenched his jaw, tightened his grip around her waist and said nothing.

The climb up was no snap.

Not having owned this property for very long, Rhune didn't know if there was a more gentle path into the ravine. He wasn't about to waste time looking. He needed to get Tess home. Perhaps there she'd come to her senses. If not, he could make her comfortable until tomorrow when he could get her to the clinic in Sterling. Holding her protectively to him, he picked his way back up the steep embankment.

Business appointment. Hah.

What could be so important that she would jeopardize her health? He scowled. This provoking behavior—this disregard for her personal well-being—seemed to be a habit with her. Hadn't her business with Wally Buckminster initially produced the same results? She'd breezed into town, hot to wheel and deal, and had forgotten to feed herself. Had wound up on an exam table. The result of *business*.

He harrumphed and heard the tiniest of moans at his side.

They were almost at the top of the embankment. Sweet mercy. In stewing about her well-being, he'd ignored it. He must have practically dragged her up the incline, and she'd not complained. "Can you make it?" he asked, slowing his pace and gentling his tone of voice.

The pain showed in her face, but she rewarded him with a genuine smile. "Don't stop now, or you'll never get me going again."

"Hang on to me. Just a few more feet. When we get to the top I can carry you through the field to the car."

Her eyes grew wide. "That won't be—"

"*Necessary*. I know." He grinned. "But, believe me, you're not going to win this one."

Tess argued no further, only increasing Rhune's concern for her. Trying not to jostle her unduly, he made one last colossal effort to propel them over the lip of the embankment, and nearly caused them both to drop to the rock-strewn path. Catching her and his breath before they fell, he scooped her into his arms before she could steady herself and protest.

He didn't need to worry. She slumped against him, silent and exhausted. She'd been a trouper, uncomplaining and strong, and he hated to see the fight go out of her. She must ache all over from that tumble. His lungs filled with the hot July air and ached from the exertion of the climb, but he strode through the tall field grasses with purpose.

Tess needed him.

At what point had it suddenly felt so natural to want to watch over her? To protect her. To care for her.

Rhune winced.

"Put me down," Tess murmured. "You'll hurt your-self."

It already hurt, this caring.

"I'm fine," he muttered. "At least this way I know where you are."

"I can see the car."

"Good. At least your vision's not double."

"I can walk from here."

"I'll let you walk into a healing bath back at Mel and Ida's. No sooner."

To his surprise, she tugged on his ear. "Your bossy bed-side manner needs work, Doc."

He ignored the fact that she was trying to get his undi-vided attention. He wouldn't look at her. Already the feel of her in his arms had begun to register. Had begun to send his thoughts into a confusing overdrive. Had begun to undo him. He didn't need to get lost in her eyes.

"Tess McQueen," he said, trying to keep his voice even, "I swear that you've been sent to test my resolve. To see if I really have the stuff necessary to face the difficulties of country doctoring." He gritted his teeth. "Well, whoever's keeping score is *not* going to see me give in to provoca-tion."

He heard her soft chuckle. Felt the puff of her breath against his neck. Prayed for the strength to withstand dis-traction. Focused on the sight of his sister's VW convert-ible, now not ten yards away. Resolved to fish—*alone*—for forty-eight hours straight as soon as this disconcerting woman in his arms left town. Solitary fishing just might distract him from the memory of the feel of her against him.

He made it to the passenger side of the car, opened the door, then helped Tess sit. Dirty, rumpled and faintly black and blue, she maintained her regal posture but looked nonetheless vulnerable. Pale and uncharacteristically fragile. That nagging feeling of protectiveness washed over him. Before it could undo him completely, he shut the car door firmly and strode around to the driver's side.

As he opened the door, he heard Tess say with conviction, "We're not leaving without the magnolia boughs."

He fought rising exasperation.

"We need to get you back to Mel and Ida's. Boone can drive out and pick the buckets up."

"Why? We're right here."

"Because..." He spoke the words slowly, patiently, as if to a child. "We need to get you cleaned up so that we can assess your condition. As a doctor, I think it's unwise to waste time right now on magnolia boughs."

He heard a muffled snort from inside the bug. "You're beginning to sound like an efficiency expert, Doc."

He felt the muscles in his jaw tense and pulse.

After a pause she said, her tone of voice far too reasonable, "Please, put the buckets in the car... or I will."

He knew she would. Or die trying. "They won't fit. I miscalculated. We should have brought Boone's truck."

"Put down the top."

"And add sunstroke to your injuries."

"You're hovering, Doc... *unnecessarily.*"

Someone had to hover if she wouldn't take care of herself. Damn, she blew his gaskets.

But he knew this argument could last forever if he didn't take action. Without looking at her, he reached into the car and unhooked the clasps that held the convertible top. With a vengeance he hoisted the ragtop and shoved it into the boot. Then he stalked across the yard of the ruined house to the well, where the buckets of magnolia boughs sat. Grabbing the handles, he stomped back to the VW, not caring that he'd slopped most of the water out of the buckets by the time he returned to the bug. He swung them into the back seat, then vaulted over the side of the car into the driver's seat.

Steamed.

If she said, *There now. That didn't take long,* he might just take out the steering wheel.

She didn't.

He had to give her credit.

Soaking in a hot bath an hour later, Tess realized she had to give Rhune credit. *Obviously* he'd not been happy with her decision to postpone the X rays, but, except for his thunderous expression, he hadn't tried to bully or patronize her into changing her mind during the entire ride home.

She wouldn't have. Caldwell, the private investigator, was to meet her at four o'clock. She needed to find out for certain what kind of a man Dr. Rhune Sherman truly was because, left on her own with him, she was beginning to form her own opinions. Opinions that were dangerously far removed from those of her sister.

Stepping out of the bath, she reached for her thick terry robe.

She needed to stop this pretense of investigating on her own. Even if her brain still refused to believe it, every fiber in her body *knew* that she continued to keep company with Rhune simply because she enjoyed being with him. Despite her bumps and scrapes and bruises, she felt alive when she was with him. Truly alive for the first time in her life. Now, that was the unvarnished truth.

Her hormones mocked her playacting gumshoe routine.

And, worst of all, she was beginning to doubt her sister's story.

Wrapping the robe around her with her good arm, she winced. The bath had soothed her body, but the pain in her shoulder had prevented her from washing her hair. She couldn't even lift her one arm to wind a towel around it to cover the twigs and leaves and bits of grass that still remained woven through it. And now the ends were soaked and covered with bubbles from the bath. She must look a sight, but the effort to raise her arm to wipe the steam from the bathroom mirror wasn't worth the confirmation. Perhaps later she could trouble Mel or Ida to brush the worst out of her hair and then hide the rest away in a bun before her meeting with Caldwell.

Right now she needed to rest. Relax. Alone in her room. Recoup her strength for the meeting with the private investigator. She had a couple of hours.

A couple of hours to get over the feeling that by meeting with Caldwell she was somehow betraying the Rhune she'd come to know.

Turning the doorknob to the bedroom, she frowned at the thought of him. Rhune. A man she'd grown to count on in the past few days. To trust. Today he'd pulled her out of that ravine, had driven her back to the bed-and-breakfast against his own best judgment, and would have fussed over her indefinitely had she not shooed him out of her room.

Some playboy.

She opened the bathroom door and found herself staring into a set of deep brown roguish eyes. "Rhune!" With her good hand she drew the robe more tightly about her. "What are you doing here? I thought I sent you home."

He scowled, the color in his eyes deepening. Intensifying. "You'll find I don't dismiss like some schoolboy." He took one step forward, she one step back. "I remained to see if you were going to be all right alone."

"I won't be alone in two more hours." She raised her chin and hoped she looked properly independent, while she gritted her teeth and thought only of finding a seat to hold her exhausted body.

Rhune raised one eyebrow. "Ah, yes. Your business appointment."

"Yes…well…now that you've seen that I'm fine, you'll excuse me."

"You didn't wash your hair."

"I beg your pardon?"

"If you have an important meeting, why didn't you wash your hair?"

"Does it offend you in some way, Doc?"

"No." He narrowed his eyes and skewered her with an unwavering stare. "It tells me that you aren't feeling as well as you'd like me to believe."

He had her there.

But she didn't want him to see that she was indeed feeling any physical discomfort. Exhaustion. Pain. The direct result of her stubbornness . . . and her drive to root out the real Rhune Sherman. Now, wanting him out of her room before he discovered the full extent of her vulnerability, she took the tack that sometimes honesty was the best offense. Straightening, she said, "It was a little difficult for me to wash my hair with one stiff shoulder. I plan to have Mel or Ida brush it later and wind it into a bun."

Rhune cocked one eyebrow, but didn't budge otherwise. "That sounds neither corporate nor efficient."

"And why should that be any concern of yours?" She didn't mean to sound imperious, but her shoulder throbbed. She wanted him *gone*.

"It isn't." His expression softened. "But I think I understand you enough to know you like your ducks in a row. Your work. Your appearance." He put a hand gently on her good shoulder and steered her back into the bathroom. "I can't imagine you feeling comfortable going into an important business meeting with unwashed hair. Come on. Let's take care of it. *Then* I'll leave and you can nap."

"What . . . ?"

"Hush." He pulled the short bathroom stool next to the edge of the large, old-fashioned pedestal sink. "I let you bully me into bringing back Belle's damned magnolia boughs. It's my turn."

"I never bullied—"

"Hush." His voice was gruff but oddly mesmerizing. Compelling. He grasped both her arms and sat her on the stool, her back to the sink. "Close your eyes."

She obeyed readily. There was something unsettling about watching him move about in the close quarters of this tiny room. Although she couldn't block him out of her other senses, she might not overload them if she shut her eyes. "What are you doing?"

"I'm going to wash your hair."

She could hear him running the water. Could smell shampoo. Unfortunately, she could feel him, too, as he brushed against her in his preparations. Her pulse skittered.

That did it. She opened her eyes. "You shouldn't be up here. The whole town will know by tomorrow."

He laid the tips of his fingers on her lips to still her protest. "Don't worry. Your reputation's ruined already." He grinned, and his dimple danced. "The word on the front veranda is that you've been seen with a less-than-savory character, your normally impeccable person rumpled and covered with field grasses." He winked. "I told you putting the top down wasn't a good idea."

She inhaled sharply and squeezed her eyes tightly closed. This would be over with much more quickly if they just didn't speak. As he tipped her head back over the sink, she didn't resist, but tried to concentrate on the latest Dow-Jones average.

It didn't work.

The feel of the warm water and his strong fingers against her scalp made her roll her eyes under their closed lids in pure pleasure. "Do you know what you're doing?" she stammered. She needn't ask. He must. Oh, Lordy, he must. "Washing someone else's hair, I mean."

His soft chuckle rumbled over her senses. "Have I had any experience in the field of hair management? Not exactly. The closest would be when I was a kid—a very little kid—and Belle made me sit still while she practiced her pin curls on me."

Tess opened her eyes and looked up at him. He paused in midshampoo to look down at her. "I can't imagine you sitting patiently," she said softly.

"I can be very patient when it comes to getting what I want."

"And what did you want from Belle?"

He laughed and began to rinse her hair. "I wanted her to let me hang around her... and her girlfriends."

Tess rolled her eyes. "I suspected you were incorrigible even then."

"She had some fine-looking girlfriends, I'll admit to that." She felt his chuckle more than heard it.

"And why are you being so patient with me?" The words slipped out before she could prevent them.

She felt his hands pause against her head. She couldn't see the expression on his face; his broad chest was in the way. He cleared his throat. "I'm the doctor, remember? *You're* the patient."

His attempt at throwaway humor didn't deter her. "It seems as though you've been more than a little bit guardian angel these past few days."

She felt him stiffen. "Don't make me out to be what I'm not." The playfulness had gone out of his voice. "Where's your conditioner?" In fact, he'd turned downright gruff.

"It should be on the edge of the tub... and I'm not making you out to be anything at all. I guess I was simply trying to thank you for your help. I certainly haven't made my appreciation clear."

He didn't answer. She felt the cool of the conditioner against her scalp. Felt him thread his fingers, slightly stiffer than previously, through her hair. Still she couldn't see his face, but she could sense a stiffness in his overall demeanor.

Something had changed. As soon as she'd likened him to a guardian angel, the playfulness, the sensuality, the warmth in the room had evaporated, leaving only this chilly awkwardness.

Perhaps he'd simply come to the realization that he was in a bathroom alone with a female patient who wore only a bathrobe. A disconcertingly unprofessional situation. Now *that* might stiffen the most seasoned of country doctors, especially one who took his profession as seriously as Rhune.

Tess smiled at the thought.

Smiled and didn't push him further. Didn't try to control that which was beyond her control. Instead, she concentrated on relaxing her own aching body, gave in to the sensations of having her hair rinsed. The tingling of her scalp. The lovely squeak of wet, clean hair. Before she'd even realized what was happening, she began to unwind so totally that even her shoulder pained her less.

Wrapping her head in a towel, Rhune helped her to sit up. "You're done." Before she could look him in the eye, he turned and busied himself recapping bottles.

"Thank you," she said softly, standing. "You've been very kind and caring."

Abruptly he turned to face her, his expression hooded. "A regular nineties hero." He made a low growling sound in his throat. "Be careful whom you trust, Tess. Too many so-called heroes have feet of clay." He wiped his hands on a towel and strode out of the bathroom.

"Now, that's a cynical thing to say." Confused by this unexpected brusque side of Rhune, Tess followed him into the bedroom. "Why are you being so hard on yourself? I was merely thanking you."

He stopped near the door to the hallway, his back to her. "I accept your thanks.... Perhaps we're both a little on edge after our morning adventure. I'd better go." The pause in his speech made it sound as if he'd intended to say something else altogether.

Something seemed to be eating at him. Something he was tempted to share.

Reaching out her hand, she touched his shoulder to stop him. When he turned toward her, she smiled and said, "Rhune Sherman, I think you're going to make a great curmudgeonly country doctor." She rose on tiptoe and brushed her lips across his cheek.

With lightning quickness he grasped her wrist and held it in a viselike grip. The look in his eyes could only be described as ferocity. "I don't think you want to do that," he growled. "Not unless you *really want* to kiss me."

Inhaling sharply, Tess took a step backward. This was not the man she'd come to know.

He released her wrist. "I thought not." Leaving Tess shaken and perplexed, he turned, opened the door to the hallway and left.

When she could finally make her body move, she hurried to the front window and looked down on the sidewalk below just as Rhune bounded off the veranda steps and right into the arms of an attractive and obviously distressed woman.

Or so it seemed.

Ah, now she understood his hurry to get out of her room. It seemed as if the good doctor had women stacked up in a holding pattern. Tess let the lace curtain fall back across the window. Well, it wasn't as if he hadn't warned her. Against her better judgment she parted the curtains again only to see Rhune slipping into the driver's seat of a strange car.

Absently she tugged at the end of the towel wrapped around her head and felt the damp weight of her hair fall down her back, as heavy as the weight holding down any hope she might have had. Hope that Dr. Rhune Sherman wasn't the mercurial playboy her sister insisted he was.

She harrumphed softly, certain now of what Caldwell was going to report.

Scowling at the ceiling, Rhune lay in his hammock, the only piece of "furniture" in the apartment above his office.

He'd bungled today. Royally.

It had started when he'd agreed to Belle and Cathryn's request to involve Tess in the gathering of magnolia boughs. He'd known the ulterior motive of those two women. They wanted to throw him together with the lovely Ms. McQueen. And he'd accepted their challenge, if only to prove to them and to himself that he was immune to the newcomer's charms.

Puerile. That's what he'd been in accepting their dare. Juvenile. Childish.

Because he wasn't immune to Tess's charms. Oh, no. Not at all. And every time he was with her, that fact got hammered home.

Take this morning.

Please.

Her accident had brought out—what had she called it?—the guardian angel side of him. Rhune ran his fingers through his hair in frustration. He was no angel. No, not by a long shot. And later in the bed-and-breakfast bathroom, alone with her, he'd almost come clean and told her exactly how unangelic a man he was.

For this was the upshot: Tess McQueen made him think of the future. Made him think of a relationship that might last. But to have such a relationship, he had to be honest about who he was.

He was no angel.

Perhaps, when he couldn't bring himself to tell her the truth in so many words this afternoon, perhaps that's why he'd shown her. With his Mr. Hyde behavior.

He snorted and reached out to push the wall with his bare foot, setting the hammock in motion.

The truth of the matter was that he'd behaved boorishly earlier not from any plan but because Tess McQueen had a way of getting to him. And he didn't like it. Didn't like the sensation of vulnerability that caring—truly caring—for someone on a personal level created. Didn't like the fact that he wanted to confess and exorcise his dark side. Didn't like not knowing what his feelings were going to be from one moment to the next.

It was turning him into a hormone-riddled Jekyll-and-Hyde to rival any in his club of adolescents.

He winced as he thought of Zach Freeman, a member of the very same Doc's Club. His encounter with Zach's mother on the sidewalk in front of Mel and Ida's this afternoon was going to require some explanation. He knew it from the look he'd caught on Tess's face as she'd glanced down at them from behind her bedroom curtains. A look that said he'd definitely toppled from any angel status he might have accrued.

He glanced at his watch. Six-thirty. Tess's meeting should be finished by now. He could walk over to the bed-and-breakfast and explain. But, damn, that's just what got him so hot under the collar. Why should he have to explain anything to Tess McQueen?

Explanation implied relationship.

And there was not—and would not be—any relationship between him and the all-too-unsettling efficiency expert. She was leaving for the world of business in a few days, and he was staying in Sweet Hope with the express desire of finding his center.

He didn't need to bollix up the process with an emotional entanglement.

"Damn!" He lowered his foot to the floor as a brake to the swinging hammock. He was going to regret this. This was another thing he hated about the spell Tess seemed to cast—it compelled him to do things he had no desire to do.

Explaining his actions had never been on his agenda.

He rolled out of the hammock, then began a search for shoes. That look Tess had shot him this afternoon from her bedroom window as she'd lowered the lace curtain haunted him. The look said clearly that he'd somehow disappointed her. Hell, he'd disappointed himself plenty in the past few years. He didn't need her getting all moony-eyed, too.

Slipping into a pair of old moccasins, he stopped at the door of his apartment. What exactly was he going to do? Was he going over to Mel and Ida's to explain the encounter with Zach Freeman's mother?

Or was he going to lay bare that which had been gnawing at him for months?

He didn't know. All he knew was that Tess McQueen had the power to unsettle him with a look. The power to coerce him into wanting to be the best he could be. And the best required honesty.

But that didn't mean he had to like it. He opened his apartment door with a jerk, then slammed it behind him.

Out on the street, Sweet Hope's evening promenade had begun. Residents waved and called to him as he made his way toward Mel and Ida's. Lord, he loved this place. For a fleeting instant he let himself wonder what it would be like if Tess decided to stay in town. Permanently. Just as fleeting, the image of her on his exam table her first night in town dispelled any such speculation. The image of her, pressed, pleated and corporate. Cool as alabaster and twice as exotic. Once old hotshot Wally Buckminster was finished with making *whatever* efficient, what was there for a Tess McQueen in Sweet Hope?

"Doc!"

The greeting startled him. He turned to see Plato standing in front of the Emporium, beckoning.

Rhune crossed the street to talk to the old man, glad for the distraction from unsettling thoughts.

Plato clapped him on the back and shook his hand enthusiastically. "Well, now, you must be mighty relieved animal control has come up with a proposal."

Rhune stared in disbelief at the other man. This was the first he'd heard of a proposal.

"You mean ole Myron didn't tell you?" Plato cackled gleefully. "Just like him. He and the boys down at animal control probably want to cook up a whopper before they release the truth. Hyperbole will stay in circulation so much better than veracity."

Rhune groaned audibly at the thought of the Sweet Hope mythmaking machine. "It was only raccoons, for Pete's sake."

Plato leaned forward and winked dramatically. "Raccoons *and* squirrels *and* woodpeckers. Found evidence of mice, too. 'Course, the crows got into the act later on."

"And what am I to do about them?" Rhune was losing patience. After all, this was *his* story. He, at least, should be made privy.

Rocking back on his heels, Plato placed his hands on his hips and, with some satisfaction, said, "Have Boone O'Malley build you a home in the clearing on the old Patterson site."

"That's the only advice animal control can come up with after three days?" Rhune asked in amazement. The hammock in his empty apartment was beginning to look like home.

"There's some people would say that's what you ought to have done from the get-go. That spot you picked was fit for no one short of St. Francis of Assisi." Plato knit his bushy eyebrows solicitously. "But I know you wanted a little solitude. Weren't ready for a thoroughly permanent residence. Weren't at that point in your journey when you come to town."

"My journey?" Rhune had the uncomfortable feeling that Plato was somehow scraping at his psyche. The man was noted for his dime-store psychology, and Rhune suddenly had an off-the-wall suspicion that the shopkeeper had been giving Tess McQueen lessons.

"You know what I'm talking 'bout, boy." Plato's voice was gruff, tinged with choked-up sentiment. "Comin' home."

Irritation pricked at Rhune. "I am home. I know it and freely admit it."

"Not yet." With a gentle smile Plato shook his head. "Before you're truly home, you have a few more things to straighten out." He nodded in the direction of Mel and Ida's bed-and-breakfast. "Over there."

Rhune flinched.

Had he just said to himself that he loved this town? Well, he'd like to amend that. He'd love this town just as soon as someone new moved in. Then *that* person—that unsuspecting newcomer—could be the butt of Sweet Hope's collective, overactive imagination. Its meddling. Its matchmaking. He glanced at Mel and Ida's. He had half a mind to turn around and head back to his apartment.

But the galling crux of the matter was that Plato was right. He did have unfinished business across the street.

With Tess McQueen.

A woman who was beginning to take up far too much room in his heretofore dormant conscience.

Chapter Seven

Clutching Caldwell's investigative report with her uninjured arm, Tess climbed Mel and Ida's veranda steps only to be met by the last person in the world she wanted to see right now. Rhune Sherman. Lounging in the rocker closest to the front door. His sprawling form made it impossible for her to avoid him.

"Hey," he said softly, rising. "We have to talk."

Tess didn't want to talk.

She wanted to fall onto her bed and go over this report once more. Wanted to let Caldwell's words sink in. She almost pleaded a headache, but the earnest look in Rhune's eyes made her pause.

"Can it wait?" she asked.

"No." He shot her a most curious look. "If we wait, it won't happen."

Taking her arm, he steered her all the way around the veranda to the gardens at the back of the house. At this time of evening the garden pathways were deserted.

"Here is fine," he said, stopping under a concealing rose arbor.

After his retreating, almost angry attitude in the bathroom this afternoon, Tess certainly hadn't expected this about-face. This unpredictability, however, appeared to be classic Rhune. She tightened her grasp on Caldwell's report. The investigator had said that the only thing predictable in Dr. Sherman's life was that he would do his job and do it well.

"Yes?" she asked, waiting, unable to imagine what had necessitated this heart-to-heart.

For the first time since she'd met him, Rhune seemed at a loss for words. Finally he crossed his arms over his chest and said, "There may have been some misunderstanding...this afternoon...about Karen Freeman...the woman on the sidewalk."

Tess looked down at the stone path as she felt the heat rise to her cheeks. How embarrassing to be confronted with her spying. "You don't need to explain," she said softly. Suddenly the scent of roses closed in on her. Became cloying. Increased her discomfort.

"I want to explain." He placed his fingers gently under her chin until she raised her head and looked directly at him. There was faint mischief in his expression. "Otherwise you might think I was angry and hurried with you earlier because I was late for a hot date."

"And you weren't?" Even though he lowered his hand, she could still feel the touch of his fingers on her chin. "Late for a hot date, that is."

A small smile tugged at the corners of his mouth. "No. The woman was Karen Freeman, mother to Zach, one of my club members. Zach had just broken his leg in an injudicious slide into second base."

An unexpected wave of relief washed over Tess. "Of course, she'd come looking for a doctor," she whispered. Caldwell had said that, of all Rhune's patients, children evoked the most compassion in him. The most commitment. He certainly had hopped without question into Karen Freeman's car this afternoon.

"We had to take Zach to the Sterling clinic. For X rays." With a rueful grin Rhune shook his head. "I haven't even officially opened my practice, and it's already evident that I'm underequipped. But that's neither here nor there. I wanted you to know who Karen was."

She looked deep into his eyes and saw no duplicity there. Hadn't Caldwell said that, with the women in his life, Rhune had been totally honest? And totally uncommitted. Yes, she believed his explanation of the woman on the sidewalk. But that didn't explain his brusqueness with her after he'd washed her hair.

"Thank you," she said, and almost left it at that. Almost. The pain in her bruised shoulder, however, egged her on. She cleared her throat. "That still doesn't explain why you seemed so upset with me earlier. In the bathroom." She watched the muscle along his jaw tense and twitch. "I got the impression that you were pushing me away. Why?" Other than the fact that Caldwell had said Rhune pushed every woman away, *eventually.*

He stiffened. "I suddenly realized you were a guest in town. A highly visible, professional woman in a place that thrives on gossip. It hit me that I'd overspent my time in your room."

He was lying. She knew it. One of the points Caldwell emphasized was that Rhune Sherman believed in the premise of consenting adults and gossip be damned. An hour in her room would not rest heavily on his conscience.

"I don't believe you," she replied in a whisper.

When he looked at her, his eyes now contained that near-ferocious cast they'd held this afternoon in the bathroom. He appeared as if he might growl. "Perhaps," he said finally, his words remarkably even, "it's that damn perceptiveness of yours I find unsettling."

She found that funny for some reason. "I didn't realize I'd been unduly publicly perceptive since rolling into town." She chuckled. "Now *that's* a tongue twister."

He scowled. "You can joke, but you have a disturbing ability to probe into a person's thoughts."

"*Your* thoughts?"

"Yes."

"I'm sorry. I thought that, all this time, we were merely conversing." That wasn't quite true. With every conversation they'd had, she'd tried to investigate the real Rhune Sherman. Funny. But she'd come up with as much as Caldwell had: that the good doctor was a true enigma. A paradox.

The look he threw her was open and unnervingly hungry. He seemed as if he were consciously willing his hands to remain at his sides. "Then perhaps it's me."

"I don't understand." She half understood, and because of the knowledgeable half, she clutched Caldwell's file and took a step backward. Away from the man who made the space in the rose arbor seem all too small.

His regard devoured her. "Perhaps I'm just responding to you as a woman."

Tess felt her eyes widen involuntarily.

"I'm attracted to you... although the chance of anything happening between us is improbable at best. A snowball's chance..." He shrugged and did his best to look nonchalant.

"And has that stopped you in the past?"

He furrowed his brow. "Let's just say *that* is the most unsettling thing about you, Ms. McQueen. You appear to bring out a little-used side of me. My chivalrous side."

"Let me get this straight! You pushed me away because I make you behave like a gentleman?"

"Let's not leak this to the town gossips," he replied, his tone heavy on the irony.

"You can try to kid your way out of this, Rhune Sherman. But since *you* initiated this talk, we're going to get to the bottom of the problem." Needing to give this elusive man her full attention, she placed Caldwell's file carefully on the rose arbor seat, then skewered Rhune with her best negotiation-table glare. "Why did you seem so angry with

me after you washed my hair? Why did you push me away?
What is it about me—*specifically*—that so bothers you?
And let's skip the nonsense about me tweaking your con-
science."

"But that's exactly the gist of the matter. You give my
conscience a good boot in the rear."

"No!"

"I wish it wasn't true." He glowered. "But every time I'm
with you, I feel like...like...coming clean, for Pete's sake.
Like telling you my life story, warts and all."

"*Every* time?"

"Well...those times I'm not already thinking about
kissing you senseless."

Tess inhaled sharply and heard herself squeak, "I thought
you said I made you behave like a gentleman."

"You don't seem to have any power over my thoughts."
Rhune grimaced. "Neither, for that matter, do I."

Tess felt her pulse flutter. "I'm confused."

"Don't be." He grasped her upper arms. "I was simply
trying to tell you, this afternoon in your bathroom when you
got that grateful look in your eyes, that I'm no hero. If you
want heroes, follow around the local fire fighters or the
highway patrol. You'll find heroes there. Now, me...I'm
just a guy who's managed to do some good professionally
while I've done some things personally that wouldn't bear
close scrutiny."

"Why are you telling me this?" Tess's words came out
almost inaudibly.

"I'll be damned if I know." Rhune released her, then
shoved the fingers of both hands through his hair. "All I
know is that when I get around you I'm afflicted with a severe case of candor."

Tess smiled. This was no act. Dr. Rhune Sherman seemed
genuinely at a loss. Her heart reached out to him. "Well,
then, Doc, except for the kissing part, what you describe
sounds like friendship."

He looked doubtful.

"I mean it," she continued gently. "Sometimes you run across someone with whom you can be yourself. You don't have to hide your flaws. That's a friend."

He narrowed his eyes. "I don't think so, McQueen. Quite frankly, you drive me nuts. Like with the way you neglect your health."

She grinned. "I never said friends didn't drive friends nuts." Oh, it sure would be easier if she and Rhune could just declare for friendship. That would take care of all those pesky little hot flashes he ignited in her. In the name of friendship, she could simply ignore them.

What was she saying? She was in Sweet Hope neither to befriend the man nor to give in to her hormonal impulses. She was here to ferret out the truth about him and her sister. And so far, even with the help of a private investigator, she'd found nothing that resembled the whole story. About either the man or his past.

Or Chelsey and her unborn child.

"Friendship would be easier," she heard him mutter.

"I beg your pardon?"

He leveled a gaze at her that was filled with purpose. "I'm not looking for any more complications in my life right now."

"Any *more?*" Was she about to get a hint of the complexity that apparently was his life?

He rolled his eyes. "You don't think a residence that's now either inoperable or in the treetops isn't complicated enough?"

"Ah, yes. Your trailer." That wasn't the complication she'd wanted explained.

"Besides, I have a practice to get off the ground. It even looks as if I'm going to have to expand and update that practice almost before I hang out my shingle. I have a town full of people I need to get to know...and I need to take some time to get to know myself."

Another hint. "What do you mean?"

He forced a sardonic smile. "That seems to be one more thing you're good at—making me think about my actions. I've never been one for much introspection."

"Such as?" Tess held her breath. Could it be that he might actually tell her something of himself? Something she hadn't been able to find out from others.

He narrowed his eyes. "Such as why I ended up in Sweet Hope in the first place."

"Are you going to tell me?" she asked in a near whisper.

"It's a long story." He shrugged in an offhand manner. She knew intuitively that he wasn't as nonchalant as he tried to appear.

"I'm not going anywhere," she offered.

Oh, no. She wasn't going anywhere. Not for a million dollars and a home of her own on the Potomac.

Not until she knew the whole truth about Rhune Sherman.

Why was this so difficult? Rhune turned and looked out over the Drakes' gardens. He'd walked over here expressly to come clean. Once and for all. So that the air was crystal clear between Tess and him. So that there were no illusions as to his fallibility. So that...what? He'd almost let the promise of a future slip into his thoughts.

No, he wouldn't think of a future with Tess McQueen.

If he came clean, she'd step back, certainly. *That* was what he wanted. To be rid of the vexing false hope concerning the ludicrous idea of a relationship between the two of them. An idea that seemed to spark, unbidden, in his mind every time the woman got close.

Oh, no, he wasn't clearing the slate to draw her closer; he was doing it to safely distance himself.

He felt her hand on his arm. Gentle. "Let's sit down," she said softly, indicating the two facing seats in the rose arbor.

When he did sit and look at her, he saw the most peculiar expression of expectation on her face. Why would she possibly be interested in his story? Apparently he could add "good listener" to her growing catalog of admirable traits.

"I moved to Sweet Hope," he began tentatively, "because it didn't appear that I was making one damned bit of difference in D.C." The old anger welled up inside him. He couldn't do this sitting down. Standing abruptly, he began to pace, the crunch of stones beneath his feet adding a staccato emphasis to his words.

Without speaking, Tess looked up at him, her hands now protectively cradling the file she'd carried with her when she'd returned to the bed-and-breakfast earlier. It made her appear all business. Dressed again in silk and pearls, sitting straight and tall, she seemed like a cool, exotic flower, unfazed by the warm and humid evening air. Regal. Untouchable.

He went on because now he couldn't stop. "The worst part of the job was patching up the kids. Ten, eleven, twelve-year-olds torn up with gunshot wounds. Kids who should be learning to fish or throw a ball around, who, instead, are busy learning to run the gauntlet of life." He clenched his fist and slammed it into the palm of his other hand. "And me, patching them up and throwing them out on the streets again."

"That's a pretty jaded perspective." She arched one eyebrow, her expression unreadable. "You're a doctor. You did what you were sworn to do."

"A doctor?" He glared at her and saw her flinch imperceptibly. "I turned into a mechanic. A very *efficient* mechanic who, while on duty, learned to turn off every human impulse except his brain and his hands. *On duty,* I became a skilled robot."

She sat immobile. Only her voice reached out to him in the soft evening air. "I know D.C. You fought against tremendous odds. But what if you and others like you hadn't been there? What if no one had attempted to make a difference?"

He didn't answer her questions. There were no answers, not to those questions. He looked out over the garden and the lengthening shadows. "Off duty," he murmured to the dying breeze, "I tried to numb myself...and became less of a man."

He didn't hear her rise, but when he turned, she was standing right beside him. "What are you saying?" she asked, her voice breathy, her face unusually pale.

There was no way he was stopping now. Hung for a pence, hung for a pound, he used to rationalize. "I'm saying that I used my personal time—what there was of it—to blot out the horror I'd witnessed professionally."

"*How* did you blot out the horror?" Obviously she wasn't going to allow him to speak in generalities.

He was going to have to spell it out. His words were bitter. "How better to blot out misery than with wine, women and song?"

Her silence spoke volumes.

"Are you judging me?" He leaned toward her. "Don't bother. I've acted as my own judge and jury."

She didn't flinch this time. "I was wondering what made you stop."

"Acting as judge and jury? I'm not sure that I have."

"No. What made you stop your self-destructive behavior." She reached out to touch him, but seemed to think better of it and withdrew her hand. "Obviously something jolted you enough so that you felt the need to turn your life around."

"Najeem," he muttered, slitting his eyes against the painful memory. "And Chelsey."

He heard Tess's sharp intake of breath. When he turned to face her, her mouth had dropped slightly open, her eyes had taken on the color of summer thunderheads. How could two strangers' names affect her so?

There was no turning back. He pushed the words from his mouth. "I'd patched up Najeem and had sent him back out onto the streets." He shook his head in frustration and disbelief even from this distance in time. "The boy had too many strikes against him already. His father had abandoned his mother and him." He ground his teeth in fury. "There is no scum greater than a man who abandons his child. . . ." Filled with sorrow for the beautiful boy Najeem, he stopped speaking.

"What happened?" Rhune started at Tess's whispered words.

He hesitated, his voice catching in his throat. "I saw him two days later when they brought him in again. This time dead." The anger threatened to consume him. "He was eight."

Tess reached out for him, but he shrugged her away.

"I took the hero's route," he snapped, his words laden with sarcasm, "and found the nearest bar. The nearest pair of willing arms."

"Chelsey," Tess breathed.

He looked her directly in the eye. He didn't want her to mistake or underestimate a word he had to say. "She wasn't Chelsey when I met her. She wasn't even Chelsey when I was about to take her to bed. I didn't know her name. Hadn't even asked. She was simply *there*. A nameless tool in my attempt at forgetfulness. That's the brilliant mechanic I'd become."

Tess's eyes were wide and filled with horror. "What happened?"

"Nothing. Nothing sexual, that is. I came to my senses. And stopped. Before I bedded Chelsey—a nineteen-year-old kid with a temper who wanted desperately to be an actress. And a grown-up."

"You found that much out about her?" Tess's voice quavered.

"Yeah. She felt the need to fill me in as she threw my clothes and me out of her apartment." He clenched his fists. "A rather ignominious epiphany."

"You *stopped* before you took this girl to bed?" Disbelief hovered at the edges of her words.

"Sounds unbelievable, I know." He slit his eyes at the bitter memory. "But bedding a nameless woman would not bring Najeem back." He shook his head. "Somehow, through the haze of alcohol and grief, I got that straight."

There was pain in her expression. "You left Washington because..."

"Because I no longer saw human beings. On duty, I saw objects of my craft. Statistics. Off duty, I saw only the means to forget. I'd lost touch with *individuals*. Human beings. And had lost the human being in myself."

Tess seemed stunned. "Why are you telling me this?" she asked, her voice barely a whisper.

"Beats me." Rhune ran his fingers through his hair, his anger ebbing, exasperation rising. "From the minute you walked into town you've been pulling miniconfessions out of me." He looked at her. Hard. "I have to say I don't like it."

"And that's why you pushed me away earlier?"

"Yeah." An uncomfortable thought struck him. "I'm not asking for absolution. Let's get that clear."

"No." Tess frowned. "I imagine you wouldn't let anyone forgive you."

"What does that mean?"

"It means that you'll always have a convenient wall of guilt to keep you safe."

This was not the reaction he'd expected from her. He'd expected her to cut bait and walk away. Or if she'd stayed, he'd expected her to tell him, in no uncertain terms, what a creep he was. He certainly hadn't expected her to probe still further. The woman was like a damned laser.

"Rhune Sherman, why are you so determined that *I*, particularly, should dislike you?"

Her question made him stand stock-still.

Life would be so much easier if she disliked him. Then he wouldn't have to give a second thought to those soft violet eyes. Nor a second glance to skin so smooth it begged to be touched. If she disliked him—truly, visibly disliked him—he wouldn't always be thinking what it would be like to kiss her. To hold her.

"Why?" she persisted.

Hell, he'd exorcised one thorny issue. He might as well go for two.

He reached for her and pulled her toward him. She was no nameless beauty. No means to forgetfulness. She was real. She made him feel and remember. A woman who disliked surprises, who loved motorcycle rides but wouldn't admit it, who fit in easily with kids at an ill-fitting age. A woman who, like now, looked beautiful and at ease in silk and pearls, or who, with a little provocation, looked like a knockout in wet shorts and a T-shirt. He knew this woman. Knew the way her eyes widened when she was startled. Knew her quest for efficiency and perfection. Knew, too, although she herself might not know it, the passion that simmered beneath her regal exterior.

He lowered his mouth to capture hers. Tasted her surprise. She was softer than he'd anticipated. And sweeter. He drew her closer. Ran his tongue over the inexpressible delicacy of her lips. Felt her open for him. Heard a low groan escape from his own throat. Felt her strong and warm and very, very real in his arms.

Felt the safe wall he'd tried to construct between them crumble and begin to fall.

So much for friendship.

What the hell was she doing? This was madness.

This kiss.

She'd wanted to wrest a confession from him, then use the opportunity to teach him a lesson of consequences. He'd confessed, but it hadn't been the confession she'd expected. She'd seen his genuine pain and had wanted to assuage it.

She'd seen, too, his hunger and had succumbed to the matching hunger within herself.

With his crazy kiss, she came alive. A lesson in consequences gone awry.

Everything and everyone fell away, except this man who held her as if she belonged with him. His arms enveloped her. She could feel the palms of his hands hot on her back, searing her senses. The low moan that escaped his throat echoed the silent moaning of her every sinew. Her eyelids fluttered, too heavy to open. She couldn't look at him. But with her fingertips against his face she could *see* him. With her tongue she could taste his need.

Against all reason she gave herself up to the kiss.

He was flawed. A man who had used sensuality as an opiate. Who had put his emotions on automatic pilot. She felt his tongue sweep her own, sending her senses into over-drive. Was *this*, for him, automatic pilot? Sweet mercy, what could he do to her if he meant it?

She willed her eyes open and pulled away. Breathless.

She could clearly see him now, his chest heaving, his eyes dark and stormy.

Her thoughts would not come rationally. "Did you mean that?" It was a stupid question, but it had slipped out on its own.

He narrowed his eyes and slowly licked his lips. And sent her pulse skittering. "Mean it?" His words were a rasp along her spine. "Let's just say I didn't mean to mean it."

She lifted her fingers to her mouth. Her lips felt swollen from the brief but thorough kiss. "I think you'd better go," she said softly but firmly. She took a deep breath. "I think I understand your lesson." Damn. She was to have been the one dispensing the lessons.

He made no move to leave, only cocked one eyebrow in question.

"Perhaps you mistook my gratitude earlier today for hero worship." She found it difficult to look at him. "Believe me . . . I'm not one to rely on first appearances. You don't have to warn me off."

He rubbed his hand along his jaw. "No," he said slowly, his expression slightly dazed, "perhaps not."

Gathering courage, she held out her hand for him to shake. "Perhaps my suggestion of friendship was prema-ture, but we certainly don't have to be at odds."

A lazy grin spread across his face as he took her hand. Despite her attempt at minimizing the moment, something had changed between them. There would never be a way to wipe out that kiss and its effect. Not with a handshake. Not with any number of rational words.

"Did *you* mean it?" His unexpected question and the accompanying twinkle in his eyes exploded her renewed composure.

"I—I beg your pardon?" she stammered.

The grin expanded to his eyes. His dimple deepened. "You heard me."

She looked down at the ground and spotted Caldwell's file at her feet. Obviously she'd let it slip, forgotten, to the ground during the kiss. She gasped in horror as she saw papers threatening to spill from the flimsy pasteboard container. How could she have been so oblivious to her surroundings? Had his kiss been that potent?

She didn't have to ask.

Kneeling, Tess began to scoop papers securely back into their holder. Papers that tried to explain Rhune Sherman but couldn't half as well as his confession and his kiss. Rhune stooped also in a gesture of help.

"Please! No! Thank you!" Her words came out a senseless jumble. "I have it."

He didn't look at the last paper as he picked it up and handed it to her. He fixed his gaze firmly, disconcertingly on her face. "The results of that important meeting?"

"Y-yes." She stood and held the recovered file safely against her middle. "I really need to review it." She winced.

"How's your shoulder?"

Her shoulder? She started. For a time she'd actually forgotten about her injured shoulder. Shaking her head in amazement, she said, "I do believe it's just a bruise."

"We'll see what the X rays say tomorrow." He turned to go. "I'll be by to pick you up at nine." He left without waiting for her reply.

A dark, heavy feeling crept over her. He'd gone. And she'd never uttered a word to tell him she was Chelsey's sister.

Perplexed in more ways than one, Tess left the garden and made her way to her room. Why hadn't she revealed her relationship to Chelsey?

When Rhune had told her about the failed night with her sister, it was as if she were the victor poised with the vanquished's throat beneath her foot. All she had to do was press. But she hadn't. Why not?

She opened the door to her room, threw the file on the bed, then began to undress. Her shoulder bothered her now.

Perhaps she hadn't exercised the power because of Rhune's obvious pain. For Najeem.

Caldwell's report had told more than Rhune had. Caldwell himself had said that all Rhune's spare time wasn't spent in wine, women and song. Rhune had traveled a long, rocky and circuitous route in his formal education. He'd come to his residency older than many of his fellow doctors. He was a man of incredible professional dedication, a man of equally incredible off-duty appetites ... and a man with a social conscience. Najeem had been his "little brother" in a nascent storefront program just outside the hospital gates.

When Najeem died, a part of Rhune Sherman had died, also.

The next day, according to Caldwell's report, Rhune had stood, unwashed, red-eyed and reeking of alcohol, before his staff superior and turned down the position of attending physician, a position offered to him not three days earlier. Apparently the hospital had chosen to put their trust in the on-duty Dr. Sherman. Rhune had taken himself out of contention because of off-duty ghosts.

Tess passed over her silk pajamas, throwing on, instead, an oversize cotton T-shirt she'd purchased from Plato.

Plato. The remarkable store owner had told her more truth about Rhune Sherman than all Caldwell's and her own investigations combined.

And this evening Rhune himself had laid bare that which he considered the worst in his past. Had laid himself open to her. Although he'd also admitted he had no idea why he felt the need to confess to her.

Perhaps it was his self-induced vulnerability that kept her from exercising her power in the end. He'd already acted swiftly as his own judge and jury. There were proscriptions against double jeopardy.

She had to call Chelsey. It was apparent, as Tess had grown to suspect, that her sister had not been totally forthright in all this.

As she dialed the Washington, D.C., exchange, her heart thumped heavily in her chest.

"Actresses are us!" Chelsey's voice rang out saucily over the line.

"Dixie Fae McQueen," Tess said sternly, using her sister's given name, "we have to talk."

"Lordy, sis, what's wrong?"

"What really happened that night with Rhune Sherman?"

The line grew dead for several long moments. When Chelsey finally answered, the sauciness in her voice was gone, replaced with an edgy chill.

"I told you...he seduced me with a lot of promises, then abandoned me. Left me pregnant and all alone." Chelsey repeated the same old song that Tess had heard over and over; it was the ever-so-slightly cracked tone that was new. As if Chelsey might suddenly be aware of her big sister's suspicions.

Tess tried to keep her frustration in check. It wouldn't do to bully Chelsey, then have her close up. The issue was not power. The issue was the truth.

Tess needed to know the truth from Chelsey.

"I received Caldwell's report."

"And?" Chelsey's voice was wary.

"There was never a hint of sexual harassment on the job."

"That was *on the job,* sis. I was extracurricular, and *he* was a different man off duty. Manipulative." Tess could hear the pout in Chelsey's words. "He took advantage of me."

"Caldwell interviewed women Rhune...dated." A euphemism if she'd ever used one. "They freely expressed that manipulation was not his style. If anything, he was brutally honest about his lack of interest in commitment." Tess softened her tone. After all, this was her sister. "Obviously, *neither of you* thought of commitment . . . or protection."

"He was the doctor, for God's sake!" Chelsey seemed to be losing it. She'd always been an emotional person, and the hormones of pregnancy had heightened her already volatile nature. "And his lack of interest in commitment is the issue here. Even with a baby on the way, he wouldn't commit."

Tess heard the waver in her sister's voice and remembered Rhune's confession tonight. Remembered how vehemently he had denounced as scum men who abandoned their children. She had to ask one certain question again. "Chelsey, honey, did you really tell Rhune Sherman about the baby?"

"Why do you keep asking me that?"

"Because, quite frankly, he seems to love children. And . . . the report . . . said that, despite his wandering ways, he wants to have a family some day."

"It did?" Chelsey's words were small. Childlike.

"Yes," Tess replied, then waited. She had only pieces of truth in this dilemma. Her sister's accusations. Caldwell's report. Rhune himself. And her own gut feelings. Something told her that Chelsey held more of the missing pieces than any of the other factors put together. And so she waited for Chelsey to reveal more.

It wasn't long before Chelsey began to sniffle.

"What's wrong, hon?" Tess couldn't stand the thought of her sister in pain. Actress or not, Chelsey's present predicament was very real and, Tess could imagine, emotionally painful. She softened her voice. "Chelsey?"

"He *insulted* me." The words hissed over the phone line as if they'd been issued through clenched teeth.

"How?" Tess asked quietly.

Chelsey didn't answer.

"How?" Tess persisted. She suspected Rhune had told her the truth, but she wanted to hear it directly from her sister.

"He seemed to think I wasn't good enough for him. Wasn't good enough . . . even to sleep with him."

"Are you telling me you didn't . . . ?"

"Have sex? No." Chelsey's words were bitter. "At the last minute Dr. Rhune Sherman decided I simply wasn't good enough for him."

"Oh, baby." Tess's heart ached for her young sister. At nineteen the whole world seemed bent on rejection. "Let me tell you what . . . Caldwell . . . told me. You happened to be right smack in Rhune's path after one of the worst days of his career. An eight-year-old boy he'd cared for deeply had died. Rhune was looking to forget."

"That was no reason to use me!" Chelsey howled.

"No, it wasn't. And he realized it. Too late, maybe, but realized it all the same. That's why he left."

"How do you know?" Accusation rang out in Chelsey's voice.

Tess sidestepped. "Rhune told his staff superior the next day that he was losing his humanity. He turned down the offer of attending physician, then made plans to take over this practice in Sweet Hope."

"Caldwell told you all that?"

"He was very thorough." Tess felt a twinge at not telling of Rhune's own confession. This was the second time today she'd failed to come forward with information. But with her sister, as with Rhune, she couldn't bring herself to exercise her full power. To her way of thinking, total disclosure would only increase the injury.

"Sherman's still a jerk!" Chelsey spat out the words in anger.

Tess didn't think so. Flawed, yes. But struggling to let the best in him triumph. "Chelsey," she said, "I think you need to move on with this. I don't think this is a matter for revenge." She checked her own rising anger and didn't mention that Chelsey, with her manipulative behavior, was not too far from the jerk department.

"He gets off scot-free?"

"Believe me...the man didn't get off scot-free." Tess sighed heavily. "But now that the truth is out, we still have the matter of the baby...and why you saw fit to use Rhune...and me. And last but certainly not least, the identity of the real father. You didn't think Rhune would deny paternity?"

Chelsey didn't answer, and Tess felt too tired to press the issue tonight. There would be time enough in Washington to sort out the details. She knew one thing for certain: her reason for being in Sweet Hope was now null and void.

She would leave tomorrow.

"We'll talk when I get home," she said, her voice weary to her own ears.

Suddenly she no longer played the role of investigator, of mediator. Even the mask of patient stand-in parent slipped. She was merely Tess, a woman who'd been sorely manipulated by her own sister. Because the truth of the matter hurt so keenly, she couldn't let Chelsey off without a warning for the future.

"From now on, you need to fight your own battles," she snapped, making no attempt to soften her words.

"You're cutting me off?"

"Dixie Fae McQueen, spare me the drama." Tess rolled her eyes. "I'm your sister. That means I'm sworn to love you unconditionally. Not be your conscience."

"Whatever are you implying?"

"I'm not implying anything. It just struck me that a nineteen-year-old pregnant and unwed woman who's willing to fall into bed with a stranger needs a hard look at the consequences herself."

"This sounds suspiciously as if you've been reading a cheap pamphlet on tough love," Chelsey grumbled.

Tess wouldn't let her sister engage her in battle. "Move on, Chelsey. Let it go, and move on. Accept the fact that you've stepped squarely into the adult world of responsibility, and start acting like an adult. Believe me, it will be your most gratifying role.''

Chelsey said nothing.

''I'll see you in a few days,'' Tess offered, consciously gentling her voice. She was angry at Chelsey, yes, but she needed to retain perspective. Hurt or not, she wasn't the one pregnant and unwed. She could afford to be generous. ''Don't forget that, tough or not, it's love.''

She heard the phone disconnect at the other end.

Inhaling deeply, she replaced the receiver in the cradle. Chelsey would come around. Tess had weathered worse snits.

It was her own future that troubled her.

There was no longer a mystery to unravel in Georgia. Caldwell had given his report. Tess had paid and released him. There would be no court date, not involving Dr. Rhune Sherman, at least, and Wally Buckminster's services would not be needed. Her own physical health had been restored.

She no longer had a reason to remain in Sweet Hope.

Why did that fact bring her absolutely no joy?

Chapter Eight

Rhune couldn't believe his eyes.

Tess was slinging a suitcase into the trunk of her BMW.

"What are you doing?" he snapped.

She dropped the suitcase with a thud into the back of the car, then whirled to face him. A flicker of regret passed over her face, then quickly disappeared. Composed once more, she exuded cool self-possession. And extended her hand to him. "My work is finished here," she said evenly. "It's time to go home."

He ignored her outstretched hand, and tried to ignore the blip of panic deep inside him. *She was leaving.*

"No pearls and silk for the road?" he asked, trying to make his words nonchalant. She wore shorts, a T-shirt and athletic shoes, her hair pulled back in a ponytail. It sure didn't look like a typical Tess McQueen traveling outfit to him.

She smiled, and his heart did a little flip-flop. "Let's just say Plato and Sweet Hope have taught me a thing or two about relaxation and comfort."

"How did you get your car?" His conversational transitions were nonexistent. He knew it. His intent, however, was to keep her from leaving, by filibuster alone if necessary.

"Mr. Martin delivered it this morning."

"Then you can drive yourself right over to the Sterling clinic to have your blood pressure checked and your shoulder X-rayed."

She arched one midnight dark eyebrow. "You're hovering, Doc."

"I thought you were staying a week. Monday would be a week. Three more days."

"I said I'd stay till my business was finished." Her questioning look told him she was confused by his volley of words. "It's finished."

"And Wally Buckminster's the only one in town that could use your services?"

She blushed. "Looks like it."

"I don't think so." After he'd spilled his guts to her as he had to no one else—*ever*—after he'd kissed her and felt it down to the soles of his feet, after he'd wrestled with the decision to come for her this morning himself or to avoid her very own disconcerting self and go fishing, asking Ida Drake to drive her to Sterling instead . . . after all that, he wasn't letting her slide out of town so easily.

He grasped her wrist firmly. "Come on. *I* need you." Sure, yesterday evening—both confession and kiss—had scared him, too, but here he was, standing on the pavement, ready to face the consequences . . . and *maybe* ready to face the possibility of exploring a relationship. "We have unfinished business."

Planting her feet firmly on the sidewalk, she refused to budge. "Rhune Sherman, don't play the caveman with me." Her voice was a warning; the look in her eyes registered shock.

Maybe he had gotten carried away. Where the hell had he thought to take her?

Releasing her wrist, he shook his head. "You thought I meant . . . ?" He pointed between himself and her. "Did I make it sound as if . . . ?"

She nodded, wide-eyed.

"Let's start all over." He took a deep breath, his mind whirring. He spotted a child's bicycle leaning up against Plato's Emporium. "*My club* . . . needs an efficiency expert. For the Fourth of July preparations. We're in charge of helping the little kids decorate their bikes."

She didn't look at all convinced.

"I know this sounds as if I'm thinking on my feet." He was. "But I'm not. I was going to ask you to help us after I took you to Sterling this morning." He tried to look scout honest.

Doc's Club *was* assembling on the village green as they spoke. The adolescents under his supervision *were* scheduled to help the younger children decorate bikes for tomorrow's parade. But Rhune had just now thought of asking Tess's help. His request for help, although ad libbed, was in no way bogus. He needed her, all right. Needed her to stay because the two of them did indeed have unfinished business.

He just needed time to figure out exactly what that business was.

One corner of Tess's mouth quirked in a half grin. "How efficiently must the kids decorate these bikes?"

"Oh, *very* efficiently." He smiled back at her.

Please, he implored mentally, if she isn't hot on the idea of staying for me, let her be swayed by the idea of being with those kids again. She'd enjoyed it at the swimming hole. He'd seen it in her eyes. And the kids had flat-out loved her. "If they waste an ounce of crepe paper streamer, Belle will have my hide."

Tess shook her head and actually laughed. "Rhune Sherman, you could quite possibly talk the moon out of the sky for your own purposes."

"That's a yes?" He saw her waver. He pressed his point. "The traffic on the interstates will be murder, what with the holiday tomorrow. Much more sensible to start back after the Fourth.''

Suddenly her expression hardened. ''I have a job to get back to.'' It sounded as if she was trying to convince herself. ''Responsibilities. People who depend on me.'' She turned to close the car trunk. ''The rest of my work didn't take a holiday while I was here.''

He reached out and gently touched her arm. ''And what about you? Do you ever take a holiday? Do you ever think about Tess McQueen and what she might want...or need?''

He seemed to have struck a chord with that line of questioning. She turned to look at him, and he detected a hint of longing in those big, beautiful eyes. A wistfulness about her sensuous mouth. He bet the efficient Ms. McQueen didn't take many holidays. Thought more of others and their wants and needs than of her own.

''What will two days matter?'' he urged. ''You can stay today and tomorrow for the celebration, then leave Sunday and be back at your desk bright and early Monday morning.'' He winked. ''You can have it all—fun *and* efficiency.''

Still she demurred.

''Come on, Tess. I'll be your funmeister and, if you must feel useful, you can give me some pointers as to how I can update my office...plus the kids, of course, need you.''

She sighed. ''This is definitely not what I planned.''

''Plans are for changing.'' He grinned. ''Heck, I bought a pond so that I could windsurf. Then I found out the pond's so protected by Georgia forest there's little or no wind.''

''So you made a Tarzan swing instead.'' Tess smiled.

''Now you're getting the idea of changed plans. Detours.'' He ran his fingers down her arm. Gazed down at her pale, slender hand that trembled ever so slightly. ''How about it? What can two days out of your busy schedule hurt?''

He thought he heard her murmur, "Too much, by far," but when he looked up he only saw her staring intently at him.

"When was the last time you decorated a bike for a parade?" he asked, pressing. "Or spit watermelon seeds? Or ran a three-legged race? Or lay on your back outdoors to watch fireworks?"

She shook her head. "You don't fight fair."

"I never intended to," he assured her, suddenly wishing he could kiss her and tip the scales even more unfairly. "Yes?"

She glanced at the trunk of her car, then back at him.

"Yes?" he asked again more emphatically.

As though it was the hardest thing in the world for her to say, Tess finally breathed, "Yes."

"Yes!"

"But . . . !" She held up her hand in warning. "Don't expect me to spit watermelon seeds in public. That's definitely beyond dignity."

"Perhaps, then, you could organize a pearl-spitting contest."

She actually laughed, and he thought he'd never heard anything so satisfying.

"And one more thing..." She grew serious. Reached out her hand to touch his arm. Compelled him to absolute stillness. "No blood pressure cuff. No X rays. If this is to be my holiday, I want a real holiday."

"Tess, I don't think—"

"My shoulder is fine," she insisted. "My blood pressure is fine. Despite what you may think, Doc, I do know my own body, and it's just fine."

"But—"

"No buts. Those are the terms under which I'll stay." She squeezed his arm and winked. *Winked!* "Deal?"

He'd been had. "Deal," he grumbled. When had he lost the upper hand in negotiations here?

Tess raised her hands in an expectant shrug. "Well, funmeister, what do we do next?"

Damned if he knew. Suddenly Rhune felt like an old dog who, after years of chasing cars, found himself in the surprising situation of finally having caught one.

What the hell did he do with her now?

"No!" Tess exclaimed, laughing. "I don't think you can thread crepe paper in your bike chain. Not without ruining your bike." Trying to unstick a roll of tape that had somehow become wadded up in an unusable mess, she looked at the disappointed five-year-old boy and the twelve-year-old girl assigned to help him. "I think we need to stick to handlebars and wheel spokes. To be on the safe side."

"But, Miss Tess, Aiden wants his bike to be *different*," Sarah explained. "Everyone has crepe paper on their spokes and handlebars." Clearly Doc's Club members took their role of advocates for the younger children seriously.

"I want to stand out," Aiden added earnestly. "So that my mama and daddy won't have any trouble spotting me in the parade."

"Well, then," Tess replied, abandoning the hopeless tape and sitting on the grass next to the boy, "the three of us will have to put our heads together to come up with something that will stand out without jamming your chain." She squinted and examined the pint-size bicycle with training wheels.

This small-town hoopla was new to her. Living in apartments and then in their condo, Tess and Chelsey's Fourth of July holiday involved cookouts on the balcony then walks to The Mall with several thousand other city dwellers to view the fireworks display over the Capitol buildings. There never had been any intimate decisions of crepe paper and bicycles or total-involvement parades.

"Could we do something with his safety flag?" Sarah suggested.

Tess looked at the five-foot dowel and attached fluorescent triangular flag that Aiden's parents had affixed to the back of his bicycle. A loving protection measure.

"Yeah," Aiden agreed enthusiastically. "Let's make it look like a giant sparkler!"

Tess chuckled. "We could try, but crepe paper doesn't sparkle."

"Mr. Moser donated some of that shiny, fringy stuff that he hangs around his car dealership," Sarah offered, brightening. "We could use that and make a terrific sparkler. Aiden's mama and daddy would sure spot him in the parade then."

"All right." Tess rose. "Point me in the direction of Mr. Moser, and I'll get us some sparkler ingredients while you two get yourselves some lemonade from Miss Belle."

Sarah stood and pointed to the gazebo in the middle of the village green. "Mr. Moser left that big white box... there... next to Doc, and Aiden's parents."

Doc.

Ah, yes, the man responsible for her being here at this very moment.

The man who, once he'd convinced her to stay, had virtually left her on her own.

Not that she was complaining. The bike decorating had been fun and the kids delightful. But Rhune's behavior had been curious. As if, once he'd convinced her to stay, he'd grown unaccountably perplexed at his own persuasion. Perplexed and standoffish.

She should talk about the good doctor's odd behavior! Her own had been strange indeed. What was she thinking when she'd agreed to stay for two more days?

Thoughts of her job had certainly flown out the window. And thoughts of Chelsey? Well, her sister needed a good dose of standing on her own two feet. But what about thoughts of Rhune Sherman, a man so flawed thoughts of him ought to send up a mental red warning flag? Had, in fact.

"Miss Tess?" She felt a small, warm hand on her arm, heard a clear, piping voice. "Do you want Sarah and me to get the sparkly stuff?"

She'd been uncharacteristically lost in thought and hadn't moved an inch toward the gazebo where Rhune still stood. "No, Aiden," she replied. "You and Sarah get your drinks." And I'll face Rhune, she added mentally.

Why did that particular prospect send a tingle down her spine?

She still hadn't answered the question of why she'd agreed to stay in Sweet Hope when there was absolutely no logical reason for her to remain. In fact, if she considered her sister and her neglected job—*others*—as she was wont to do, reason compelled her to return to D.C.

But Rhune had definitely struck a chord when he'd asked her if she ever thought of Tess McQueen and what *she* might want or need. She rarely did. Consider her own desires, that is. And the temptation to do so this time had proven too powerful.

She kept telling herself that her own desires simply involved a weekend of small-town fun. Nothing more. Nothing faintly reckless.

As Tess cautiously approached the gazebo, Rhune turned and fixed her with an unexpected languid brown gaze that took her breath away.

Heavens.

In taking forty-eight hours of rest and relaxation for herself—for her overworked mind and body—had she left her heart and emotions vulnerable?

Squelching that troubling thought, Tess squared her shoulders and met Rhune's regard with what she hoped was a decidedly no-nonsense one of her own.

"Tess." His voice reached out to her, warm and unsettling. "I want you to meet someone." Even more unsettling was the way in which he reached out to her, took her arm, pulled her to his side in a disturbingly proprietary manner.

And, despite her best intentions, she fell under his spell. With a peculiar compliance, she moved easily to his side. Felt his hand remain on her arm and made no move to extricate herself.

Oh, Tess. What have you done?

She'd taken the plunge into unknown waters by remaining in Sweet Hope; she would now see where the strange current would take her. That realization thrilled her as much as any real submersion in a racing stream ever could. She swallowed hard and blinked at the handsome couple standing before her.

"And this is Cathryn Matthews." Rhune's voice intruded upon her reflections. "She and Jacob were two of the people who held this town together in the aftermath of last year's tornadoes."

Tess frowned self-consciously at her inattention. "I'm sorry. I was woolgathering."

The tall, dark man standing next to the petite, blond woman smiled and extended his hand. "I'm Jacob Matthews." He nodded at the pretty woman beside him with a look of unabashed love. "Cathryn's husband. You've been working with Aiden, our son."

Tess extended her hand. "Ah, yes. You must be the pastor of Grace Everlasting."

"One and the same." Jacob Matthews grinned an all-American grin.

A mischievous look passed over Cathryn Matthews's face. "And you must be the damsel our knight errant Doc, here, keeps rescuing."

Rhune flashed Cathryn a warning look as irritation made Tess bristle. "I would hope I've come to be known as more than a woman in need of a man's help."

Jacob laughed. "Tess McQueen, the whole of Sweet Hope knows that you're a high-powered corporate figure from the important city of Washington, D.C." He leaned forward and lowered his voice. "But what impresses most of the good folk in this town is that you've the capability of keeping Doc in a state of near constant agitation."

Cathryn reached out and gently pressed Tess's arm. "Now, *that's* an accomplishment worth gossip."

Rhune reddened. "Jacob and Cathryn," he offered, as though trying to restore some semblance of dignity to the conversation, "wouldn't rest until the individual residents of Sweet Hope had received the funds necessary to rebuild after the storms."

Knitting her brows, Cathryn looked around at the buildings rimming the town green, some of which were in obvious disrepair. "It's a crime the municipal funds haven't come through, however."

"What do you mean?" Tess's ears pricked up at the mention of a problem. Her whole character seemed hardwired to solve problems. She loved a challenge, and the working out of one now could make her forget that she was fast becoming a topic of town gossip.

"Just that," Cathryn replied. "It's been a year now since the tornadoes, and, although individuals have received help, the town itself has yet to receive its federal aid."

"The wheels of government seem to grind very slowly," Jacob added with a grimace.

Tess scowled. "Haven't your municipal officials pressed your representatives in Washington?"

"They've pressed, all right." Rhune's voice was loaded with sarcasm. "Seems, however, little ole Sweet Hope isn't quite powerful enough to be a meaningful thorn in our elected officials' sides."

Rubbing her hands together, Tess mulled over the germ of an idea. "Sometimes it's more effective *not* to go through channels."

"Do you know someone who could help?" Rhune's face registered surprise.

"Why, Dr. Sherman," Tess teased, "you're always accusing me of being a high-powered corporate efficiency expert. What good is all that power and efficiency if I haven't cultivated some very useful contacts?"

Cathryn grinned. "What do you have in mind?"

Now pacing, Tess tapped her chin with her index finger. "I don't want to make any promises. Not before I make a few inquiries." She looked at the three, who stared at her. "Could you get me a list—as soon as possible—of the funds still outstanding?"

"Sure." Jacob looked eager to get on it.

Ooh, how she loved a challenge. "I'll see if we can't make that thorn in your representatives' sides considerably more painful."

"But it's the day before a holiday," Cathryn objected. "Won't Washington, D.C., be closed down?"

Tess narrowed her eyes with glee. "I have a fax, I have a modem... *and* I have the home phone numbers of people who owe me."

With a look of pride Rhune slipped his arm around her shoulders and squeezed. "That's my girl!"

Tess stared at him wide-eyed as she heard both Cathryn and Jacob chuckle.

Rhune seemed to catch himself immediately. "That's just an expression, you know."

"Of course." Tess tried to level a withering stare, but found his arm, which still rested across her shoulders, a considerable distraction. Surprisingly, she found she could only smile.

"If you could help," Cathryn said with a twinkle, "the O'Malley women might mount a grass-roots campaign to make you mayor."

"I haven't promised anything," Tess protested, holding up her hands. "I think, however, I might be able to get the government glacier moving again."

Jacob looked her straight in the eye and deadpanned, "If you could just do that, you've got my vote."

"There is no mayoral race in Tess McQueen's future." She loved these people. "You all seem to forget I'm leaving Sunday."

Cathryn and Jacob looked at each other, and a thoroughly disbelieving look passed between them.

Rhune leaned close and whispered in Tess's ear, "It's not *you all.* If you're going to be mayor of Sweet Hope, it's *y'all.*"

His breath tickled the side of her face, sending a lovely little frisson across her shoulders where his arm *still* rested. The man just kept getting closer and closer. She raised one eyebrow imperiously and turned to look at him, and found herself the recipient of the most devastating smile she'd ever seen. Wickedly devastating.

Oh, my.

"*Y'all* need to get busy," she drawled pointedly, "if I'm to help you at all."

Jacob took his wife's hand. "Cathryn and I can handle retrieving the necessary information. We can have it to you in a couple hours, tops." He grinned. "You and Rhune stay with Doc's Club. The kids need you."

Now, why did Tess get the distinct impression that Pastor Jacob Matthews was firmly on the side of the notorious matchmaking O'Malley women?

She looked at Rhune, as if he might want to accompany Cathryn and Jacob.

"Hey, the kids need us." He shrugged innocently. "And I spy my sister passing out lemonade and fresh peaches to the workers. I wouldn't want to miss fresh Georgia peaches."

The mischievous look in his eye coaxed. The sensuous lilt in his voice drew her under his spell. And that dimple... that dimple thoroughly undid her.

With each moment she spent in Sweet Hope in the company of Dr. Rhune Sherman, the more difficult she found it to concentrate on her Sunday journey northward.

Carefully clutching one perfect peach in each hand, Rhune flopped down on the grass under the shady branches of an oak tree. Young Aiden Matthews flopped beside him and examined the one peach he held in his own hands.

"If I took *two* peaches, Doc," the boy said seriously, "my mama would say I was a little piggy."

One imperious eyebrow raised, Tess sat down ever so regally beside Aiden. "Believe me, if Doc's mama were here, she'd say he was most certainly a little piggy, too."

As he held her with a look, Rhune bit into one peach and let the cool juices run down his chin. He grinned as he slowly chewed the sweet fruit, then swallowed. "Have you no cravings? Have you no romance?'' He waggled his eyebrow roguishly. "Have you never seen *Tom Jones,* lass?''

"I'll Tom Jones you," Tess replied, rising up on her knees, then leaning over to swipe the juice off his chin.

Dropping the half-eaten peach to the ground, he caught her wrist. Jacob Matthews had been right earlier. Tess McQueen was capable of keeping Rhune in a near constant state of agitation. Lord, but she was beautiful, and he'd had just about enough of holding back.

He pulled her closer to him.

Flames rising in her cheeks, she broke away laughing. Under her breath she murmured, "Rhune Sherman, please . . . the child."

"Oh, that's okay, Miss Tess," Aiden assured her quite soberly. "I'm used to seeing girls fall all over Doc."

Tess eyed the boy in open-eyed wonder.

My, but she was a stunner when she was flustered. Those violet eyes held the promise of passionate storm. Or stormy passion.

"Wh-where did Sarah go?" she asked finally in an obvious attempt to wrest control of the situation.

Aiden bit into his peach, then spoke around the mouthful. "She went to help Bitsy Miller finish her bike decorations." He swallowed. "After Bitsy saw my sparkler, she wanted one, too."

"And that doesn't bother you?" Rhune asked. "That someone's copying your original?"

"Nope." Aiden shook his head emphatically. "Bitsy's mama makes really, *really* good chocolate chip cookies, and Bitsy always shares 'em with me."

Chuckling, Rhune reached out and ruffled Aiden's hair. "A pragmatist if I ever met one."

Aiden wrinkled his face in question, but was too preoccupied with the juicy peach to speak.

Leaning back on his elbows to finish his second peach, Rhune sighed. How he loved the kids in Doc's Club. With a sharp pain he thought of Najeem and clenched his fists. If only that particular boy could have had a chance at an afternoon of bike decorating and peach eating amid the safety of a community that loved and protected him.

Rhune scowled. In leaving D.C., had he abandoned future Najeems? Could he have made a difference if he'd stayed? Or would the off-duty price have been more carousing attempts at forgetfulness? More Chelseys.

"Are you all right?" Tess's voice close at hand startled him out of his troubling reverie. She knelt next to him on the grass.

He looked up into her face and saw genuine concern. "Yeah," he replied far too gruffly, rising. "We need to get Master Aiden, here, to some water for washup, or his mama will read me the riot act."

Ignoring Tess's quizzical glance, he held out his hand for the young boy, who hopped up and took it immediately. He looked down at the beautiful, innocent face of the child staring up at him. If he ever had the opportunity for children, he would never—*never*—squander it.

In the meantime, he would enjoy the kids of Doc's Club...and think of a way he might help the Najeems of nearby Atlanta.

Turning to Tess, he affected a lighter tone than he felt. "Are you coming, too?" He looked at Aiden's and his own peach-stained T-shirts, then at Tess's still spotlessly clean clothes. "Perhaps not." He grinned. "You ate that peach very efficiently."

Tess rose to her feet. "Oh, I'm human, too." She held up shiny fingers. "My hands are sticky."

Rhune felt an involuntary shiver run through his body. *Sticky* could be most agreeable...under certain circumstances. And with the right person.

He tried to tamp down the rising feeling that Tess McQueen was the right person. Now wasn't the right time for the right person. He had too many personal demons to exorcise.

"Doc?" Aiden tugged at his hand. "Why do you suppose God made peaches so messy?"

Rhune shrugged. "To prepare us for life," he replied in an uncharacteristically philosophical tone. He was beginning to understand that life was seldom tidy.

What had gotten into Rhune Sherman today? He'd blown hot and cold ever since he'd convinced Tess to stay in Sweet Hope for the Fourth of July festivities. As she followed him now to the fountain in the center of the town green, she tried to get a handle on the mercurial doctor.

He seemed in almost as much conflict about his feelings for her as she was about her feelings for him. That much was apparent from his smoldering glances one minute and his gruff dismissals the next.

Perhaps she'd made a mistake in staying.

No. She looked around at the town green, now strewn with children of all ages and brightly decorated bicycles. She felt the hot Southern sun caress her shoulders. Felt her normally intense demeanor relax amid the fragrance of sunbaked vegetation and peach. She had earned this break from her workaholic schedule. And who knew what she must face on a personal level when she returned to Washington? The truth in Chelsey's story still remained to be untangled.

No. She hadn't made a mistake in tarrying. Instead of giving in to those nagging feelings of guilt, she would cherish these couple days of unfettered freedom.

She only wished she didn't find Dr. Rhune Sherman so dangerously attractive.

The twelve-year-old girl, Sarah, who'd been helping Aiden with his bike earlier, joined them at the fountain. Without ceremony she plunged her hands and arms into the burbling water. "Whoever thought of bringing peaches to bike-decorating day ought to be shot," she exclaimed with the exasperation of a middle-aged matron. "Half the kids are now dyed red and blue from a combination of juice and crepe paper."

Rhune seemed to snap out of his curmudgeonly trance. "Why, Miss Sarah, you sound as if you had the makings of a schoolmarm . . . or an efficiency expert."

Sarah blushed at the teasing. Obviously, even twelve-year-old girls were not immune to Rhune's charms.

Rhune looked up at Tess and grinned devilishly. "Caught you looking, Tess McQueen," he murmured, his words pure provocation.

"Don't you wish," she sputtered, flicking the water in the fountain's pool dismissively.

Now, she really hadn't meant the water to splash Rhune. But it did.

And Sarah and Aiden stepped back, their mouths open, their eyes full of expectation.

With a sensuous growl Rhune sent a spray of water her way. The cool droplets nearly sizzled on her skin. She yipped, not so much in reaction to the unexpected shower but to the look of blatant longing in Rhune's eyes. The pendulum had swung again. . . .

And now the formerly cool doctor was hot.

She should have acted the mature adult and put an end to the horseplay immediately. But she'd been mature for so very, very long. Years. Ages. Aeons. The kid in her just slipped out and, laughing, smacked the surface of the water with both hands, sending a veritable tsunami in Rhune's direction.

Howling in mock rage, he lunged for her, caught her and himself off-balance and pulled her fully into the shallow fountain to the shouts of glee from Sarah and Aiden.

It doesn't take long for children to gather around the out-of-the-ordinary. Especially if the out-of-the-ordinary involves adults in ridiculous situations. And Tess had to admit that she and Rhune, reclining as the centerpiece in the town fountain in the middle of Sweet Hope green, looked ridiculous indeed.

She didn't care. She felt *alive*. The efficiency expert in her had disappeared. The kid in her leaned her head back and spit a perfect arc of water between her front teeth.

Rhune stared at her in total shock.

The crowd of giggling children parted as Cathryn and Jacob Matthews stepped to the fountain's edge. Jacob's expression mirrored Rhune's, but Cathryn smothered a laugh.

With a mischievous twinkle in her eyes, she held out a manila folder. "We have the information on federal aid that you requested. Were you perhaps going to submit it to Naval Affairs?"

Chapter Nine

Did the fact that a woman could recline, spitting water, in a public fountain and still maintain her dignity constitute grounds for falling in love? Rhune couldn't say for sure, but why else would he be standing before Tess's door this evening with no other excuse or reason but that he *had to see her?*

As he raised his hand to knock, the door opened, revealing Tess dressed in understated elegance. On the surface, she was obviously too sophisticated and too sleek to fit into life in Sweet Hope ... so why did he continue to picture her nowhere else but right here?

And when would that arresting violet gaze cease to jolt him?

Probably never.

"Hello." Her voice was warm, soft and welcoming. She flushed slightly. "I wasn't expecting anyone. I was on my way out."

His pulse beat a tattoo at the base of his jaw. "Can I interest you in dinner?"

"Sure." She smiled, and he went all mushy inside like some schoolboy with a crush. "Shall we go to the Hole-in-the-Wall and hear what they're saying about us tonight?"

Oh, he *knew* what the town was saying about them tonight. He grinned at the thought. "And how did you make out with your calls this afternoon? About the missing federal aid. If you get any results at all, the town will be talking about you constantly."

Closing and locking the door to her room, she sighed in a satisfied way. "It seems that all my contacts who owe me have contacts who owe them." She rubbed her hands together. "Most rewarding. Sweet Hope town officials might even hear something as soon as next week."

"You're good," he said. She was, he thought a touch gloomily. Far too good for a tiny town to hold her.

She slowed in her walk down the bed-and-breakfast hallway and tilted her chin proudly. "That's not all." She appeared incredibly self-satisfied.

"Have you cleaned up the national debt?"

"Even better." Reaching the head of the staircase, she rested her hand regally on the banister. "Esther from the Hole-in-the-Wall has been crazy, trying to find a groom for the top of Maria and Manuel's wedding cake."

It amazed Rhune that Tess cared.

"I remembered I have a friend who runs a wedding specialty shop in D.C." She paused in her descent of the staircase. "I called her this afternoon and had her overnight one of every cake-top groom she has in stock. There should be one in the bunch that stands up to public scrutiny."

Rhune chuckled. "I can see your Sweet Hope mayoral campaign slogan now—The Woman Who Gets Things Done."

Tess tilted her head imperiously as she swooshed through the old Victorian foyer and out onto the wide veranda. "Laugh, Dr. Sherman, but some things are too important to leave undone."

He shook his head. He was in trouble. This woman pulled strings in him he didn't know were internally attached. Certainly in none of his medical studies had he come across any anatomical evidence that showed the direct relationship between a beautiful woman doing a kind deed and the pure, physical blips he now felt deep in his heart.

He was in trouble for sure.

"I'm going to the Hole-in-the-Wall for supper," Tess said to Ida Drake, who sat in a rocker on the veranda. "If I should get any calls."

"Then take this shawl, dear." Ida rose quickly. "They keep the air-conditioning over there at absolute zero."

"Thank you," Tess replied, taking the shawl and smiling gently at the older woman's gesture of kindness.

Once they were on the sidewalk, she said, "You were right. Ida and Mel have coddled me beyond belief." She fingered the shawl, and her voice sounded far away. "And you were right also that it would be very good for me."

Something wistful in her tone caught his attention. "Back in Washington, don't you have someone to coddle you?"

She exhaled sharply. "Just the opposite. It seems that both in my job and in my family life, I'm the one who does the coddling."

For an instant that pesky thought—the one that said it would be wonderful to care for a woman like Tess—reared its persistent little head. He was drawn to her; there was no doubt about that. But this recurring secret thought went beyond mere attraction. This thought tapped into an unexpressed longing he had to make a genuine connection with a person he could trust not to take advantage of his vulnerability.

He harrumphed.

"I beg your pardon?" Tess looked at him in question.

"I was just thinking," he said, covering, "that you shouldn't have to coddle a nineteen-year-old sister."

Tess sighed. "Normally, I'd agree. But this particular sister finds herself pregnant and unmarried."

"And you were wondering if you were going to have to raise this child as you raised your sister."

Tess stopped short. As she turned to him, he could see disbelief dawning in her eyes.

He reached out and touched her arm. "You never thought of that possibility?"

She shook her head mutely.

"I'm sorry." He tried to backtrack. "I don't even know your sister. If she's anything like you, she may turn out to be a very mature nineteen-year-old."

Tess's lovely violet eyes became clouded. Troubled. "On the contrary, ever since she reached adolescence, she's tried to prove to me and to the world that she's nothing like me. She refused to go to college. Chose instead to strike out on her own."

He took both her hands in his. "You can be a very intimidating woman, Tess McQueen. The ease with which you accomplish things could be daunting to a younger sister. Perhaps she's been trying to carve out her own niche in the world."

"Perhaps." She tightened her grip on his hands almost imperceptibly. "What am I going to do?"

He brought her hand to his lips and brushed her knuckles gently. "You're going to watch your sister have her baby. You're going to encourage her. You're going to watch your sister raise her baby, and you're going to love them both." He tried to make his words as gentle as possible. "You're going to let your sister live her life...and you're going to live yours."

"You make it sound so easy."

"Easy it won't be."

He wished he could make it easy for her, but he knew from experience—Najeem especially—how uneasy caring could be. Perhaps much of his emotional detachment with the women in his life had come from the deep-down truth that he was capable of caring too much. And he pulled away before it could cause him pain.

As epiphanies went, it bordered on the cliché, but it startled Rhune nonetheless.

"Perhaps," Tess said, "I should look at this baby as one of those detours in life you talked about."

He scrunched his brow in question.

"You know...you said that sometimes the detours turned out to be more interesting than the planned route."

"I said that?" He reached to open the door of the Hole-in-the-Wall Café.

"You did." She smiled at him, with her eyes more than with her mouth. "And it made sense."

He was glad something of the past few days in Sweet Hope made sense.

Tess stared in disbelief at the mashed potatoes on the plate in front of her. They had been flattened and formed into a lopsided heart. The gravy had been carefully poured into indentations that looked suspiciously like $T M + R S$. She closed her eyes, then looked again. Hard. The effect certainly was of a carving on an old tree or a park bench.

That Esther.

She heard giggling and muffled laughter. When she looked in the direction of the cook and the dinner patrons at the counter, the entire crew looked far too innocent.

"Is there something strange about your mashed potatoes?" Rhune asked cautiously. Snickers broke out anew at the counter.

"Not at all," Tess replied, stirring the silly spuds with her fork, then placing a dollop in her mouth as if there had been absolutely nothing unusual about them.

"Aww, Miss Tess," complained a regular at the counter, "you've turned out to be no fun at all."

Rhune flashed a grin at her across the table. "I think you have the hang of dealing with them. I'll gladly sign over my position as new kid on the block."

"You forget I'm leaving day after tomorrow."

"Perhaps," he said, the one word hanging—a vexing enigma—in the air.

There was no *perhaps*. He would not be saying *perhaps* if he knew who she was. She'd dug herself into a hole by not telling Rhune immediately about her relationship to Chelsey. She would have to tell him, certainly, before she left Sweet Hope. But when? And how would he react?

Oh, she knew how he'd react. And the thought pained her deeply.

She blinked to ward off the threatening sting of tears.

"Are you all right?" Rhune reached across the table and touched her hand.

She dabbed at her eyes with her napkin. "Yes. I must have inhaled some pepper," she lied. She sat up ramrod straight in her seat. "Before our meals came, you were about to tell me an idea you had for a youth exchange?"

He beamed. "It's just in my head at this point, but I'd like to go beyond Doc's Club. The kids I work with now are going through a normal rocky period in their lives because of their age. But they all have their families, the church and the community as a safety net. I'd like to set up a program for kids at risk. Rural kids. City kids. Suburban kids. Geography wouldn't matter. What would matter..."

Tess sat back in her seat and with fascination watched Rhune's animation. He was an incredibly handsome man—a fact she hadn't allowed herself to dwell on when she'd had him under investigation. With his looks and with a career that had the potential to bring him a considerable degree of wealth, he could be living the fast and easy life. Or, at least, the secure life. Instead, he chose to sit in a tiny diner and discuss his plan to help kids no one else wanted to help. The man—no matter how unorthodox his personal life had been—had a conscience. Even his unexpected confession concerning her sister had, instead of outraging Tess, pulled at her heartstrings. Yes, there was a real man underneath the cover-model good looks.

Tess was glad Rhune couldn't tell how attractive that made him to her.

"Of course, I could use an efficiency expert to help me with the organization part," he said pointedly, skewering her with a deep brown gaze.

She felt her cheeks flush under his scrutiny. "Are you trying to convince me to relocate to Sweet Hope?"

It was his turn to look uncomfortable. "It's just that... strictly as your former physician...of course...I think our town has been good for your health. You said so yourself earlier. If you go back to your workaholic ways, you'll surely land yourself in your D.C. doctor's office. And I've talked to her. She's not about to recommend Tarzan swings and Fourth of July parades as treatment."

No, she wasn't. Tess smiled. Her Washington physician was as no-nonsense as Tess herself.

"Besides..." His voice had become very still. Very intense. "I think you and I have unfinished business."

Tess blinked.

Grinning—a heart-stopping flash of white in a finely chiseled face—Rhune pressed on. "Look." He pointed to the half-finished mashed potatoes on his plate. "The whole town recognizes it. We'd be fools not to explore it."

"It?" Her racing pulse somehow had slowed her brain.

Edna the waitress loomed over them, freshening their coffee. "Birds do it. Bees do it. Even monkeys in the trees do it." She leaned down and winked at Rhune. "If Tess doesn't want to do it, I'm available, honey."

"Thanks, but no, thanks, Edna." Rhune ran his fingers along his jaw thoughtfully. "I hear tell your husband won first prize in riflery at last year's state fair."

"Oh, pooh." Edna fluttered her hands as she moved to the next table. "What's a little buckshot between friends?"

Rubbing his backside, Rhune grimaced. "That's not even funny," he muttered under his breath.

Tess fingered her napkin. "I'm flattered, I admit."

"But?"

"But I'm not... at liberty to explore a relationship right now."

"You lied?"

She started.

"You have a significant other in D.C.?" he added.

"No. Not that." She looked him right in the eye and wished that she'd cleared all this up immediately after his confession. "It's just that you don't know me."

"And that's precisely the point. I'm asking for a chance to get to know you better." He reached across the table and took her hand in both of his. "I do know that you're strong and intelligent and very beautiful. And trustworthy beyond belief."

She inhaled sharply, wishing he'd stopped at beautiful.

The man at the next table leaned over and offered up a stage whisper. "Ask her to turn her efficiency-expert skills on your trailer and them varmints."

"Oh, for Pete's sake," Rhune exclaimed, throwing up his hands in exasperation. "Can't a body have any privacy in this town?"

"No!" came a chorus from the diners.

Tess welcomed the witnesses and participants. This conversation was wandering into dangerous territory. The last thing it needed was privacy.

Rhune, however, rose and picked up the check. "Finished?"

She'd lost her appetite. "I need to get back to my room. I have a ton of work still." She hoped he'd take the hint.

"I'll walk you back." The pressure of his hand on her elbow did nothing to cool her thoughts.

On the contrary, her thoughts jumped wildly and erratically to thoughts of his touch. His intimate touch. Previously, the mere remembrance of her mission, of Chelsey, was enough to throw cold water on such thoughts. Now, after Caldwell's report, Rhune's confession and Chelsey's recantation, the recollection that she'd not been straight with Rhune only fueled her longing with thoughts of what if.

What if?

Ridiculous to even ponder. When Rhune Sherman found out who she really was, there would be no more offers to explore a relationship.

* * *

Something had been released, and Rhune was at a loss to stop it.

From the moment Tess had agreed to stay in Sweet Hope for the Fourth of July weekend, his thoughts had turned to *what if*.

But Tess McQueen was unlike any other woman he'd ever met. Pursuing what ifs—of any kind—with her was tantamount to entering uncharted territory. Sure, he could envision his hormones running amok. And, sure, he could imagine a brief affair so torrid it would singe his synapses. But did he want a *brief* affair with Tess? *Brief* being the operative word.

No. Definitely not.

And that uncharacteristic response put him in the damnedest situation he'd ever faced. As he'd reluctantly admitted to her, the minute he was in her company he was afflicted with three of a confirmed bachelor's most deadly sins: candor, chivalry and thoughts of a long-term relationship.

He glanced at Tess walking beside him in the sweet, warm evening air. She, too, seemed lost in thought. Did she, by any chance, feel the same attraction? The same elemental pull? The same conflict? There were moments when her expressive eyes told him she did.

They walked in silence back to the bed-and-breakfast, then, against her perfunctory protest, he walked her to the door of her room. The hallway was empty; most of the other guests were enjoying the evening air on the veranda.

"Will you help with Doc's Club in the parade tomorrow?" he asked, just to lengthen the parting.

"If they need me." She glanced up at him, her face intense. It almost seemed as if she were about to say something else. Something quite important. Instead, she sighed softly and repeated, "If they need me."

He could drag out the moment with small talk if he had to, but suddenly that seemed pointless. Every fiber in his being called out to touch her. To kiss her. To show her rather than to tell her that she belonged here. In Sweet Hope. With him.

Her eyes widened as if she could read his thoughts.

He reached out to touch her cheek, and, with a little intake of breath, she leaned ever so slightly into his touch. She closed her eyes, and for a moment her lashes rested thick and sooty on her cheeks, in marked contrast to the alabaster of her skin. He wondered what the flicker of those lashes would feel like against his own skin. Little butterfly kisses. The prelude to lovemaking. He felt himself harden.

"Tess," he whispered.

Her eyes fluttered open. One corner of her mouth lifted in a demi-smile. "You make my name sound so sensuous."

He trailed his fingers down her petal-smooth cheek, along the strong outline of her elegant jaw, down the long, graceful column of her neck. Her soft, barely audible moan combined with his lower, harsher one.

Ah, so she was not immune to the spark and sizzle between them.

"You, Tess McQueen, are a very sensuous lady."

He slipped his hand behind her neck. Threaded his fingers through her thick, glossy hair. Felt her tremble. Felt his own pulse quicken. Felt need grow within him.

She parted her lips.

He lowered his head to claim her.

This was not what he had planned for his new life. This was not the next logical step. This was crazy. This was . . .

Hot.

Heady.

And compelling.

He explored her lips, her tongue, her mouth as if this were his first kiss ever. She responded by opening to him, by twining her fingers in his hair, by pressing her firm body against his. She showed by her touch, by little mewing sounds, by her warmth, that something had been released in her, also. She kissed him with the fervor that he felt.

And thus, the passion-driven cycle was charged and recharged.

Had she been the reasonable one, had she demurred, he could have held back, but the woman in his arms was no longer a hold-back kind of woman. He groaned and pulled his mouth from hers.

"Tess," he murmured as he tasted the flesh of her cheek, the lobe of her ear, the pulse at the hollow of her throat. He was a man famished.

For her alone.

For Tess.

She ran her fingers over the planes of his face, touched his tongue and his teeth as he flicked little love nips along her skin. Ran her hands over his chest. Branded him with her heat through the very fabric of his clothing. Kissed his throat. Made the hairs rise on the back of his neck as she fluttered her breath along his skin.

Tess.

He moved his hands down her back and over her well-rounded bottom. Pulled her hard up against him. Heard her gasp when she encountered his passion. Groaned as he felt the pressure of her breasts against his chest.

The heat of their kiss seemed to simmer the elusive woody fragrance that she wore. It wafted about them, weaving a spell, ensnaring them. An exotic sorcerer's brew, but the sorcery was theirs alone.

The world didn't exist except for this kiss. This soul-drenching, magic kiss.

Oh, Tess. He buried his face in the hair that spilled around her throat and over her shoulder. He inhaled her. "You must stay," he murmured, almost intoxicated with the *yes* feel of her in his arms.

"But I can't," he heard her whisper as she sank against him in a surrender that belied her words.

"I will convince you," he promised, drawing back to look in her eyes.

"But you don't even . . ."

"Know you?" he finished for her. He wrapped his arms more tightly around her. "*This* is knowing you, Tess. We fit, you and I."

Mutely she shook her head, and he saw tears at the corners of her eyes. He lowered his lips to brush away the wetness and felt her eyelashes flutter against his skin. Butterfly kisses. Kisses that made his passion rise again.

"Tess," he breathed against her face.

"Oh, Rhune." She sighed, touching his lips with her fingertips. "This was not supposed to happen."

This was not supposed to happen. But it had. She had let it happen. And it had brought her to life.

All that had gone before this kiss wasn't life. This kiss was different even from the one they'd shared before. Because this kiss had come after Rhune's confession, after Caldwell's report, after Chelsey's recantation. And after all that, Tess had allowed herself to want this man.

But the wanting was a mere shadow of the having.

He was right. They fit, he and she, in a way that she might have pooh-poohed only days ago. She would have to stop scoffing at incurable romantics.

"You're right," he agreed, a thoroughly undeterred grin on his face. "This was not supposed to happen." He kissed her lightly on the nose. "But it did, so now what are we going to do about it?"

The wild, newly released side of her wanted to invite him into her room, wanted to explore his body, wanted to see if they could perhaps fly.

She heard a faraway ringing and smiled. So it was true that, when it happened, you heard bells.

He looked chagrined. "I think it's your phone."

How awfully prosaic.

She fumbled with her keys, managed to get the door open, stumbled in a daze to her bedside, then lifted the receiver. "Hello?"

"We have to talk." Chelsey.

"Could I call you back?"

"No."

Tess exhaled slowly.

Rhune stepped to her side, ran a hand over her hair, kissed her forehead. "I'll pick you up at ten tomorrow morning," he murmured, his voice low and husky.

Tess nodded, more than sorry for the interruption.

"Who's there?" Chelsey asked, her tone one of suspicion.

"I'm all ears," Tess replied evasively. "What's on your mind, little sis?"

Rhune's face registered understanding. After one final, lingering, feather-light caress of her face, he left the room, and Tess felt his absence like an ache.

"When are you coming home?" By the petulance in Chelsey's voice, Tess could tell this would not be one of their better conversations.

"I'll be home late Sunday night." Tess tried to maintain at least a veneer of patience, but it was a struggle. Her senses were experiencing the shock of reentry—from the stratosphere of desire back into the gravitational forces of a pseudoparental relationship. "Are you all right?"

Chelsey began to whimper. "What am I going to do?"

"Are you all right? *Now,*" Tess persisted. "Is your health okay? Is the baby okay?" It was hard to read the signs long distance. Was this conversation a matter of concern, or was this just a pity call?

"I'm fine," Chelsey snapped. "But how am I going to manage after the baby is born?"

Tess resisted the urge to ask why her sister hadn't considered these consequences before she'd participated in unprotected sex. Instead, she tried to make her voice reassuring. "You'll manage. You're strong. Hey, you're my sister, aren't you?" She paused. "Is there any chance the real father can be called upon to help?"

She'd tried to keep her voice even, but she must have put a tad more emphasis on the word *real.* Chelsey picked up on that. "I didn't expect you'd track Sherman down after I'd named him," she muttered.

Tess was stunned. "You didn't expect I'd want to make him own up to his responsibility?"

"He was convenient simply because he'd left D.C."

"You had no intention of marrying him or having him support you and the baby financially?"

"Not at the beginning."

Shocked, Tess remembered how, once the investigation had begun, Chelsey had participated wholeheartedly. How her projected scenarios of revenge had, at times, seemed downright gleeful.

"But as things progressed," Chelsey continued, "I thought how a prosperous husband wouldn't be all that bad."

"Dixie Fae McQueen!" Tess exploded. "Have you given one thought to the welfare of this child?"

"Sure. You feed it. You clothe it. You give it a roof over its head. *You* did it."

And I might just have to again, Tess thought as Rhune's words of warning popped into her head. "Those things are secondary to love and selflessness, little sis," she said softly.

"Can't you drive back home tonight, Tess?" Chelsey's voice faltered. "I need you. You're my rock."

"Chelsey..." Tess took a deep breath. "I'm taking some time for myself. Twenty-four hours."

"But you never have before."

No, she never had before. But that was before she'd spent time in quirky little Sweet Hope. Before she'd met the most wonderful assortment of meddlesome people in the world.

Before Rhune.

She straightened her shoulders. "Well, I'm doing it now. I've been invited to stay for the Fourth of July celebration, and I'm staying."

"Is that man I heard earlier the reason?"

"Chelsey, the whole town is the reason. This place is like somewhere outside of time. There's a little bit of magic here."

"You're not thinking of staying, are you?" Panic filled Chelsey's voice. "What would happen to me then?"

Tess pinched the bridge of her nose. She felt a tension headache coming on. "When I get home, we need to talk about how *you* will cope with your future. I'm willing to help you go back to school to obtain marketable skills so that you can support yourself and your child." She paused. "And that way it won't matter if I work in Washington or transfer elsewhere."

"You are thinking of moving!"

"In my line of work, you go where the jobs are." That had always been true in the past. But tonight, after that kiss, Tess couldn't help but amend her former axiom. Tonight she was more willing to concede that she should go where her heart was.

And her heart, it was turning out, longed for Sweet Hope. And Dr. Rhune Sherman.

Chapter Ten

July fourth.

Tess clutched the package the express company had just delivered and jogged across the town green to the Hole-in-the-Wall Café. She glanced at her watch. Nine-forty. Rhune had said he'd pick her up at ten. She needed to hurry because she didn't wish to miss one minute of this day she'd chosen for herself.

Just for herself. For no one else.

All Chelsey's railing last night in the phone-call-that-would-not-end had not deterred Tess from taking this one day. For years now, in her work and at home, she'd taken care of others' wants and needs. Today, no matter what tomorrow brought, she'd take care of her own.

That resolution gave her a heady sense of recklessness.

She hugged the package to her side. Well, she did have one small errand to do for someone else before she embarked on her totally selfish day. Slowing to a dignified walk before the café, she peered through the plate-glass window.

The regular morning crew was there. She opened the door to a chorus of "Tess!"

How could you not love this place?

She marched to the end of the counter and set her package on it. "Esther. Edna. Do you have a minute?"

"Sure do, sugah," Esther called out, hanging up her spatula.

Edna stuck her pencil in her hair and her pad in her pocket and moved to Tess's side in expectation.

Tess opened the package, then carefully unwrapped a dozen tiny cake-top grooms and stood them on the counter. "There. I think we should be able to find a suitable man for the top of Maria and Manuel's wedding cake."

"Where did you get all these?" breathed Esther.

"A friend in Washington owns a wedding supply shop."

"Ooee." Edna sighed, picking up one of the tiny figures. "You must have gorgeous men in D.C. It'd be hard to pick from these darlin's."

"The point is," Tess replied, "finding one that suits Manuel. And since I don't know the man, you ladies will have to help me out there."

"Why, here he is!" Esther exclaimed, holding a handsome, dark-skinned figure up to the light. "Won't Maria be pleased!" She leveled a look at Tess. "Honey, you don't even know these lovebirds, and you went to all this trouble. Bless you."

Tess flushed. "It was no trouble. It just needed to be done. And after the welcome Sweet Hope gave me, I figured this was small payback."

Edna grasped her hand. "Small payback, indeed. Cathryn Matthews was in here braggin' on how you're trying to get some movement on those federal funds. She was joking about runnin' you for mayor."

"Joke or not," Esther said with a wink, "you've got my vote. And, I swear, you'd get Maria's."

The attention was beginning to embarrass Tess. "Well, we found a suitable cake-top groom. Now I'll just wrap the others up and return them to my friend." She began to re-wrap the other figures.

"Hold on one minute," Edna said, picking up a russet-haired groom. "I think you ought to hold this one out for future use." She handed it to Tess.

Tess's eyes widened in recognition.

There was no need to point it out, but Edna continued, "If you painted in a wild tropical shirt peeking out from that tux, isn't this our Doc?"

It was. The spitting image.

Tess arched an eyebrow. "Even if it were," she began cautiously, "why would I want to save him?"

The two women burst into peals of laughter.

"Lordy, child," Edna chuckled, wiping a tear from her eye. "Smart and with a sense of humor, too." She kissed Tess on the cheek then bustled over to the service sideboard to pick up a fresh pot of coffee. "Why, indeed," she sputtered as she swooped past Tess on her way to tend to her customers.

Esther carefully rewrapped the groom for Maria and Manuel's cake. "You just save that auburn-haired devil, girl, and don't overthink it. Remember how much trouble we had finding a suitable groom for this wedding."

"But..." Why did she always feel so swept away in Sweet Hope?

"No buts, sugah." Esther placed the wrapped figurine in her apron pocket. "And thank you, Tess McQueen. You've proved your heart is here. In Sweet Hope." She smiled a warm and grandmotherly smile. "Now, scoot. As soon as breakfast is over, we're closing for the festivities."

The Fourth of July festivities. Tess had almost forgotten, with all the unsettling talk of grooms and weddings. She looked at her watch. Ten o'clock. Rhune would be waiting for her back at Mel and Ida's. She quickly finished packing the tiny figures, then hastily waved her hand in goodbye to Esther, Edna and the remaining breakfast patrons.

As she trotted across the green her pulse picked up, not from the exercise, but from the anticipation of spending an entire day with Rhune. An entire day with no other agenda but to enjoy herself.

As she pulled up in front of the bed-and-breakfast, such a sight met her eyes. By the curb Rhune sat astride that enormous black Harley. A powerfully compelling man on a powerful machine. The breeze ruffled his sun-streaked hair. The morning brightness made him squint ever so slightly like some rugged poster model for wilderness camping supplies. But his shirt... his shirt nearly blinded her. Cut from the wildest fabric of red, white and blue hibiscus blossoms, it was the loudest shirt that Tess had ever seen. A tropical shirt extraordinaire. Her blue jean shorts, white T-shirt and red bandanna chosen in honor of the day looked mighty tame in comparison.

She grinned. Always expect the unexpected from Doc, she mused. Today it was most definitely difficult to picture him as a small-town physician. Today he looked every inch the rogue. Unfettered and definitely dangerous.

"I thought I'd been stood up." His voice was a husky rumble.

"No." She patted the box she held. "I had an important delivery for the Hole-in-the-Wall." Thank goodness for the box. It provided her trembling hands with something to grasp.

"Hop on. We're late." They might be late, but his smile was lazy and thoroughly unhurried.

"Why?" She unlocked her car parked next to Rhune's motorcycle, then placed the box on the back seat. "I didn't think the parade started until eleven."

"Oh, but we have an important part in the parade. We need to get there early." He flashed her a dimpled grin, and Tess hoped her part didn't involve standing face-to-face with Rhune Sherman for any length of time. If it did, she'd be a goner. "We have to act as a buffer," he explained, "between the high school band and the little kids on bikes."

"How?" Her voice came out a squeak.

He patted his Harley. "We ride between the two groups. Just you and me on the bike."

She gulped. She was to spend the parade on that big, powerful, vibrating machine, hugging the likes of Rhune Sherman? No way.

"Yes, indeed," he said with a mischievous twinkle in his dark brown eyes. As if he could read her objections on her face.

She stepped gingerly to his side.

"Aw, McQueen," he teased, "give it a try. I don't bite." His eyes became smoky, his regard smoldering. "Not until the sun goes down, that is."

The sensation of tiny icy fingers played down her back. Just *what* had she gotten herself into?

He unhooked the helmets from the back of the bike, tucked one under his arm, then placed the other on her head. As he fastened the chin strap he smiled a slow, sensuous smile, and Tess could not get rid of the thought of those lips pressed hungrily against her own last night. Could not erase the memory of those strong hands claiming her body. Felt again the longing he'd unleashed in her.

She thanked her lucky stars today's festivities took place in broad daylight amid the entire population of Sweet Hope. Her runaway hormones would be safely chaperoned, at least.

When Rhune had secured his own helmet, Tess cautiously mounted the motorcycle behind him. To touch him no longer bore the innocence of their first ride. To touch him now was to call up a moment of shared passion. She touched him nonetheless . . . and allowed herself to savor a momentary sensation of possession.

Oh, my. The emotional pitfalls of today were going to be most difficult to dodge.

The parade and speeches successfully over, Rhune contemplated skipping the picnic. Reflected on the consequences of whisking the beautiful Ms. McQueen off to his pond for a private swim to cool his overheated senses.

Parading through town with her lithe body nestled close against him had not been easy on his well-intentioned restraint. Not easy at all. On second thought, what were the chances he could easily restrain himself if he were to get her alone at his secluded swimming hole?

Slim and none.

And today he'd definitely vowed restraint where Tess was concerned. This day of togetherness was not designed to frighten her off with the intensity of his desire. Today he intended to convince her to return regularly to Sweet Hope so that she and he might explore the possibility of a relationship. Slowly. Maturely. In harmony with his new life and his new focus.

Good luck, he mentally chided himself.

He parked the Harley under the shady branches of a giant oak at the edge of the green, then turned in the seat to look at Tess behind him. "First we feast," he said, grinning, "then we play."

Her violet eyes widened sensuously. The word *foreplay* came unbidden to his mind.

Oh, he was off to a fine start at forbearance.

He inhaled deeply, then tried again. "Belle and her family asked us to join them for the picnic . . . and then I signed us up for the three-legged race."

"You *what?*"

He'd known he'd get that reaction from her. Removing his helmet, he swung one leg over the front of his bike to dismount. He then turned to her and unfastened her helmet. Surprisingly, she let him.

He grinned. "The pearl-spitting contest was booked solid."

She tried to suppress a smile, but couldn't quite. Keeping her disconcerting violet gaze upon him, she removed her helmet, freeing that rich cascade of hair. Rhune's fingers itched at the imagined texture of it.

It was going to be one hell of a job to rein in his desire today.

With infinite grace, Tess dismounted, one midnight dark eyebrow cocked imperiously. "Are you planning to be bossy and controlling all day, Doc?"

He slid an arm around her shoulder and grinned. "Only where you and your time are concerned, darlin'. Only then."

Turning her in the direction of the festivities in full swing on the green, he felt her relax and nestle against him. The sudden, overwhelming proprietary feeling that washed over him nearly took his breath away. It had never felt so right being with any woman as it felt *right* now, being with Tess McQueen.

He had a premonition this was going to be no ordinary day in his life.

It was difficult to notice his surroundings when he was in Tess's company. The post-parade hubbub swirled around him, muted, as he thought of Tess and Tess alone. She consumed his consciousness, his senses. He took only vague note of families spreading picnic blankets. Couldn't have told you whether the sun shone or if the sky was overcast. Felt no pangs of hunger from the scents wafting from the food tent. Felt nothing but Tess, warm and real, at his side.

He'd told her about the worst in him. About Najeem. About Chelsey. The lowest point in his life. And, surprisingly, she'd encouraged him not to build a wall around his emotions because of that dark moment. If the truth be told, he'd taken a few bricks out of that wall for Tess, and the resulting feeling was one of expectation. Laced with a terrible new feeling—vulnerability.

"There's Belle." Tess's voice filled with lilting anticipation. A girlish excitement. She waved to catch his sister's attention.

Rhune shook his head to banish his intense reflections. Keep it light, Sherman, he warned himself. Today is for innocent fun. He extended his hand to Boone O'Malley as his brother-in-law approached.

"Well, now, I'm glad to see you two here." Boone shook hands heartily. "From the town gossip I kind of expected you'd eloped by now."

Tess tipped her head saucily. "We would have, but we had an argument. I wanted him to change *that shirt* before we stood in front of the justice of the peace."

Rhune's mouth dropped open. She certainly was getting the hang of handling the Sweet Hope spotlight.

Boone winced as he looked at Rhune's shirt. "I thought the raccoons—"

"You've never heard of mail-order catalogs and overnight service?" Rhune cut him off. He, quite frankly, had had enough razzing on the subject of raccoons.

Five-year-old Margaret O'Malley came running through the crowd and flung herself into Rhune's arms. "Uncle Rhune!" she exclaimed, her eyes flashing. "We have to drink Co-Colas all day today because all the drinking fountains are busted."

"Are they, now?" He nuzzled his niece. "What a hardship on you."

Belle joined the group. "We were waiting for Tess to arrive." She winked. "Surely she can get the drinking fountains fixed. What's a little municipal water problem compared to finding a groom for Maria's cake?"

Tess laughed. "Esther talked?"

"No, I heard it from Maria herself." Belle reached out to gently squeeze Tess's arm. "I'll introduce you this afternoon. She's thrilled."

Rhune looked at Tess with a mixture of awe and pride. "I call her The Woman Who Gets Things Done."

"More than that," Belle replied, "she does it without stepping on anyone's toes. In a small town, that's what counts above all else."

Tess appeared lost in thought. "About that water..."

Margaret O'Malley squirmed in Rhune's arms. "Aunt Tess, don't you dare fix the water. Not till I've had at least eight Co-Colas."

The adults laughed, but was he the only one who'd seen Tess stiffen at the child's uninhibited use of the word *aunt?* A preposterous childish presumption. Funny. Rather endearing. And a little too close for comfort.

"Come along," Belle urged. "We've laid blankets under a tree. Cathryn, Jacob and their brood will be along any minute."

Margaret wriggled to the ground, and the three O'Malleys began to make their way through the crowd.

For a fleeting moment as they were left alone, Tess appeared far too sad for this holiday.

"Are you thinking about your sister?" Rhune asked softly.

She turned her face up to him, and he could see her eyes glistening with tears she obviously tried to hold back. "Yes." She blinked. "Friends asked her to join them. I don't know if she will. She can be very stubborn."

"Must you spoil your day, then, because of your sister's willfulness?"

The corners of her mouth turned up in a faint smile. "I forget you're a proponent of tough love."

He reached out to stroke her hair. "Enjoy today, Tess. Deal with your sister when you get back to D.C. Her situation will keep."

Her smile broadened. "You're asking a lot. I'm the kind of person who likes to have yesterday, today and tomorrow all neatly under wraps."

"I know." He gently brushed the moisture away from one corner of her eye. "That's the whole point of getting you to stay in town today. To get you to enjoy the moment."

Unexpectedly, she rose on tiptoe and planted an inexpressibly soft kiss on the corner of his mouth. "Thank you," she whispered, and set his pulse to racing.

His problem was just the opposite from hers. He'd lived his entire life in the moment, while there had been times he should have heeded his past actions as well as the future's consequences.

It was a lesson he needed to relearn daily.

You couldn't live more for the moment than by being tied to a too-handsome, grinning rascal at the starting line of a three-legged race.

"You do know we're in this to win." His voice rumbled in her ear, a sexy tease, as he wrapped one strong arm around her waist.

"Absolutely." It didn't matter that she found his muscles rippling under her own arm, hand and fingers a terrible distraction. Whatever Tess McQueen undertook, it was always with the intention of winning.

"You need some practice?" The chuckle in his voice compelled her to look into his eyes.

"Oh, no," she replied flippantly, trying not to get lost in his brown regard. "Every Saturday the Speaker of the House and I and two other representatives run three-legged races on The Mall." She lifted her chin and smiled sweetly into his face. "I'm a real pro."

She liked the feel of his soft laughter as it resonated through his body, then, because she was pressed against his side, through her own. Was it some warped symbolism that had her now physically bound to him? It was certainly most unsettling how, in parallel, as the days, hours and minutes passed, she increasingly saw herself as bound emotionally to Rhune Sherman and his life here in Sweet Hope.

"Ladies and gentlemen, start your engines!" The organizer's voice boomed over the racers.

Rhune gave her a squeeze. "This is it, Tess McQueen. Do or die."

It was absolutely ridiculous how rapidly her pulse danced in anticipation of this race. She'd become more and more keyed up as the day progressed. Of course, parading through town on the back of that megamotorcycle had initially jump-started her senses.

"On your mark!"

And then lounging on the picnic blankets with the irrepressible O'Malley-Matthews clan, Rhune hovering sexily by her side, had certainly raised her temperature and her pulse rate.

"Get set!"

And now she was physically bound to the overwhelming hunk....

"Go!"

Lost in thought, she was thoroughly unprepared. Had she been alone, she would have been standing at the starting line, breathing the other racers' dust.

But Tess was not alone. Consequently, she found herself suddenly dragged into action by a force that could only be described as a runaway locomotive.

"Come on, Tess!" whooped the mad engineer strapped to her side. Casey Jones move over. Rhune Sherman had more energy than the sum of four ordinary mortals.

Her competitive nature kicked in. He'd rescued her from high blood pressure, leaping green lizards and a gully on his property, all of which immediately became grist for the town gossip mill. Never let it be said that he had to carry this race, too.

The spectators' cheers and taunts ringing in her ears, Tess concentrated on the rhythm of Rhune's and her joined stride. She could do this. She was a team player.

She'd never, however, had such a distracting teammate.

With every step she took, the sensation of movement doubled. Her body bound to his. Her muscles working in unison with his. Their breathing synchronized. Their laughter entwined. Their goal, one and the same.

"Oh, baby," Rhune growled with satisfaction. "I think we've got it!" His words, double meaning and all, slithered over her senses, igniting a spark that fueled her energy reserve.

"Then let's bring it on home, darlin'," she shouted with uncharacteristic glee. *Darlin'?* Where had the drawl come from? Tightening her grip around his middle, she thrilled to the undulation of his straining muscles. Where had any part of her unusual behavior come from in the past few days?

No time for introspection.

Rhune and she were gaining on the lead racers, a couple of members of Doc's Club, adolescents so light the wind fairly blew them across the course. But Tess and Rhune had the power of bullheadedness on their side. Separately, they were stubborn individuals. Bound together, they unleashed a dynamo of obstinacy.

It helped, too, that adolescents, no matter that they'd agreed to run such a crazy race, were compelled by their age to maintain their cool.

Rhune and Tess obviously harbored no such restraints.

Grunting and groaning and giggling shamelessly, their arms wildly flapping, they bore down upon their only real competition. The kids glanced for a startled moment over their shoulders, then quickly sidestepped to let Rhune and Tess barrel toward the finish tape held by Boone and Belle, who cheered in a most brazenly partisan manner. Margaret O'Malley and Aiden Matthews jumped with childish abandon at the adults' sides.

Unaccustomed to strenuous exercise, Tess's lungs burned. Every muscle ached with the attempt to coordinate her movements with those of another. She hiccuped from laughter. And still she clung to Rhune.

Warm, hard, compelling Rhune. The man for whom fun was a life-style choice.

With one final desperate lunge, he and she broke through the tape and into a wall of bystanders who, with arms outstretched, were determined to keep the entrants from falling and breaking their foolhardy necks. Even so, Rhune and Tess slipped out of the grasp of the well-intentioned onlookers and tumbled in a heap onto the cool, sweet grass.

Tess heard the voice of Homer Martin. "Never did see a pair more suited to be a team."

Another voice teased, "You talkin' 'bout Sherman and McQueen, Homer, or about mules?"

"Is there a difference?" Homer countered.

Still attached to Rhune at the thigh and calf, Tess rolled awkwardly to look squarely at him lying sprawled and laughing on the grass. Were they two stubborn mules who wouldn't admit that they belonged together?

He rose on one elbow, reached out for her, pulled her into a bear hug. Planting a resounding kiss on her cheek, he declared, "We did it, McQueen! We did it!"

Or were they adults, both holding back, both trying to be mature and responsible?

Tearing her gaze away from his face filled with rascally jubilation, she concentrated on untying the two colorful bandannas that joined them. Her fingers trembled. How responsible had she been to leave Chelsey alone for the holiday weekend? How mature was it to leave her own emotions open and vulnerable to the far-too-attractive and compelling Dr. Sherman, a man, by his own admission, flawed?

"Let me help you." Rhune placed his hands firmly over hers and quelled her trembling. "You seem to have the post-race shakes."

Undoing the bandannas, he helped her to her feet. The crowd seemed to fade into the background. Rhune filled her line of vision. Rhune. A man filled with fun and the ability to seize the moment. She wobbled, and he caught her.

"Ah, Tess," he crooned. "Who would have pegged you for a three-legged champ?" His dimple danced. "You're a woman of hidden talents. What other secrets are you hiding from me?"

Tess shivered. For the life of her, she couldn't return his grin. Not as she thought of the very real secret she kept from him. With each opportunity she missed to tell him the why and the wherefore of her presence in Sweet Hope, the larger the lie seemed to grow.

The more difficult it was to come clean.

Leaning against the red, white and blue bedecked gazebo in the middle of the green, Rhune gazed up into the darkening sky and saw the first star of the evening. How did that old children's chant go? *Star light, star bright, first star I see tonight. Wish I may, wish I might . . .*

What would he wish for if given the opportunity?

Tess.

He'd wish for Tess to stay in Sweet Hope.

Sighing, he looked across the green at the families scattered on blankets, listening to the band concert, and waited for Tess to return. She and Belle and Cathryn had taken a contingent of children for sparklers. Had left him alone for a few moments with his thoughts after a day of parading and feasting and playing.

And Tess.

How he would miss her after she left for Washington, D.C., tomorrow. How he wanted to ask her to stay. But what right did he have to ask anyone—least of all Tess—for anything after he'd said *no* in too many different ways to too many different women in his past? He'd been on the other end of being pressured. If Tess hadn't suggested remaining in town, it wasn't in her plans. She simply didn't feel the pull strongly enough. From experience he knew the feeling, and because of that knowledge he wouldn't beg.

He felt a hand slide down his arm. Tess stepped in front of him, carrying a lighted sparkler. "Happy Fourth," she said, an enigmatic smile playing about her sensuous lips. "Let the fireworks begin."

In the gathering darkness, her features illuminated by the tiny hissing flare, she took his breath away. "Did you enjoy your detour?" he finally managed to ask.

"My holiday in Sweet Hope?" She closed her eyes and hugged herself. "I loved it." When she opened her eyes, she stared directly at him. "Every minute of it."

So had he.

The little sparkler she held sputtered and died. "I hope the fireworks are good," she said wistfully.

"Belle says they're some of the best in the South. Very daring. Orchestrated by old two-fingered Joe."

"For goodness sakes, Rhune." Tess swatted him, coming alive. "That's a terrible thing to say. And patently untrue, I'm sure."

"Let's hope so." He grinned. The Sweet Hope myth-making virus was beginning to affect him, too. "I do know where the best seats in the house are, if you're interested."

"Where?"

He pointed to the two-story building that housed his offices at the edge of the green. "Over there. On the rooftop." He bent close to show her. His face close to her face.

His arm over her shoulder and pointing along the other side
of her head. To give her a bead.

Sure.

He bent close to feel the softness of her skin. The tickle
of her thick, rich hair. To inhale her exotic woody fragrance. To memorize the essence of her. For the time in the
future when she'd gone.

Tess's eyes widened as she turned to face him. "Should we
invite the O'Malleys and the Matthews family?"

"'Fraid we can't. The rooftop has only a three-foot guard
wall around it. Not tall enough to be safe for little kids."

But just enough to provide privacy.

Rhune Sherman, he mentally chided himself, this is not a
prudent course of action. What happened to the plan to take
it easy, take it slowly? He suddenly counted on Tess to be the
sensible one.

She paused for just a fraction of a second. "Why, that
would be lovely," she breathed.

So much for prudence.

He inhaled, deeply and slowly. "We could stop at my
apartment on the second floor and get a blanket and a
cooler of soft drinks," he offered, recouping, and warming
to this faintly dangerous idea by the minute. "If we start
over there now, I bet we could be on the rooftop before the
fireworks start."

"Sure." The single word hung in the air. The look in her
eye said that she knew full well they were taking a risk.

The way his pulse picked up in anticipation proved his
previous mental caution to be hypocrisy, plain and simple.
This was Tess McQueen's last night in town, and he wanted
her all to himself. She might decide to move on, but he
planned to make damn well certain she didn't forget him,
risk or not, when she did.

Placing his hand on her elbow, he began the process of
weaving their way across the crowded green. Almost at the
street, she made a movement as if to extricate her arm from
his grasp, but, instead, she reached for his hand. Threaded

her fingers with his. Smiled up at him. His heart seemed to come to rest in his throat.

"So," she said, a hint of mischief in her voice, "I finally get to see the infamous bachelor's pad."

"Infamous bachelor or infamous pad?"

"Is there much of a difference?"

Rhune grinned. "That you'll have to decide for yourself." With her hand in his, they crossed the almost deserted street.

Suddenly his old reputation—the one that pegged him for a carefree bachelor—seemed trite and wearisome. Suddenly the feeling that he'd always heretofore tamped down rose within him: the longing to make a lasting, genuine connection with a woman who seemed right for him and only him.

His whole being cried out that Tess McQueen was that woman.

In the past, his lovers, upon leaving, had sworn he'd someday meet a woman who would tame him. Rhune smiled. Why, now that he'd met a woman capable of that task, did he not feel the slightest bit tame?

Oh, no. If anything, he felt wilder and more alive than at any point in his life.

As Rhune opened the street-level door to his walk-up, Tess squeezed his hand. Compelled him with her touch to look at her. "Back at the races, Homer Martin called us mules," she said softly, an inscrutable look in her eyes. "Are we?"

"In what way?" He knew full well how he resisted acknowledging what was right before his eyes. The obvious. What everyone in town seemed to recognize. He needed to hear her misgivings.

Smiling, she flushed and looked down at their clasped hands. "Perhaps you and I are caught in parallel ruts." She looked up and waved her free hand dismissively. "Oh, I know your life seems very little like a rut...but people have put us in deep tracks by labeling us. You're the bad boy. I'm the straitlaced professional." She harrumphed softly. "Neither label is completely true, but we each seem to find some comfort in hiding behind them. Our respective shields. As long as we're shielded, we don't reach out to the one who could pull us out of that rut.''

''Like mules, too stubborn to give? Even if giving would be for the better.''

She nodded silently.

''Well, Tess McQueen, I don't know about you, but the knot in my stomach right now tells me I've stepped out from behind my shield.''

Just admitting it aloud made him feel dangerously vulnerable.

Chapter Eleven

Tess stared in disbelief at the barren loft apartment. This was no playboy's pad. This was a monk's cell.

"You live here?" she asked incredulously, eyeing the refrigerator and the hammock, the only two furnishings in the enormous single room.

He grinned and closed the door behind them. "What did you expect? Black walls? Lava lamps? Exotic harem pillows?"

"I guess I didn't expect anything so...so temporary."

He pulled a small plastic cooler from the top of the refrigerator, then opened the fridge and began filling the cooler with ice and soft drinks. Peeking over his shoulder, Tess could see that the only items in the refrigerator *were* ice and soft drinks.

"Don't you cook?"

His voice echoed from inside the fridge. "Why should I when the Hole-in-the-Wall's right down the street?"

"Have you always lived like a nomad?" She couldn't believe the austerity of this room. Perhaps she had expected harem pillows.

"Let's just say I haven't ever felt the pull to live otherwise." He stood and skewered her with an intense brown gaze that made her believe he might now harbor second thoughts. On what? Living the life of a solitary nomad, or bringing her up to his place?

"Not till now." He reached out to caress her cheek, and his touch told her that his second thoughts did not involve bringing her up here. Oh, no. His smoldering regard said that he wanted her here. Alone. With him.

"What made you change your mind?" she asked with a tiny catch in her throat.

His eyes twinkled mischievously. "Now, *that's* a topic for conversation tonight." He handed her the cooler. "Hold this. I'll get a blanket."

He walked across the room, then disappeared through a doorway on the far wall. Tess could see a bathroom, could hear Rhune opening and closing what must be closets.

She sighed. Sometime tonight she must steer the conversation to the truth. At some point she must tell Rhune that she was Chelsey's sister. Must tell him of Chelsey's accusations. And of her—Tess's—response. If she didn't, then this day, from beginning to end, would have been a lie between him and herself.

The feelings she held for him wouldn't countenance a lie. Love?

She barely dared speak the word before she could speak it in light of the truth. Wasn't that what love meant more than a physical attraction, more than passion—an honest commitment?

She started when Rhune reentered the room holding a folded blanket.

"Ready for the fireworks?" he asked, ushering her to the door.

He couldn't know how his words held a prescient double meaning. And no, she wasn't ready for the fireworks her confession was certain to bring. As they entered the hallway, then made their way up the narrow stairs to the roof, Tess fought a battle within. She *would* tell him the truth, but first she would have this one last evening with him.

He would be angry, yes. How much more angry could he be if she first took this evening for herself?

Rhune pushed open the door at the top of the stairs, and a million stars seemed to rain down upon them as the strains of band music floated up on the sultry night air. He turned, then took her hand to help her step onto the roof. In the starlight he was a shimmering prince leading his princess to the sorcerer's ball. She certainly felt the enchantment in every fiber of her body.

"Do you come here often?" she asked in an awed whisper.

He bowed over her hand and brushed his lips over her skin. "Not much. Alone, it seems a waste of magic."

So he felt it, too.

Leading her to the center of the roof, he released her hand so that he might spread the blanket. When he'd done so, he made a low, courtly bow. "M'lady, the royal box."

She hadn't missed the roguish grin. Nor the dimple. With a fluttering pulse, she carefully sat on the blanket, leaned her head back and drank in the stars. As Rhune lowered himself to her side, the band below broke into "The Stars and Stripes Forever."

"I don't care if it's hokey," he said, chuckling. "The Fourth of July chokes me up."

In surprise, Tess looked at him. "You, too? I thought I was the only one—"

"To feel the pull of a brass band and patriotic songs? The pull of country and of family...and of belonging? No, I feel it, too."

Since when had they begun finishing each other's thoughts?

"And what does family mean to you?" she asked, truly curious.

"Right now, it's the O'Malleys and the Matthewses and the extended family of Sweet Hope." He reached out to stroke her arm. "But someday I want my own personal family to be added to those families. Me as husband. My wife. Our rug rats. The whole nine yards."

She sighed. "Me, too."

His fingers, feather light on her arm, sent a tingling sensation throughout her entire body. "So, Ms. McQueen," he murmured, "the bad boy and the proper professional aren't so different after all."

She grinned. "Who would have thought it?" Suddenly the night seemed very warm. And very close.

As if reading her mind, he reached for a soft drink in the cooler. "Do you want a drink?"

"Sure." What she really wanted was for this evening to never end.

"What else do you think we have in common?" His voice enveloped her in the duskiness.

"Don't protest."

"Why would I?"

She pressed the cold, wet soft drink can that he'd handed her to her overheated cheek. "I think we both, in our own ways, want what's best for others. Me, for my sister and my clients. You, for your patients. For the kids of Doc's Club."

"Don't make me, at least, out to be a saint." She heard a faint growl underlying his words.

"I don't intend to." She took a draft of the soda as she thought how to best phrase her next statement. "I think, however, that in doing what's best for others, we sometimes neglect ourselves."

He stiffened beside her. "Perhaps that's true in your case, but I certainly haven't led a self-denying life. Not off duty, that's for sure."

"Still hiding behind the bad-boy shield?"

He turned to her, and she could tell that he definitely did not like her probing. He said nothing, however. Only stared at her in stony silence.

"You just told me you'd like a family." She reached out and gently touched his arm. "How could you give that to yourself if a part of you refused to allow relationships to grow?"

"What are you getting at, Tess?"

She inhaled sharply, then let her breath out in a long, low sigh. "I'm asking if you're ready now to let a relationship grow.... I guess I'm asking your intentions, Dr. Sherman."

If he never said another word, the look in his eyes told her exactly what his intentions were.

The explosion of the first fireworks above them saved Rhune from an immediate answer. The night sky filled with red, white and blue, and Tess looked upward, the expression on her face one of absolute and childlike delight. Slipping his arm around her shoulder, he drew her down so that they lay on their backs on the blanket, Tess's head pillowed on his shoulder.

How could he find the words to tell her that part of his intentions included keeping her just like this beside him for as long as she would stay?

She flinched at one of the sonic booms, all noise and very little show. "I don't care for those." She nestled into his embrace.

If she snuggled up each time one of those minibombs went off, he'd order up a menu of fireworks composed of nothing but those noisy little devils.

The air hissed then exploded into a shower of silver nuggets. Tess laughed as she turned her face upward to look at his reaction. He could see the light show reflected in her eyes. Could see, too, a reflection of the longing he felt.

He lowered his mouth to hers.

She responded with fire and passion.

To kiss Tess was like kissing no other woman. To kiss Tess was to kiss his destiny. It took his breath away to think that, body and soul, his life belonged with another. For reasons that logic could never explain.

She pulled her mouth away from his. Ran nibbles of kisses down his jawline. Whispered his name. Made his blood run hot and cold at once.

He groaned and pulled away, still holding her firmly in his arms. "Tess McQueen, I'd better tell you my intentions before they're self-evident."

The rockets exploded overhead, drowning out her response. But her mischievous grin told him that she was well aware of the physical evidence of his passion. Her fingers tracing sensuous, lazy circles on his chest told him, too, that she was here to stay. That his desire hadn't frightened her away.

Damn. He needed to harness his runaway emotions. He needed to regain control or the evening would be over before it began. He didn't want quick-and-done with Tess. He wanted slow and lasting.

Tess deserved fervently slow and everlasting.

The band below struck up "I'm a Yankee Doodle Dandy." It was the opportunity to redirect the pace of the evening that Rhune needed. Clasping Tess's hands in his, he sat and pulled her to a sitting position with him. "Dance with me."

She cocked one eyebrow. "*To dance* is your intention?" The corner of her mouth quirked in a compelling invitation to forget the dance and resume the kiss.

He rose, pulling her tightly to his chest. "I have to be able to talk to tell you my intentions. And lying on that blanket with you stretched out beside me...well, I can barely think, let alone talk."

She laughed in delight. "But we can't dance to this."

"James Cagney did. I think I can manage a decent two-step."

"This is crazy!" she exclaimed, her eyes flashing with happiness as he swung her into step with the music.

Yes, this was crazy. Tonight was crazy. This whole week had been crazy. *And,* he finally had to admit, he was crazy.

Crazy in love with Tess McQueen.

The music swirled around them, providing an invisible lotion that massaged his senses. Overhead, a shower of emeralds crackled, hissed and sputtered in much the same way his synapses sang with the feel of Tess in his arms.

He looked deep into her eyes, and paused in the dance. "Stay in Sweet Hope."

Fluttering those smoky thick eyelashes, she demurred. "Why?"

"Because you belong right here...with me. I want you to stay. Need you to stay."

There. He'd finally said it. He held his breath.

"I want to stay," she whispered.

With a whoop he swung her around then back into the rhythm of the dance.

Laughing, she withdrew one hand from his, then smacked his chest. "But there are so many things that must be worked out first." Her eyes grew very dark and very serious.

This was no time for serious. He dipped deeply, almost swooping her off her feet. He held her inches away from the surface of the roof. "Tell me one," he commanded, grinning, he knew, like a fool.

She'd said she wanted to stay.

They could negotiate the small stuff.

She laughed. "Do you always dance so recklessly?"

"Always," he growled. Pulling her upright and hard against him, he began to move in a rhythm that had very little to do with the music from below. This music, this rhythm was of their own making. Hip to hip. Belly to belly.

Slow.

Sexy.

And overpowering.

Passion pumped like blood through his body. He nibbled on her earlobe. "Say you'll stay in Sweet Hope, and that will satisfy me for tonight."

Drawing back, she shot him a look of pure instigation. "You're a man who satisfies easily."

He felt the restraints within him snap one by one.

"You have a lot to learn about me, Tess McQueen." His words rasped with his effort to hold back.

She kissed the corner of his mouth. "Then teach me."

He pulled her roughly to him. Covered her mouth with his. Found her tongue. Found that she wanted him as much as he wanted her. His mouth claimed her. His hands claimed her. And everywhere he touched her, she burned.

He wanted her to stay.

And she wanted to stay.

Those two facts provided sheer release.

Still kissing her, still stroking her, he guided her slowly back to the blanket. When his foot felt the cooler, he pulled her carefully down to the surface of the roof.

Not carefully enough.

The cooler tipped, spilling ice all along the edge of the blanket.

She laughed huskily. "Is that a sign we should cool things down?"

If they were smart they would.

Not heeding *smart*, he lay on his back on the blanket and pulled her on top of him. "Oh, baby," he murmured. "I can't deny I'm hot."

With the most sensuous of smiles, she reached for one of the spilled ice cubes. "Then let me cool you off." Her offer promised no relief from the heat.

Hovering over him, she slowly licked the ice cube until the water trickled over her tongue and lips and down her chin. Then, holding him absolutely still with her gaze alone, she touched the ice to the pulse in his neck.

Rockets thundered overhead.

He shuddered as his body surrendered to her power. With one hand she traced an icy hot path down his throat, across his collarbone. With the other she unbuttoned his shirt, slowly, slowly, slowly as his body ached and burned and grew hard with desire.

She pushed the fabric of his shirt aside, ran that devilish ice cube around first one nipple, then the next. Pressed her hot lips and tongue to the cold flesh.

He groaned and rose to his elbows. "Fair is fair," he growled, reaching for an ice cube.

Oh, the look in his eyes!

A look to match the pounding of her heart.

Never taking his gaze from Tess's, Rhune traced her lips with ice. A delicious shiver ran through her body. Fueled rather than quenched the heat that pulsed within her. Taking the cube away, he leaned forward, ran his tongue over her lower lip. Ran the ice down her arm.

Oh, fair was not fair.

She dropped the nearly melted cube she held. Reached for him. Slid her hand behind his neck. Twined her fingers in his hair. Leaned into his kiss. Felt her body yearn.

She had thought she'd been swept away earlier. On the motorcycle. On the Tarzan swing. In the race. But this... *this* was swept away.

He lowered her so that she lay under him on the blanket. Desire drenching his expression, he gazed down at her. "I have wanted you almost from the very first moment I laid eyes on you."

She stretched and smiled up at him. *"Almost?"*

"Ah, but you're a demanding woman, Tess McQueen." The tender way in which he said her name sent a dizzying current through her. He bent and kissed the hollow of her throat.

Wrapping her arms around his neck, she arched to him. Heard a tiny moan escape her lips. Wanted nothing more than to be close, so very close to him. Wanted to feel his touch claim her. To feel her senses soar. To lose herself in him.

Fireworks exploded overhead. A wash of blues and greens and lavenders.

Strains of the *1812 Overture* pulsed in the air.

As he planted superheated little kisses on her face, on her neck, on her shoulders, his hand moved possessively over her body. Claiming her. Changing her forever. Her heart danced in a wild, abandoned rhythm.

Rhune.

Rhune.

Rhune.

His name throbbed within her mind. He was right for her. They were right together. She had never felt this way before.

She felt his hand slide up under her T-shirt. Felt the night air caress her belly as his long fingers caressed her breast, his thumb coaxing her nipple to a hard, tingling bud.

So this was how it felt to lose one's very self.

"Tess," he whispered as he bent to suckle her. "Tessss...."

Her heart lurched madly as she reached to push his unbuttoned shirt from his shoulders. He shrugged free, and she reveled in the strength and warmth of his flesh beneath her fingers. The ripple of his muscles. The hardness of his spine as he bent to kiss an excruciatingly slow molten path over her breasts and down her belly.

"Let me take this off," he murmured huskily as he lifted the T-shirt over her head. Then, placing his hands on either side of her shoulders, he hovered over her and bathed her with a look of sheer hunger. "You are so beautiful, my Tess."

His words washed over her, a caress. But she was greedy for his touch. She wound her arms behind his neck, pulled herself to him until the heat of his bare chest seared her bare breasts and belly. Where her hips pressed against his, she could feel the hardness of his need.

Sonic booms shattered the air overhead.

The sound of brass instruments drowned out the thudding of her heart.

Lying down, he pulled her alongside him. His intoxicating male musk enveloped her. As his mouth captured hers, she felt him unsnap her jean shorts. Felt his hard, warm hand slide underneath the fabric and cover her pulsing womanhood. Felt little frissons of electricity begin deep within her. She arched her body, utterly helpless to stop or control the current of desire.

"Rhune," she murmured, a plea against his lips. Her flesh prickled.

As their tongues joined in erotic play, he lovingly stroked and stoked the heat between her legs. Her blood surged wildly.

With a sharp little cry, she threw her head back. He kissed her neck, his breath hotly fanning her skin. She bit her lip to stifle yet another cry as she soared through the heavens. Between her legs, her body burned with his relentless caress. She opened her eyes to the night sky as a million shards of light erupted overhead, mirroring the explosion within her.

She gasped and clung to Rhune as she fell to earth.

He caught her. Caught her and covered her with soft little kisses. Kissed her and crooned her name as if it were love itself. Wrapped his arms around her and cradled her with infinite tenderness despite what must be inordinate need within himself.

She touched his face with her fingertips, and he looked at her. Looked at her and told her with his eyes that she was the most desired woman in the world.

Her heart took a perilous leap. "Come into me," she whispered, almost voiceless from want.

Rhune's gaze raked Tess's body with a searing possessiveness as he reached into the pocket of his jeans. She heard the muffled clatter of foil packets falling to the blanket. Heard the snick of his zipper. Felt more than saw him shrug out of his remaining clothing. Closed her eyes as he tugged her shorts down the length of her legs.

Froze in disbelief as she felt an ice cube touch the arch of her foot. As she wriggled to be free, he subdued her with hot kisses to her belly. With one hand he forged an unforgettable icy trail up her calf, over her knee, up the inner part of her thigh. With the other he caressed her hair, her shoulders, her breasts, all the while sending little flicks of his tongue over the flesh on her torso.

Delirious with need, she called his name, reaching out for him. Searching for his pleasure points.

He moaned and took her hands, encouraging her to explore. A heady invitation.

Her gaze followed her hands as she ran them over his hard, smooth body. Over his arousal. The starlight and fireworks made him shimmer like one enchanted. The sight of his flesh against her flesh mesmerized her. The real world spun dizzily away, leaving them in a sphere of their own creation.

For one breathless moment he positioned himself over her. She reached out and placed her hands on his hips. Said yes with her eyes. With her name on his lips, he entered her, and they were one.

Together they found the age-old tempo of lovers bringing their desire to completion.

Burying her face in the corded muscles of his neck, she moved with him in harmony. Riding the wild crescendo. To the liberation of her mind and body.

As the rockets boomed their climax overhead and the band thundered its finale below, Tess felt her whole being flood with the sensation of soaring. Above the earth. Above the everyday. Into an ether rich in love.

Gusts of ecstasy buffeting her, she was unable to control her outcry of unfettered delight.

Crying her name, Rhune shuddered his release and pulled her to him in a crushing embrace.

And they lay still.

In the quiet of the night. Without the previous accompaniment of fireworks and band. Under the stars. The cicadas their only serenade. They lay as lovers. Spent. Clawing need replaced with the rich, warm honey of caring.

Rhune shifted to his side and pulled Tess into the protection of his embrace. "My sweet lady," he murmured, brushing a wisp of hair back from her face. "You leave me breathless."

She could only manage a low purr as she nestled against the hardness of him and reveled in the softness of his words. If it could be, she would remain in Sweet Hope forever.

With Rhune.

The man she loved.

He looked down at her cradled in his arms and wondered that he had ever been afraid to commit. He wanted this beautiful, passionate and giving woman in his life forever.

Tess.

The woman he loved.

He gazed up at the starry sky. "I think the fireworks stopped because they couldn't take the competition. Knew they were only second best."

She rose on one elbow and, smiling, pressed a finger to his lips. "You are such a phony, Rhune Sherman. All tough and solitary on the outside. All soft and oozing poetry on the inside."

He chuckled. "Tess McQueen, you bring out sides of me I would never dream possible. Perhaps I can gain fortune and fame in the medical annals by documenting my post-McQueen multiple personalities."

Bending, she kissed him softly, then murmured against his lips, "Just as long as your fame doesn't take you from Sweet Hope."

"May I interpret that concern as a decision on your part to remain here?"

She inhaled deeply. "You may. If Sweet Hope wants to remain charmingly inefficient, there must be work for me somewhere in the metro Atlanta area."

"Yes!" He rolled her over on her back. "And don't forget your mayoral campaign."

"I'd forgotten about that." She laughed, a beautiful, from-the-heart sound, then ran her fingertips down his face. "You seem to have the power to make me forget." Suddenly a look of concern passed over her features.

He kissed her forehead and tried to smooth the wrinkle between her eyebrows. Tried to bring back the laughter. "What is it?"

Her eyes darkened. She stiffened in his arms. "You do make me forget. Everything. Too much."

"What?" He didn't like the serious tone her voice had taken.

"There are things you need to know about me."

He sighed. "Oh, Tess, there are things you need to know about me, too. But tonight can't we just know this—that we fit? That we belong. Together."

"Just for tonight, seize the moment?" She seemed to relax.

"Just for tonight, seize and share the moment," he assured her. "We can iron out the small stuff on a day-to-day basis."

She harrumphed softly. "Small stuff."

"Come here." He pulled her closer to him. "I want to tell you that this has been the most incredible Fourth of July of my entire life."

She snuggled even closer. "Oh, I think we're in agreement on that. I especially liked the fireworks."

"Which ones?" He nuzzled her neck.

"The homemade ones." She sighed. "Doc?"

"Yeah?"

"Can we stay up here forever?"

"Not on your life." He chuckled. "Sweet Hope's close enough to Interstate 75 that the traffic copters fly over at dawn. Now, if you don't mind baring all on the six-o'clock morning news..."

"I guess you're right," she answered, stretching. "Hey!" She rose to her elbows. "What's this?"

Rhune grinned sheepishly as he noticed that she'd rolled onto his stash of condoms. "I brought extras," he admitted. Moonlight danced rakishly over his considerable supply.

"Red, white and blue?" She sifted them through her fingers. "And one lime green?"

"That one glows in the dark. We'll have to wait for the moon to go behind a cloud."

She pummeled his chest playfully, then leaned her head against his shoulder. "You are a man too much for words."

He breathed deeply of the night air. Of starlight and magic. What could be better? He held the woman of his dreams in his arms. And she'd agreed to stay with him in Sweet Hope.

He sighed.

Anything else was just small stuff.

Chapter Twelve

It was well after midnight when Tess and Rhune began a
slow walk back to the bed-and-breakfast. Rhune firmly
grasping her hand, Tess felt as if her feet barely skimmed the
ground. As if Rhune were the only force that kept her teth-
ered and earthbound. Ever since their lovemaking on the
roof, she firmly believed she could soar.

"Do you know," Rhune said with a chuckle, "that when
I first saw you lying on my examination table in that black
suit, with your skin so pale, and your hair fanned out
around you, my first thought was that you were an exotic
creature who'd dropped from the sky."

"And here I *have* been trying to fly all this time." She
smiled and gave him a quick, hard hug. "Perhaps you knew
more about me than I knew about myself."

"Well, what did you know about me that I didn't know
about myself?"

Tess froze. Too much. Far too much.

She pressed her palms flat on his chest. Looked up into

his eyes. "Rhune? Can we talk about Najeem . . . and Chelsey?"

He stiffened, and his eyes went cold. He reached for her. Hugging her to him, he resumed walking. "Not tonight, Tess. I don't want to look back tonight. I want to look forward."

She couldn't argue that. But she would, before he left her tonight, spill the horrible truth.

He seemed to brighten. "You know, I had a thought. I'm always having *a thought* when you're around. Cherry bombs of revelation. I guess I'll have to get used to them. This one was about my trailer."

"What about your trailer?" She leaned her head against his shoulder. His optimistic voice soothed her.

"If I can secure it against animal invaders, I'd like to turn it into a retreat—supervised, of course—for the kids. Perhaps if I expand the youth program to include kids at risk, it could be a headquarters. A fresh-air headquarters, so to speak."

Tess sighed. He was not afraid to dream. That was one of the things she loved about Rhune: his ability to seize the moment and expand upon it. To wring from it everything good and fun and worthwhile.

"But where will you live?" she asked, chuckling softly as she thought of his nomadic spirit. "Will you pitch a tent under the stand of magnolias until the weather turns cold?"

"No." He kissed the top of her head. "I'll be fine over my offices, in the loft apartment . . . for the time being."

"For the time being?"

"Well . . . it wouldn't hurt to discuss with Boone O'Malley . . . and with you . . . the possibility of building a home in the magnolia grove."

"No, it wouldn't hurt," she murmured, and closed her eyes. She could listen to the comforting sounds of his nesting plans forever. Especially since they seemed to include her.

He stopped and turned her to face him. "Until then, I think it might be wise to buy a bed."

"A bed?"

His dimple danced in the pale light of the street lamp. "I know you're a woman of many talents, Tess McQueen, and I'm a very adaptable man. But I think my hammock might just be too much for even the likes of us."

At the hint of renewed lovemaking, Tess's knees weakened and her pulse picked up. Slipping her arms around his neck, she offered up her mouth. The freedom to show him her desire proved heady indeed, and the privilege of expecting to receive his passion in return, headier yet.

Rhune lowered his mouth to hers, then slowly teased her with a feather-light kiss.

"Not fair." She ached for more. Standing on tiptoes, she gently nibbled on his lower lip. She could feel his smile. And then his need as he covered her mouth with his.

Ah, but his kisses were satisfying.

Hot and deep and lingering. Kisses that claimed. Kisses that bared his soul and hers. Kisses that promised tomorrow and tomorrow and tomorrow.

He ran his hands down her sides, sending prickles of pleasure throughout her whole body. He cupped her bottom, pulled her to him. Hard. She lost herself in the hardness of his body. In the searing softness of his kisses.

She was his. Body and soul.

Surely he would recognize that when she must tell him who she was.

Breathless, she pulled away. Drank in every feature of his face, in case...*in case* he didn't understand, and all that was left to her was a memory. A memory of eyes deep and caring one minute, roguish and seductive the next. Of a mouth quick to smile and even quicker to pleasure. Of features strong and noble. Noble, yes. Plato would agree with her. A man who struggled in the classic sense against the worst in himself, who tried to make of himself the best he could be, was certainly noble.

Would he see her struggle as noble? Or would he see it as betrayal?

He kissed her tenderly on the bridge of her nose. "Why the furrow?" he asked, his words cosseting. "Having second thoughts?"

"Oh, Rhune, no. Never." She embraced him, burrowing her face against his throat. "Never."

"Then I'd better get you home before Auntie Mel and Auntie Ida refuse to let you see me again."

She released him except for one arm around his waist. "I'd tie the bed linens together and escape out the window."

Laughing softly, they began to walk again, their steps the steps of lovers reluctant to part.

The moon had risen, and the night bore a silvery cast. Enchantment, thought Tess, her mind moving sensuously, slowly. Pure enchantment. "You told me," she said aloud, "that Sweet Hope was a little like Brigadoon. That it would wrap me in its spell and that, before I knew what was happening, I'd never want to leave."

"And has it done that?"

She touched him with her free hand just because she had the license to do so. "You did that."

Suddenly in the night sky a cloud slithered across the moon, throwing Main Street into darkness. The cicadas seemed to pause. And Tess shivered.

"Tess!" Ida Drake's voice rang out sharply from the veranda of the bed-and-breakfast. "Oh, Tess, dear, please hurry." Her words crackled with worry.

Rhune's face became a mask of concern. He gripped Tess's hand as they both broke into a run across Main Street.

The porch light illuminated an agitated Ida descending the veranda steps. What could have her in such a state? Tess's thoughts flew to Chelsey.

"Oh, Tess, we couldn't find you." Ida wrung her hands. "There's been a call from a hospital in Washington. The number's by the phone in the foyer. They said it was extremely urgent that you call back. Immediately."

"What's happened?" Tess felt fear rise in her throat. "Is it my sister?"

Ida reached out for Tess's free hand. Tugged both her and Rhune up the steps. "They didn't say. The message was only that you should call immediately. And that it was urgent. *Extremely* urgent."

Dear God, it was Chelsey, she knew it. Why had she left her alone?

What had Tess done by seizing today for herself?

Dread hammering on her spine, she gave both Ida's and Rhune's hands a quick releasing squeeze for support, then raced into the house.

Rhune had seen the joy on Tess's face turn to alarm, and vowed she wouldn't go through this alone. Her happiness was his happiness now, her despair his, as well. He'd grown gruff with her when she'd suggested he was her guardian angel, but the overwhelming feeling within him now was to protect her. To shield her from whatever difficulty she now faced. That was unfair, and he knew it. He couldn't wholly protect her, although that was his most fervent wish. Neither would she want his overwhelming protection. But he could stand by her. Work out the problem with her.

Together.

He was unused to sharing another person's life. But with Tess it felt right.

Leaving a fluttering Ida Drake on the veranda, Rhune bolted through the doorway to see Tess standing, a look of frustration on her face, at the telephone table at the far end of the foyer.

Holding the receiver limply in one hand, she turned to him. "I can't get it to go through." The words caught in her throat.

Quickly moving to her side, he could see why: her hands trembled. She had probably misdialed. "Let me," he offered, taking the receiver from her hand. Cupping it between his ear and shoulder, he dialed the number she held out to him, then took her still-shivering hands and pressed them between his own. He only wished he had as easy a remedy for the waver he saw in the depths of her eyes.

"Mount Mercy Hospital. Obstetrics. How may I help you?" The voice at the end of the line was crisp. No-nonsense.

"I'm calling for Tess McQueen," Rhune replied. "She received a message to call this number. That it was extremely urgent."

"What was the name again?"

"Tess McQueen." He felt impatience rise hot.

"One moment, please."

Rhune handed the phone to Tess. "Someone should be on the line shortly." He wrapped his arms around her and held her in a light, protective embrace. Unrealistic as it might be, he'd do his damnedest not to let the world hurt her.

Waiting, she shook almost imperceptibly. "Hello. Yes, this is she." She stiffened. "Yes...yes...I understand... I'll catch the next plane out." Her voice had become thready, her facial expression drawn. "I *do* understand. Thank you...goodbye."

She held the receiver and stared blankly into space even after Rhune could hear the disconnect tone. Carefully taking the receiver from her hand, he replaced it in the cradle. "Tess, what is it?"

"My sister lost the baby."

"What's her condition? Were there complications?"

"The doctor assured me she'll be fine." She pushed by him. "But I should have been with her."

He reached out for her hands. They were icy cold. "I'll get you to the airport, but I won't let you blame yourself in any way."

She swung her gaze upon him, and her eyes were glittery with tears. "Why not? While I was playing, my sister was losing her baby."

He ached for her. "It's not your fault."

"How can you say that? I pushed her away in the name of tough love."

"For God's sake, Tess. I'm a doctor. If I know nothing, I know that love doesn't cause miscarriages."

Tess pulled away from him, biting the knuckle of her hand. "She's so young. And now so alone. I have to get to her."

"Of course. I'll help." He was more worried about Tess's self-blame than he was about her sister's condition. Her sister was in good hands. She'd recover. Tess's emotional state, on the other hand, was extremely fragile. He wouldn't push her now. He'd do what he could to get her to D.C. "Go pack what you need in a carry-on bag. I'll be right up. Ida can call the airport and reserve a seat on the next flight out."

With a look of anguish she tore through the foyer and up the staircase.

He hurried to find Ida. He didn't want to leave Tess alone for long. She needed him. Needed every ounce of support and reassurance...and love...that he could show her.

Having enlisted the older woman's help, he charged the stairs two at a time. This was not an emergency. The emergency was over. Out of their hands. The critical problem now was to convince Tess that she should not shoulder guilt over the loss of her sister's baby.

He found the door to Tess's room open. Found her throwing things into a small bag. Found her weeping. He strode to her side and enveloped her in his embrace.

She pushed against his chest. "Please, Rhune. I know what you're trying to do...but I have to get to my sister. She needs me."

"Yes, she does," he murmured into her hair. "We all need you, Tess. But at the moment you have needs, too."

She pulled back, and he could see frustration in her eyes. "I indulged my needs today, and consequently my sister was alone when she needed me most." She slumped against him. "Oh, Dixie Fae," she moaned.

He brushed the hair away from her face, wiped her tears with his hand. "We'll get you to Dixie Fae, I promise." He kissed her forehead. "Take only the essentials. I'll drive your car and the rest of your belongings to D.C. Heck, the way I drive, I might beat you."

"But your practice is scheduled to open Monday."

"For Pete's sake, Tess McQueen, would you stop worrying about other people?" He lifted her chin so that she had to look at him. "We'll work it all out. *We* being the optimum word."

Ida Drake stuck her head into the room. "The first available seat is on the six-o'clock flight this morning. I reserved it. Even with the drive to Atlanta, you don't have to hurry. You won't get any sleep tonight, but you don't have to hurry."

"Always good news-bad news." Rhune grinned ruefully. "Thanks, Ida." He turned to Tess. "So now we can get you to your sister with plenty of time to convince you that, at every opportunity you take a break for yourself, the world is not going to fall apart."

"But she lost the baby."

"Very sad, yes." Sitting on the edge of the bed, he pulled Tess next to him. "But not the end of the world. And no reason for you to beat yourself up."

Tess inhaled sharply. "She's my sister, but she's also like my daughter."

"And so you feel her pain doubly."

"More than that. I would take on the world to protect her."

He felt his heart contract. "For the first time in my life," he said, his voice a low rasp, "I know exactly what you mean."

Tess looked deeply into Rhune's eyes. Could he possibly feel the same way about her?

She glanced at her watch. Two o'clock. The fact that they need not rush didn't assuage her anxiety. She wanted to rush. Wanted to fly to her sister's side. Dixie Fae, with that ridiculous stage name, Chelsey Wellington. A repudiation of who she was and where she'd been. Rebellion, plain and simple.

She rose and began to pace. Impetuous Chelsey. Her sister. Her almost daughter. As difficult a young woman as she'd been, Tess loved her mightily. Chelsey had needed her, and Tess had failed her.

"Are you packed?" Rhune's voice came to her from what seemed a great distance. "Can I help with anything?"

She started. "No. I have what I need. I just wish I was on that plane and landing at Dulles."

He rose also, then came to stand next to her. He took her hands in his. Stilled her nervous body with his quiet strength. "I always find that time passes more quickly if you keep moving." He stroked her hair. "Why don't you take a shower and change. I'll go round up some coffee for us. Then I'll drive you to the airport, and we can pace there." He grinned in an obvious attempt to cheer her. "At least they have moving sidewalks there. We can pace much faster."

She attempted a smile. "Okay." There was absolutely no point to her present pacing.

As soon as Rhune left in search of coffee, Tess entered the bathroom, turned on the shower, then undressed. Waiting for the water temperature to even out, she lifted her T-shirt and pressed it to her face. The scent of lovemaking filled her nostrils. Rhune's scent and hers commingled. A heady fragrance and one that pulled pangs of guilt from her.

If she'd only come clean with Rhune immediately after Caldwell delivered his report, she and Rhune probably would have parted, if not friends, then two adults who openly and honestly understood one another. And *if* she'd left Friday as she'd intended, she and Rhune would never have made love. Instead, she'd have been home with Chelsey when her sister needed her most.

She touched the T-shirt again to her face. Ah, but, knowing all this, would she have missed the night of passion on the roof with Rhune?

Throwing the T-shirt to the floor in frustration, she stepped into the shower. Under the warm and enveloping cascade of water, she chastised herself for having conflicting feelings still. Her sister needed her, yes. But she needed Rhune.

Rhune.

He now helped her get back to the woman who'd been a major part in his life's upheaval.

Tess turned off the water. She must tell him. She didn't know if they'd be able to salvage any part of their relationship, but she must tell him the truth. She was Chelsey's sister, and she'd come, if not to seek revenge, at least to seek the truth. And having found it, she'd begun her own trail of lies. How just was that? Was that any tribute to her love for her sister... or her growing love for Rhune?

For love Rhune she most surely did. She'd come to Sweet Hope expecting to find a cad and had, instead, found a man of such complexity it would take a lifetime to figure him out.

Sighing, she reached for a towel. There had been a moment when she'd dreamed of a lifetime with him. But now...?

"Tess!" His voice rang out from the other room. "I'm back. I have coffee. Ida had already made a pot. And biscuits." The sheer optimism in his voice brought tears to her eyes. "Take your time. I'll save you a crumb."

She quickly toweled herself dry, then reached for her robe on the hook on the door. Wrapping herself in the thick terry, she remembered Rhune's use of the word *we*. How he'd said it was the optimum word.

Such a tiny word.

Would it be strong enough to hold up to her confession?

It would have to be. She was about to tell the truth. Squaring her shoulders, she opened the door to the bedroom. What she saw made her blood run icy, then hot.

A small round table and two antique chairs sat in the bay window overlooking the street. She'd used that space to work on her files. Rhune had obviously tried to maneuver the coffee and biscuit tray onto the table without disturbing her work papers and briefcase. But the briefcase had fallen. Had spilled its contents across the bedroom floor, including Caldwell's report.

Rhune now crouched over the papers, holding the investigator's open file in his hands. This couldn't be. He would now never believe that she'd been about to tell him all.

He looked up at her, his face filled with question. "What is this, Tess?" His eyes had suddenly gone very dark. "It looks like an investigator's report, and my name is on it." He rose, his body stiff. "Do you have all your lovers investigated?"

"No... of course not... no. I've wanted to find a way to explain all this." She prayed fervently that he would see the truth in her explanation. The larger truth. That she'd done what she'd done out of love for her sister. That she hadn't expected to fall in love with him.

"I'm listening." His words were hard and cold. His eyes even colder.

There was no easy way to begin this. No way to soften the truth she had to tell. She could only jump into the middle and pray he'd stick around to hear her out.

"I'm Chelsey Wellington's sister." The words seemed to explode in the room.

The look he gave her was one of frozen disbelief.

She forged ahead, needing now to get it all out in the open. "Chelsey Wellington is her stage name. Her real name is Dixie Fae McQueen."

"The sister who lost the baby?" What was he thinking? His face told her nothing.

"Yes. She tried to involve you in the patrimony, and sent me and an investigator on your trail."

"But I never—"

"Slept with her. I know. She finally confessed as much." Tess took a deep breath. "After I confronted her with the investigator's report... and the story you told me of Najeem and Chelsey."

A fire seemed to burn in the depths of his eyes. He smacked the files in his hand. "You had this report with you that night in the garden. And you let me spill my guts."

"Yes." How cruel that one little word sounded.

"Until then you thought I was the father of your sister's child?" His words were raw, scraped of all emotion.

"I thought it possible."

His face became an inscrutable mask. "And you came to town for revenge." The bridled anger in his voice raked her senses.

"No, Rhune. I came to town for justice. I came to learn the truth."

"And when, pray tell, were you planning to confront me? With your suspicions. With your identity."

Her palms felt cold and clammy. As uncomfortable as the rock that seemed lodged at the bottom of her heart. "I'd planned to tell you as soon as I arrived in Sweet Hope. But I fell ill . . . and you were nothing that I expected. I thought it best to learn more about you before I acted."

He took a step forward, glaring at her with burning, reproachful eyes. "Or perhaps you thought the sweetest revenge would be to have me fall for you—hard—and then leave. As you thought I'd done with your sister."

"No!" Dear God, is that what he thought?

He thought he'd been sucker-punched.

He thought he'd been proven the biggest chump in history.

He thought all his wariness about his increased vulnerability had blown up in his face. He was furious that he'd allowed his guard to drop.

He'd been had. Plain and simple. By an obvious master—or should he say mistress?—of the game. And the horrendous realization came from the fact that this time it hadn't been a game to him. This time he'd not just fallen and fallen hard. This time he'd laid himself open.

He loved her.

He felt sick. Sick at heart. He wanted to leave. But greater than the pull to hole up somewhere alone to lick his wounds was the desire to understand how a woman he thought he loved could betray him so seamlessly.

What an incredible sting operation.

He shook his head as if, once the cobwebs had been shaken out, all this would turn out to be a confusing dream. But, clearheaded, he still saw the stricken look on Tess's face that said she'd been found out. That said this was no dream.

"Ask me anything," she said softly. "I'll explain anything and everything until you understand it all."

"Who was the real father of your sister's child?" he snapped, a chill like hoarfrost hanging at the edges of his words.

"I don't know. Chelsey wouldn't tell me." Tess raised her hands in a helpless gesture. "And now, with things the way they are, I may never know."

This was crazy. He should walk out the door right now. But she fascinated him with her incredible acting skills. Like sister, like sister he presumed. "Why did she name me?"

"Partly the revenge of a woman scorned. She felt rejected when you wouldn't bed her." Tess rubbed her arms hard as if she were freezing. "Partly because it was convenient that you'd left town. She said she hadn't really counted on me going after you. To make you live up to your responsibilities."

"Ah," he replied bitterly, "Tess McQueen, the avenging angel. A very efficient avenging angel, I might add. You certainly ran me through."

"You must remember that Chelsey's more than a sister to me. She's very much like my daughter. The pull of the protective lioness is incredibly strong." Her voice wavered.

For a moment he almost fell for the sincerity of her plea. For a fleeting moment only. He forced himself to remember that this woman had calculated harm against him from the beginning. Had used him as she'd thought he'd used her sister. Had decided to deal with a perceived wrong with another wrong.

He slit his eyes and tried to see her as he'd seen her only hours ago. The woman he loved. He looked away. It hurt too much to try. "You never let me take the stand in my defense."

She put her hand on his shoulder, but he shrugged it off. "In a way, I did," she replied in a low, tormented voice. "After your confession in the garden, I confronted Chelsey. Made her tell me the truth. The truth as it pertained to you. Yesterday morning, if you recall, I was prepared to leave. I'd come to the end of the story—in Sweet Hope, at least.''

He turned upon her, a primitive grief gnawing at his belly. "What made you stay?" Now, this should prove a most interesting part in the tale, he thought bitterly. "You knew I wasn't the father of Chelsey's child, but that I'd *almost* fallen in bed with her. Based on that knowledge, what plans did you make for Saturday? Not quite the rack. Just the thumbscrews, perhaps.''

Very convincing tears appeared at the corners of her eyes. "I never meant to hurt you. Even when I believed Chelsey, I only wanted you to face up to your responsibilities. Then later . . . as I came to know you . . . as I came to care for you, I wanted more than anything for the truth to be different than my sister's story.''

He couldn't answer her. So much did he want to believe her that he feared opening his mouth and betraying all logic.

She looked down at her hands. "I wanted to stay Saturday for me," she said, her voice so low he could barely hear the words. She raised her head to look at him. Her nostrils flared as if she were trying to keep tears at bay. "I wanted to stay because I'd fallen in love with you."

He could feel the muscles in his jaw twitch with the anger he needed to keep in check. "And you expect me to believe that, after all your lies?''

She didn't answer.

He glared at her. "What do you want from me, now that I know who you are, Tess McQueen?''

"I want you to forgive me.''

Terrible, terrible regrets assailed him. "*That* I'll never be able to do.''

Chapter Thirteen

The bottom fell out of Tess's world.

She hadn't dared to hope Rhune would still care for her after her confession, but she'd prayed he'd find it in his heart to forgive her.

He'd just now sworn, with great conviction, that forgiveness was not a possibility. And that seemed, to her, as if the door to her future had just slammed shut.

Standing cold and unyielding in her bedroom, he was not the warm and loving Doc she'd come to know. The steely look in his eyes told her that no amount of persuasion on her part would bring that old familiar Doc back. Still, she had to try. She couldn't surrender her hopes and dreams without a fight. Couldn't simply walk away, leaving behind the man who'd made her soar—heart, mind and body.

"Rhune." She stiffened her resolve. "Put yourself in my place."

The corner of his sensuous mouth, now thinned in anger, twitched. His eyes had become two sharp slits in his face. Not a particularly encouraging response.

Tess, however, forged on. "If Belle told you that a man had slept with her then left town after learning she was pregnant, wouldn't you want to find that man? Learn the truth? Have him own up to his responsibilities? Wouldn't you be single-minded in your search?"

"Let's get one thing straight," he snapped. "My problem isn't with you believing your sister. Nor is it with your campaign for justice, as you insist on presenting it." His frown deepened. "I take issue, however, with your failure to come clean with me from the moment you arrived in Sweet Hope. To my mind, that failure contaminates every-thing... *everything*... you've said or done since your arrival."

It wouldn't hurt quite so much if she simply could not see his point.

But she did. Clearly.

Had, in fact, previewed it in her mind as she'd struggled with the inner conflict of picking the right time to tell him the truth. Obviously, by delaying, she'd picked the absolutely worst time.

"Why didn't you tell me exactly who you were, Tess?" This time he spoke her name in a contemptuous hiss.

"Because, from the moment I first saw you, I couldn't wholly believe you were the man my sister said you were."

"And so you had me investigated." A tiny visible shudder ran down his jawline and corded neck muscles.

"I thought that, to be fair, I had to be thorough."

He cocked one eyebrow suspiciously. "And what did your investigator tell you?"

"That you worked hard. That you played hard. And that, although you might not be perfect, you were a man with a conscience."

He snorted with derision. "I could have dug up worse on me."

"I wasn't looking for *worse*. I was looking for the truth as it pertained to my sister."

"And you thought the investigator had found it?"

"I thought he'd found a part of it. I believed that you—in your life in Sweet Hope—held a greater part. And that Chelsey, with her silence, held an even greater part still. For myself, I needed to see these parts made into an understandable whole."

"For yourself?"

"For myself," she repeated softly, looking him directly in the eye. "For, by that time, I was beginning to fall in love with you."

Looking away as if her regard seared him, he moved to the bay window, parted the lace curtains, then stared at the street below. "In the garden that night, you already doubted your sister's word. You held a report in your hands that cast further doubt. *And* you claim to have been falling in love with me." He whirled around, fury sparking in his eyes. "Why didn't you tell me who you were then?"

She'd asked herself that same question a dozen—no, a hundred dozen—times. Her answer still didn't satisfy her. "I was afraid."

He started toward her, then stopped abruptly. "Afraid of what?"

A tiny revelation burst inside her. All this time she'd thought she'd been afraid of his reaction. But her fear had been something far more elemental. Something deep within her. A realization that made her far too vulnerable. "I was afraid," she whispered, "of the power of the attraction I felt for you."

Crossing his arms over his chest, he tipped his head back. Gazed hard at the ceiling. Inhaled and exhaled deeply. Seemed to fight a reply.

"And then," she ventured, "you told me about Najeem and about Chelsey. I recognized that you had, in a sense, bared your soul to me."

His head snapped upright. His dark regard almost frightened her. "I would have thought *that* the perfect time to swoop down for the kill."

"It crossed my mind." Her words sounded blunt and cruel; however, she was finished with half-truths. "But I thought it would be a case of throwing salt in an open wound."

"Ah." He rubbed his jaw. "So you were afflicted with a small case of conscience."

"Yes." She winced. "More than that, I wanted to use the new information from the investigator and from you to wrest the truth from my sister. In fact, immediately after we left the garden, I called Chelsey to confront her."

"You want me to believe that the focus of your undercover work then turned on your sister."

She felt despair rear its ugly head. "You make me sound so cold and calculating. So manipulative."

"Be honest, Tess. Doesn't this scenario sound like the work of a cold and calculating manipulator?"

On the surface, yes, it did. But if he could only see deep in her heart, he would see another perspective altogether. She reached out to touch him, but, thinking better of it, pulled back. "I admit to poor judgment. But I will never admit to wanting to manipulate or hurt you."

He *must* believe her on that point.

"I find that hard to believe."

She took a step forward. "Rhune..." Speaking his name with all its implications of lost happiness pained her. "Think about the woman on the Tarzan swing. The woman picking magnolias. Decorating the kids' holiday bikes." She paused when a flicker of longing cut through his dark and forbidding regard. "Do you think that woman was playacting? Or do you think that woman had truly fallen under Sweet Hope's spell?"

The flicker of longing disappeared from his eyes, and he answered her question with his own brusque and brutal question. "And the lovemaking? Was that an act?"

"Dear God, no!"

"How can I know for sure?"

She took another step toward him, this time reaching out and pressing her hand to his arm. He didn't shrug it off or move away, only stared at her with a judge's cold appraisal. "You *know*," she fervently assured him. "You know for sure, Rhune Sherman, that my passion came from the depths of my heart. As surely as you know how our lovemaking affected you, you know how it touched me. No amount of acting could have covered my real feelings.''

He started.

She had touched a raw but honest nerve.

At that moment Ida Drake popped into the room. "Time is running out, my dears. Will you be taking Tess's car to the airport, or will you need to borrow mine? Surely, Dr. Sherman, your motorcycle isn't suitable.''

Rhune turned abruptly to face Ida. "You and Tess will have to decide. I'm afraid I won't be able to drive after all.'' He walked across the room to leave.

He couldn't leave. Not like this. Not when she had to leave town. And this mess unresolved.

Ida stared in amazement at Tess, who tried to impart without words her need for help.

"Wh-why...'' the older woman sputtered, staying Rhune's exit with a touch of her hand. "I'm afraid the only help I can offer is the use of my car. I have a terrible case of night blindness.''

"Then perhaps Mel could drive.''

Behind Rhune's back, Tess shook her head furiously.

Ida seemed to understand. At least that Rhune was to drive Tess to the airport. "I'm afraid Mel took a sleeping pill upon retiring. A full brass band couldn't rouse her.''

The set of Rhune's shoulders spoke of exasperation. "Then a cab.''

"Absolutely not.'' Ida ruffled like a mother hen. "I won't have a guest of mine subjected to a seventy-five-dollar ride to the airport. I implore you, Dr. Sherman, to aid *my guest.*'' The older woman certainly knew how to twist a man's chivalrous conscience.

"I'm sure someone else in town...''

"Oh, there's no time now,'' Ida clucked. "You take Tess's bag down, and Tess and I will check the room one more time for essentials.'' She all but shooed him from the room.

Clenching the muscles in his jaw, Rhune reached for the carry-on bag on the bed. With a glance at Tess that said, in no uncertain terms, that this was a favor to Ida, he turned unceremoniously and left the bedroom.

He stalked down the hallway, seething.

How had he allowed himself to be talked into this folly? With the bomb that Tess had just dropped on him, he had no desire to sit in the same car with her for the hour's drive to the airport.

Hell, he had no desire to spend another minute in her manipulative—no matter that she denied manipulation—company.

His anger simmering, he swept through the bed-and-breakfast out to the sidewalk, where he cooled his heels under the still-dark sky, impatiently awaiting Tess's appearance with her car keys.

Tess.

How could that woman have taken him in so thoroughly?

She'd admitted that she'd come to town to track him down. Admitted that she'd hired an investigator. Admitted, too, that she'd knowingly withheld her identity. And then she had the unmitigated gall to want him to believe that her sleeping with him wasn't an act of revenge. If he believed that, he was a candidate for oceanfront property in Arizona.

Pacing the sidewalk, he fumed.

How could he have been so gullible?

He stopped short. He knew how. He'd loved her. The idea froze him to the spot. And now he'd lost her.

He didn't know what pained him more: the idea of loving the wrong woman or of losing the dream of the right woman. He shrugged that troubling thought off. He refused to place Tess McQueen—efficiently calculating Ms. McQueen—even remotely close to the category of *the right woman.*

The click of heels on the veranda made him turn. Tess aimed the keyless entry remote at her BMW, and the big car chirped in response, the doors unlocked and the alarm de-activated. Rhune snorted. Even her car was a slick big-city model and fit in trusting little Sweet Hope no more than did its owner.

"I'll drive." He held out his hand for the keys. It wasn't a polite offer. "I know the shortest route."

He slid behind the wheel of the luxury car and knew immediately it had been a mistake not to take Ida Drake's car instead. Not only would he have to drive a full hour to the airport with Tess in the car, he'd have to drive a full hour back, seated in a car that was pure Tess McQueen. Efficient. Elegant. High tech. And powerful. The faint scent of her perfume that lingered with the scent of leather was enough to raise the hairs on the back of his neck.

This was a mistake. Once the woman was out of Sweet Hope, he needed no further reminders of her.

He glanced at his watch. They really didn't have time to make the switch to Ida's car.

"Is something wrong?" Tess asked.

Yeah. He could name a hundred and one things. "Nothing," he answered, clipping the word short. He started the engine, shoved the car into First, then pressed the accelerator. In only minutes they roared out of Sweet Hope.

He hoped she didn't expect to make chitchat. They'd each said what had to be said back in the bed-and-breakfast. Now he needed time to absorb his stupidity.

"I'm assuming you no longer want to drive my car to D.C." Her voice cut into his thoughts.

"You assume right." He studied the road with the intensity of a *NASCAR* driver, hoping she'd take the hint and accept the ride for what it was. A ride and nothing else. No more talk. She'd told her preposterous story and seemed to be sticking to it. What could he do but turn away?

"Perhaps I can pay one of the mechanics from Homer Martin's garage to drive it up and fly back." The hopeful lilt in her voice begged him to engage in small talk, even.

He didn't reply. He had too much on his mind.

She'd lied to him from the beginning.

He could forgive her the overwhelming sense of protection she felt for her sister. He'd felt that way earlier. About Tess. About keeping the one he loved out of harm's way. He could forgive her hiring an investigator. The world was filled with bums and sleazy characters, and his own track record hadn't been spotless.

But even with all his faults, he'd always been honest. He couldn't find it in his heart to forgive her the lies.

Despite his best intentions, he glanced surreptitiously toward the passenger seat. His heart caught. She looked so small, slumped against the door. And so defeated. That wasn't the can-do Tess he knew. For an instant he let himself believe that she sure was taking this brouhaha hard. He forced his eyes back to the road and to his driving.

Hell, she'd caused the brouhaha. Let her stew in her own juices.

"Rhune...?"

"I don't want to talk."

"I'm not asking you to talk." Her voice was soft and so damned sincere. "I want to tell you that I'm sorry."

The simplicity of her apology almost undid him. In fact, her relative silence since they'd entered the car almost undid him. He'd expected...what? Histrionics? Tears? A prolonged argument? Whatever he'd expected, it hadn't been this simple, seemingly heartfelt apology.

It almost undid him.

Until he thought of the simple truth he'd expressed to her in the bedroom earlier: By lying to him from the start, she'd contaminated everything she'd said or done from that point on.

He was too tired and in too much pain to begin again fresh.

She reached out and laid her hand on his arm. "Did you hear me?"

"Yeah." He made as if to fine-tune the air-conditioning and shrugged off her hand. "I heard you."

"Then I guess there's nothing more to be said."

"Not a thing."

After a pause she added, "Perhaps, after I make sure my sister's all right, I could fly down to pick up my car. It wouldn't be for a week or two. Maybe then you'll want to talk."

The idea of her returning was repugnant to him. "I'll talk to Homer Martin to make certain he can spare one of his crew to deliver your car. That way you won't have to leave your sister or your job in D.C."

There. He hoped that cut off any conversation about her returning to Sweet Hope. Cut off any promise that he'd ever want to discuss this matter again. Hell, it hurt too much now. Why would he want to reopen an old, festering wound?

They drove the remainder of the way in silence. Curbside at the airport, Rhune stayed in the car while Tess got out with her carry-on bag and briefcase. The briefcase that held the damned investigator's file that had precipitated this whole hellish fiasco. The beginning of the end. The end of the most passionate night of his life. The end to their blossoming relationship. And to his gut feeling of having finally found a lasting connection.

As he watched her walk, straight-backed, into the terminal, he almost wished he'd never discovered that file. What was the saying? Ignorance is bliss. Well, hell. He'd most assuredly been blissful in his ignorance.

And had he ever been ignorant.

A traffic cop motioned for him to move along.

He might as well get back to Sweet Hope, pick up his fishing equipment and make a day of it on his pond. He certainly wasn't about to get any sleep. Monday, his practice opened to a full schedule, so Patsy Sinclair, his receptionist, had informed him. Good. He'd lose himself in the practice of medicine.

On the plane, Tess stared at the phone on the back of the seat in front of her. She looked at the crumpled paper Ida Drake had pressed into her hand just before she'd left the bed-and-breakfast.

Rhune's home and office phone numbers.

Glancing at her watch, she estimated that Rhune should be well back at his loft apartment by now. Her movements robotlike, she slipped her credit card into the slot, lifted the phone, then dialed Rhune's home number. Closing her eyes, she waited.

And waited.

She could picture him lying in the hammock, ignoring the call. Knowing that she was on the other end. The thought made her feel ineffably sad. She hung up. She'd let him cool off for a few days, and then she'd try again.

She couldn't afford to think of Rhune now or of her own aching heart. She had Chelsey to think of.

Tess had been home for slightly over a week, Chelsey for several days now. If Tess had to pick which woman was coping better after her ordeal, she'd most definitely pick Chelsey. Her younger sister seemed almost relieved to have the dilemma of pregnancy taken out of her hands.

Quite frankly, the matter only added to Tess's sorrow.

She lifted her sunglasses and squinted at the view from her balcony. She hadn't been back to work since coming home from Sweet Hope. One of the benefits of being a former workaholic was that you accrued a hefty vacation bank. She took a drink of her iced tea and tried to return her attention to the bestseller in her lap.

It was a fruitless attempt.

Restlessness wearing at her like an ill-fitting shoe, she rose and padded to the telephone, checked her personal planner, then punched in the number for the Hole-in-the-Wall Café.

Edna answered.

"Hey, it's me." Tess felt better just being linked by a phone line to Sweet Hope.

The waitress's drawl sounded like home. "Honey, we've got to stop meeting like this."

"I know." Tess smiled weakly. "But Homer Martin called earlier to tell me he has more work than he can handle. That he can't possibly spare a worker to drive my car to D.C."

"My, my," Edna sympathized. "That surely does put you in a bind. But what can I do about it?"

"Would you perhaps like a minivacation?"

"Me? Darlin', any trip that's longer than twenty minutes sets me to noddin' off. Your big old Beemer would arrive in D.C. lookin' like a pretzel, and you wouldn't want that, now, would you?"

Tess sighed. She really didn't give two hoots about that car anymore. Right now, however, it was her only connection to Sweet Hope. "Would you ask the regulars at the café if anyone would be interested? I'll pay expenses, the flight back. And I'll even provide a day's worth of sight-seeing. I'm an excellent tour guide."

"I'm sure you are, sugah. But folks around here are just as busy as bees. What with work and crops and...what all. Tempting as your offer is, I doubt you'd get a nibble."

"Are you being straight with me?" Tess wouldn't put it past the matchmaking residents of Sweet Hope to be in collusion.

"Scout's honor."

Right.

"Edna, are you trying to tell me that I'll have to return to Sweet Hope if I ever want to see my car again?"

"I sure am." Edna's voice brightened considerably. "I'm telling you that ... and I'm also telling you to call Doc. He looks sorrier than a hound with the mange. He looks so bad no one in town's had the heart to even gossip about him."

That bad.

"I've called his apartment," Tess confessed. "Several times. I think he has the phone off the hook."

"Then call his office. Patsy will put you through."

"Oh, Edna, that's so unprofessional."

Edna hooted. "Do you want professional, Tess Mc-Queen, or do you want Doc back?"

There was no contest.

"I want Doc back."

"Then get off the line, girl. I've got no power to get him back for you. You've got to do it for yourself. Now, shoo." Edna chuckled. "And good luck."

"Thank you." Tess hung up. "I'll need it," she murmured to the walls.

With a great deal of hesitation she checked her personal planner again, then punched in Rhune's office number.

"Dr. Sherman's office. Patsy speaking. How may I help you?"

"Patsy, this is Tess McQueen."

"Tess! How is your baby sister doing?"

"Fine. Thank you for asking." The grapevine still worked, she could see. "Patsy? Could you put me through to Dr. Sherman?"

There was an uncomfortable pause. When finally the receptionist spoke, she sounded crestfallen. "Tess, you know right well I would if I could. But Doc has asked *specifically* that we not accept any calls from you. None whatsoever."

Tess's heart nearly broke. Dear Lord, he'd cut her off as if she were nothing more than a pesky bill collector.

"*But...*" With that one word Patsy sounded downright cheery. "I see a way out of this dilemma."

"You do?" Tess wished someone did.

"Yes. Now, you get yourself on a plane as soon as you feel you can leave your sister. When you get in town, you just call me, and I'll schedule a Jane Doe appointment with Doc for the very last spot of the day."

"You'd do that?" Tess felt emotion well up inside her at the lengths to which Sweet Hope residents would get involved. She made a mental note to kick herself if she ever complained of their meddling again.

"I sure would do that. Doc's been a bear since you left town."

Ah, what a lovely thought.

"Patsy, thank you. I'll most definitely be in touch." As she hung up, it seemed as if her knowledge of soaring had returned.

Sure, this was a big chance. There was no guarantee that Rhune would be any more amenable to listening to her now than he had been a week ago. But in a week's time she'd done a lot of thinking. And now she thought she saw a way to use that honesty Doc was so proud of to make him realize how much he and she belonged together.

She needed to pack.

But first she needed to talk to Chelsey.

Her sister wouldn't be happy. How had she been so lucky to get a sourpuss at each end of the journey? But Chelsey and she needed to begin forging a new relationship. Tess was the young woman's sister. Not her mother. From this point forward they needed to interact as peers.

Perhaps Tess hadn't done Chelsey any favors by always trying to protect her, by expecting her to follow the sensible route of studies and career that Tess had followed. It was time for both of them to pursue their individual paths.

Tess had come to realize that she wasn't responsible for her sister's happiness. But she was responsible for her own. And her own involved following her instinct. Taking into consideration her own wants and needs.

She wanted to set things right with Rhune.

She needed him in her life.

And now, with the matchmakers of that tiny Georgia town in her corner, Tess felt sweet hope in her heart for the first time in over a week.

"Chelsey!" she called out as she fairly flew through the condo.

Chapter Fourteen

Rhune was running late. One more patient—he glanced at the new chart on the exam door, skimmed the unfamiliar name—and he could go home.

Some incentive.

Home was a hammock amid a pile of empty pizza boxes. Home was pacing the floor all night, wondering if he had indeed bitten off his nose to spite his face. Home was solitary and joyless.

It was his work that kept him going.

He had a patient who needed him. He inhaled deeply. For the next twenty minutes he'd be all right.

Staring at the chart, he opened and closed the door. "I see you've been experiencing undefined chest pains, Miss... Deacon?" Extending his hand, he looked up into arresting violet eyes.

"McQueen." With a hint of a smile, Tess slipped her hand into his, and he felt the electricity down to his toes. "Tess McQueen. From Washington, D.C. Your receptionist must have misunderstood the name."

"Misrepresented the name, yes," Rhune mused, slowly removing his hand from hers. He cocked one eyebrow. "Is this some kind of joke?" Leave it to the good folk of Sweet Hope to set up something like this.

Tess's beautiful features became very still. "Not at all. I've been experiencing severe pain. Here." She folded her hands over her heart.

He expected to see a faintly mocking cast in her eyes, but, no. He saw only sincerity and real emotional pain. Pain that mirrored his own.

Stiffening his resolve, he made his words gruff. "I have a practice to run, Tess." Her name on his tongue now tasted bitter. "I don't have time for games."

"This isn't a game." She skewered him with a regard that bespoke the utmost seriousness. "And I happen to know that I'm your very last patient of the day. All I ask is my twenty minutes."

"This will get us nowhere." Admit it, Sherman, he thought. You're afraid. Afraid that if she remains, the conversation will indeed lead somewhere. To a renewed understanding? And then where will your precious bruised ego be?

"If we fail to reach an understanding," she ventured, "I'll leave this office and Sweet Hope for good."

Now, why did that not cheer him?

"Okay." Resting against the small sink in the exam room, he crossed his arms over his chest in what he hoped was uncompromising body language. "Twenty minutes. I'm listening."

A small smile of what looked like relief crept across her sensuous lips. "I'd like to run through a little exercise. Sort of like truth or dare, but without the dare option. I call it truth and comprehension." She cocked one midnight dark eyebrow. "Before I begin, I want to make certain that you'll be totally honest with me."

"Me? Be honest with you?" He bristled. She certainly had her nerve. "I'm not the one here who has a problem with the truth."

"Then I can count on your sterling candor?" She didn't seem in the least bit rattled. In fact, there appeared a disconcerting twinkle in her eye.

"Absolutely," he replied cautiously. He always suspected a conversation that began with one party insisting upon total frankness.

"Good." She became very serious. "When I came to Sweet Hope, I had no intention of developing a relationship of any kind with you. I kept my identity a secret because I thought the element of surprise would be to my advantage. Would give me an opportunity to observe the real you."

"You came to spy on me."

"Yes."

Her admission without any hesitation startled him.

"When you first saw me," she continued, "did you want to form a relationship of any kind with me?"

"Absolutely not." There. He could certainly answer that question honestly.

"Why not?"

Now, *that* question was tricky. He frowned. "Because I'd come to Sweet Hope to start over. Especially in the realm of personal relationships. You were under my care as a doctor. A relationship with you wouldn't have been professional."

He didn't have to tell her that right from the beginning he'd had the suspicion that an affair with Tess McQueen might be like nothing he'd ever experienced before. Explosive and not easily controlled or denied. Something to be avoided if he wished to maintain his equilibrium.

Tess tented her fingers under her chin. "It's admirable that you were so professional. Were you always so politically correct in choosing relationships?"

He threw up his hands. "Tess, this is silly. You're starting to sound like the district attorney."

"*Truth.*" She glanced at her watch. "My twenty minutes is far from over. Let me make this quick. Do you admit to making errors in judgment where relationships were concerned?"

"Yes. But I never misrepresented myself. I never lied." He winced. He wasn't proud of the fact that sometimes he'd been brutally honest. Unnecessarily so. Honesty could cut both ways.

"Hold on to that thought. The one where you said yes to making errors in judgment. Remember it when I get to the part in my summation where I talk about *to err is human.*" She almost smiled. "Next question."

He regretted ever agreeing to this conversation. Not conversation. Inquisition. He heaved a sigh and settled back against the sink.

"Tell me how you've felt this past week." Her suddenly sober gaze held him with a too-familiar look of hurt and longing.

"Honestly?"

"Of course."

"Rotten." There was no harm in admitting that. Who wouldn't feel rotten after they'd been used and lied to?

"Me, too," she said softly, almost as if to herself. "I'd just started getting the hang of living."

Her admission made his heart constrict. He'd tried not to consider that she might feel genuinely devastated by their breakup. The thought of her hurting had the power, even now, to pull at his protective instincts. Still, it was foolish to attempt to go back. "Tess." He wanted his voice to sound firm but not cruel. "After what happened, we're simply not going to make it."

She cut him a curious look that said she might know something he didn't. "Let's talk about what happened."

"This is old territory. I don't want to go over this again."

A tiny furrow appeared between her brows. "Not what happened after you found the file."

"Then what?" The woman was a provocation, jumping around with conversation changes. Keeping him off-balance.

"What happened that week I arrived in Sweet Hope." Until now she'd sat sedately on the edge of the exam table. With a sinuous grace she stood, then stepped directly in front of him. Less than two feet away from him, she defied his personal space. Unsettled him beyond reason. "If you had to describe in one sentence how you felt that week, what would you tell me?"

He inhaled sharply. "Am I still under oath, Counselor?"

The corners of her mouth quirked in a half smile and presented a vexing image of kisses, hot and satisfying. "Yes, indeed," she declared, a little catch in her voice.

He tried to look away, but the force of her gaze compelled him to look directly at her. "I won't lie, Tess. I felt whole for the first time in my life."

She didn't speak. In fact, her eyes suddenly glittering with unshed tears, she seemed to be having difficulty speaking.

A terrible sadness descended upon his heart. He reached up and wiped away a tear from the corner of her eye. "What is this accomplishing... besides making us both miserable?"

Closing her eyes, she inhaled deeply. When she again opened her eyes, she'd managed to quench the tears. "I want you to think about what we had... and what we lost. I want you also to think about how we're both very human, very fallible individuals struggling to do what we think is right."

He felt a twinge in his conscience. Sometimes—in his personal life—he hadn't struggled quite hard enough to do what was right. Sometimes expediency or personal need had taken over. Since she hadn't asked about it, there was no need to admit that small truth.

She turned from him and stepped as far away as she could in the tiny room. When she spoke, she didn't turn around. "I've always been the wunderkind in the workplace. Always dedicated. Always efficient. Always conscious of not screwing up. In fact, one of my supervisors wrote in her evaluation that she'd like to be present if and when I ever did take a tumble. She said it certainly would be memorable."

She turned back to face him, and he saw her lower lip tremble. "Well, I took my tumble, and it certainly was memorable."

For a fleeting moment he had the strangest urge to reach out to her and reassure her that, as debacles went, hers wasn't any more catastrophic than some of his.

She raised her chin. "Rhune, I'm guilty of incredibly poor judgment, I admit. But I think a woman who's head over heels in love for the very first time should be allowed some margin for error...especially if she's sorry from the heart."

He didn't know how to respond. His head urged him one way, while his heart urged him quite another. "Tess...I..."

She touched her watch to check the time. "What do you know, my twenty minutes are up." Unshed tears clinging to her lashes, she brushed by him. "If you'd like to continue any thread of this conversation, I'll be having supper at the Hole-in-the-Wall before heading back to Washington." She turned at the door. "If you decide not to come, I'll understand. I won't like it, but I'll understand."

Far too quickly she was gone.

Now what should he do?

He'd been steamed with Tess the way Chelsey had been steamed with him after he'd walked out on her. The overriding issue in both cases, he hated to admit, was a severe case of bruised ego. A feeling of being used. A feeling, too, of being judged and somehow coming up unworthy.

That was ludicrous.

If Tess had thought him unworthy, if she'd only been out for revenge, would she be back in town now, asking his forgiveness?

But could he believe her sincerity and risk the hurt that came with caring?

He smacked the phony file down on the counter, then ran his hand over the back of his aching neck. Should he lay himself open again and take a stroll by the Hole-in-the-Wall, or should he play it safe and go home to another pizza?

Twisting the straw in her iced tea, Tess gazed out the window over Main Street and the town green. She certainly was going to miss this town.

"It doesn't look like he's going to show, now, does it, honey?" Edna plunked herself beside Tess in the booth and reached for Tess's hand. "Too bad. We all had such high hopes for the two of you."

Tess tried not to cry. So determined had she been that Rhune and she would work things out, she hadn't given in to a good cry in all the time since she'd first left Sweet Hope.

But now it looked as if Rhune didn't want to carry on any thread of their previous conversation.

"Oh, Edna, I really made a mess of things."

Edna squeezed her hand. "It was a messy situation from the start. And the way I see it, no one was blameless. Doc included. Surely he has to see that."

"I don't know that he has to." Tess sighed. "I don't know if I would, in his place."

"You told him you were sorry?"

"From the heart."

"You told him you loved him?"

"Yes."

Edna frowned. "You reminded him that no one's perfect?"

"That, too."

Shaking her head, Edna rose. "Honey," she said, patting Tess's hand, "after all that, I'd have expected Doc to be a smarter man than to throw away the chance of his lifetime."

"Who says I have?" a gruff voice behind Tess asked.

She turned to see Rhune standing slightly behind her seat in the booth. Never in her life had she seen such a welcoming sight, heard such promising words. Her pulse picked up.

"My, my," Edna cooed. "Seems I have some customers who need attention. I'll just leave you two."

Rhune slid into the booth opposite Tess.

There were several moments of awkward silence. "I'm still angry with you," he said finally.

"But?" She couldn't suppress the smile in her heart.

"What makes you think there's a *but?*"

"You're here." Oh, yes. And his presence was definitely a good sign.

He looked out the window. When at last he turned his gaze upon her, the steely chill was gone. In its place was a deep velvety regard tinged with longing. "I'm still angry with you," he repeated. "But my anger isn't going to last forever. It would be a pigheaded shame if, when my anger is finally gone, you were gone, too. Forever."

"Ah." Tess inhaled deeply, then exhaled very slowly. "Let me get this straight. You're still angry with me . . . but you want me to understand that you might not always harbor such feelings."

"Yes." He looked so terribly sober.

She grinned. "Dr. Sherman, am I being put on the back burner, so to speak? Not quite put in the deep freeze, but not being chosen as the main dish, either."

He opened his mouth, then closed it abruptly. He beetled his brows, clearly taken aback.

Tess chuckled softly. His mere presence after their horrible dark moment in the bed-and-breakfast a week ago emboldened her. "What does this mean, Doc? That I should go back to Washington and wait for you to stop being angry?"

He seemed to conquer his discomfort. Looked her squarely in the eye. "It means I'd like to forgive and move on."

"Move on?"

"You're not making this easy, Tess." He reached across the table and took her hand in his. "I had to dig deep into my gut feelings about you. And my gut feelings tell me that you came to town to protect your sister. That you came to town searching for the truth."

"You no longer believe I came solely to exact revenge upon you?"

He smiled ruefully and shook his head. "The woman who can find an easy place among difficult kids is not vengeful. Neither is the woman who goes the extra mile in nudging her contacts in Washington to help a tiny little town in Georgia. Nor the woman who finds the perfect cake-top groom for a couple she's never met." Pausing, he lowered his arresting brown gaze over her like a caress. "Nor the woman who makes love with such passion."

She felt heat rise to her cheeks. "And what about the fact that I lied to you?"

"I can't deny that hurt like hell. Still hurts." Shadows flickered in his eyes. "But I tried to put myself in your situation . . . I sure would be afraid of losing what we had."

"You would?"

"I am." He stroked her hand and made an attempt at a lopsided grin. "That's why I'm here."

Tess's pulse raced. Her heart thumped wildly. She felt an excited flush creep into her cheeks. "And where do we go from here?"

A slow, sensuous smile crossed his features. "For one thing, Ms. Sherman, we finish the exam you cut short."

"The exam?"

"You ran out of my office without the prescription for your chest pains."

"Ah, yes." Tess cocked one eyebrow. "Will you prescribe a week in Sweet Hope under Mel and Ida's care?" She certainly hoped he would.

"I had something more permanent in mind."

She shivered in sheer anticipation. "Such as?"

"I'd been seriously thinking about this before our . . . messy detour."

"This?" She didn't find this gradual denouement easy.

"Tess McQueen . . ." His voice played erotically over her entire being. His gaze, filled with smoldering passion, ignited her senses. He drew her hand to his lips. It seemed as if the world paused. "Would you marry me and remain in Sweet Hope?"

She exhaled sharply. "You're not worried that we won't take further messy detours?"

He shook his head ruefully. "Oh, I know we'll probably take more detours than stick to the plan."

"And that doesn't scare you?"

He rolled his eyes. "Scares the hell out of me."

"But you're asking me to marry you anyway?" She leaned forward across the table. "That's crazy." But what delicious madness.

The longing in his eyes reached out to her. "What can I say?" His voice was a husky rumble. "I'm crazy in love with you."

"I love you, too," she whispered.

"But will you marry me?"

Joy flooded her. Tears pricked at her eyes. Somehow she managed to untie her tongue. "Yes!"

A cheer went up from the crew and regulars of the café. Bemused, Tess and Rhune turned to discover that the entire restaurant had been focused on the little drama unfolding at their table.

"Let me be the first to congratulate you." Edna bustled to the table and kissed them both soundly. She winked at Tess. "Whoever said a good groom was hard to find?"

"I'm making the cake," Esther declared. "A bride and groom in a forest of green frosting, attended by a congregation of woodland animals."

"I always did say those two made a good team," Homer Martin chimed in with a cackle. "Stubborn as mules, but a fine team."

"I knew they were right for each other before you knew they were right for each other." Plato's voice rose above Homer's. "Saw it in their eyes."

"You old fools," Patsy Sinclair scolded. "*I* was there from the very first moment they laid eyes on each other...."

The conversation degenerated into a hubbub of cheerful argument, each diner trying to lay claim to the beginning of the magic. Sweet Hope myth in the making.

Standing, Rhune pulled Tess to his side. "I think this is where we make our getaway."

"Where to?" The possibilities made her blood sizzle.

"What would you say to a moonlit ride out to the magnolia grove on my property? We could lie under the stars and plan a homestead."

Edna brushed by again and pulled the check from Rhune's hand. "It's on me. Now scoot before this crowd starts plannin' your firstborn in graphic detail."

With a chuckle Rhune gently pulled Tess to the door, then out into the warm summer night. "How does it feel to have had a marriage proposal by committee?"

"When Patsy faked my name to get me an appointment with you, I swore never to complain of Sweet Hope's meddling again."

He pulled her to him. His voice husky, he declared, "Tess, I can't promise our relationship won't be a rocky road. We're two very strong people, if you hadn't noticed. We're bound to go head-to-head more than just this time."

Tess wrapped her arms around his neck. "Just promise that, as this time, when you cool off, you'll listen."

Drawing back, he viewed her skeptically. "That's assuming I'll always be the hothead. Do you plan never to get angry with a thing I do?"

She tipped her face to his saucily. "Do I look as if I have an angry bone in my body?"

His grin was pure, delicious wickedness. "I'm the doctor. Let me feel."

She smacked his chest. "Before I submit to any exams with ulterior motives, I want that ride in the moonlight. On your Harley."

"Before I give you that ride, I want a kiss." He bent to where his mouth hovered temptingly over her own.

"Kiss the man!" came a chorus from inside the Hole-in-the-Wall.

She did.

And the thought came to her mind as she soared with the feelings of shared pleasure that, if Rhune turned out to be as good a groom—as good a husband—as he was a kisser, then she was a woman blessed indeed.

Amid applause from the café crowd, Rhune pulled away. "Care to finish this in private?"

She could only smile her assent as they walked to his motorcycle parked at the curb.

Having secured her helmet, she mounted the big bike behind Rhune, then slipped her arms firmly around his waist.

He turned to look at her. "Ready?"

Was she ever.

Epilogue

With a whoop, Rhune lifted Tess, yards and yards of wedding lace and all, into his arms, kissed her soundly as her arms went around his neck, then stepped over the threshold of the wedding suite at Mel and Ida's bed-and-breakfast.

He'd always said this place was perfect for a romantic entanglement.

And entangled he most certainly was. With intentions of loving Tess McQueen Sherman—as challenging as that might prove to be—all the natural days of his life. And beyond, if that were possible.

He lowered her gently to the floor, then pulled her into his embrace. The circle of his love. He gazed into her wide violet eyes and could scarcely believe his good fortune. They were at last husband and wife.

At last and to last.

He had found the connection that made him whole.

He gently removed her headpiece and veil. "That was a wedding to end all weddings," he murmured, feeling the lush weight of her hair fall over his hands.

She rose on tiptoe and brushed her lips along his jawline, sending shivers of anticipation to the very depths of him. "It gave new meaning to the term *community involvement,*" she purred.

Ah, what the sound of her, the feel of her, the sight of her, the very heady scent of her did to his body.

With a soft hum of pleasure, he began to undo the tiny pearl buttons that ran in a very long row down the front of her gown. "I especially liked Belle and Cathryn's touch," he whispered, bending to nibble her earlobe. "The Tess For Mayor fliers in the wedding program."

She laughed softly and tugged at his cummerbund made of the best tropical fabric money could buy. "I loved the arch of raised fishing rods when we came out of the church."

He chuckled. "Boone's idea, I'm sure." He undid the last button, then slipped his hand inside the gown, over the warm and silky softness of her skin.

He heard a low moan escape his throat. Felt himself grow hard.

With a teasing sparkle in her eyes, Tess slipped the bow tie of matching tropical fabric from around his neck, then let it fall to the floor as she concentrated on freeing him from his tux. "Do you think they'll leave us alone for the honeymoon?" She swept aside the fabric of his shirt and planted hot little kisses across his chest.

He felt his knees weaken.

"They'd better," he growled. "Although Homer and Plato threatened to serenade us tonight." Shrugging out of his shirt and tux jacket, he pulled Tess against his bare chest.

Oh, my. She felt his heat sear her own partly bared flesh. Desire for this man, her husband, flooded through her. She lifted her mouth to his.

He kissed her with a passion that swept her away. No longer would she resist that swept-away feeling. No longer would she deny her own wants and needs. Where Rhune was concerned, she would seize the moment. The present moments, the future moments and all the moments in between.

She felt his hands slide over her arms as he freed her from her gown. Felt the air caress her skin. Felt his touch claim her. His kisses bathed her in a delicious intoxication. Her senses soared.

"Happy?" he murmured in her ear.

"Mmm." She reached for the top button on his trousers and heard his sharp intake of breath. "What do you suppose they're saying about us over at the Hole-in-the-Wall?" she asked dreamily as she managed both button and zipper.

"They're saying we're crazy to stay in town under their scrutiny for our honeymoon." He growled low, then swooped her into his arms. "And even crazier to concern ourselves with anything other than making love tonight." His eyes sparkled with mischief.

"Are you telling me to stop talking?"

He cocked one russet eyebrow as he carried her to the bed. "Doesn't it seem in the least bit strange to you that the conversation on our wedding night revolves around the town and its residents?"

"Not when you consider that it was Sweet Hope that brought us together with its magic."

"Perhaps." With the most smoldering of gazes, he laid her gently on the bed. "But I thought tonight we could concentrate on some original McQueen-Sherman magic."

She grinned up at him. "What did you have in mind?" She had several things in mind, each more provocative than the next.

Stretching out alongside her on the bed, he propped himself on one elbow, his nearness dazzling her. He flashed her his most seductive smile, and his dimple danced in provocation. "Something Sweet Hope myth is built on."

With a sigh of utter contentment she wrapped her arms around him and surrendered to the possibilities.

* * * * *

The first book in the exciting new
Fortune's Children series is

HIRED HUSBAND

by *New York Times* bestselling writer
Rebecca Brandewyne

Beginning in July 1996
Only from Silhouette Books

Here's an exciting sneak preview....

Minneapolis, Minnesota

As Caroline Fortune wheeled her dark blue Volvo into the underground parking lot of the towering, glass-and-steel structure that housed the global headquarters of Fortune Cosmetics, she glanced anxiously at her gold Piaget wristwatch. An accident on the snowy freeway had caused rush-hour traffic to be a nightmare this morning. As a result, she was running late for her 9:00 a.m. meeting—and if there was one thing her grandmother, Kate Winfield Fortune, simply couldn't abide, it was slack, unprofessional behavior on the job. And lateness was the sign of a sloppy, disorganized schedule.

Involuntarily, Caroline shuddered at the thought of her grandmother's infamous wrath being unleashed upon her. The stern rebuke would be precise, apropos, scathing and delivered with coolly raised, condemnatory eyebrows and in icy tones of haughty grandeur that had in the past reduced many an executive—even the male ones—at Fortune Cosmetics not only to obsequious apologies, but even to tears. Caroline had seen it happen on more than one occasion, although, much to her gratitude and relief, she herself was seldom a target of her grandmother's anger. And she wouldn't be this morning, either, not if she could help it. That would be a disastrous way to start out the new year.

Grabbing her Louis Vuitton totebag and her black leather portfolio from the front passenger seat, Caroline stepped gracefully from the Volvo and slammed the door. The heels of her Maud Frizon pumps clicked briskly on the concrete floor as she hurried toward the bank of elevators that would take her up into the skyscraper owned by her family. As the elevator doors slid open, she rushed down the long, plushly carpeted corridors of one of the hushed upper floors toward the conference room.

By now Caroline had her portfolio open and was leafing through it as she hastened along, reviewing her notes she had prepared for her presentation. So she didn't see Dr. Nicolai Valkov until she literally ran right into him. Like her, he had his head bent over his own portfolio, not watching where he was going. As the two of them collided, both their portfolios and the papers inside went flying. At the unexpected impact, Caroline lost her balance, stumbled, and would have fallen had not Nick's strong, sure hands abruptly shot out, grabbing hold of her and pulling her to him to steady her. She gasped, startled and stricken, as she came up hard against his broad chest, lean hips and corded thighs, her face just inches from his own—as though they were lovers about to kiss.

Caroline had never been so close to Nick Valkov before, and, in that instant, she was acutely aware of him—not just as a fellow employee of Fortune Cosmetics but also as a man. Of how tall and ruggedly handsome he was, dressed in an elegant, pin-striped black suit cut in the European fashion, a crisp white shirt, a foulard tie and a pair of Cole Haan loafers. Of how dark his thick, glossy hair and his deep-set eyes framed by raven-wing brows were—so dark that they were almost black, despite the bright, fluorescent lights that blazed overhead. Of the whiteness of his straight teeth against his bronzed skin as a brazen, mocking grin slowly curved his wide, sensual mouth.

"Actually, I *was* hoping for a sweet roll this morning—but I daresay you would prove even tastier, Ms. Fortune," Nick drawled impertinently, his low, silky voice tinged with a faint accent born of the fact that Russian, not English, was his native language.

At his words, Caroline flushed painfully, embarrassed and annoyed. If there was one person she always attempted to avoid at Fortune Cosmetics, it was Nick Valkov. Following the breakup of the Soviet Union, he had emigrated to the

United States, where her grandmother had hired him to direct the company's research and development department. Since that time, Nick had constantly demonstrated marked, traditional, Old World tendencies that had led Caroline to believe he not only had no use for equal rights but also would actually have been more than happy to turn back the clock several centuries where females were concerned. She thought his remark was typical of his attitude toward women: insolent, arrogant and domineering. Really, the man was simply insufferable!

Caroline couldn't imagine what had ever prompted her grandmother to hire him—and at a highly generous salary, too—except that Nick Valkov was considered one of the foremost chemists anywhere on the planet. Deep down inside Caroline knew that no matter how he behaved, Fortune Cosmetics was extremely lucky to have him. Still, that didn't give him the right to manhandle and insult her!

"I assure you that you would find me more bitter than a cup of the strongest black coffee, Dr. Valkov," she insisted, attempting without success to free her trembling body from his steely grip, while he continued to hold her so near that she could feel his heart beating steadily in his chest—and knew he must be equally able to feel the erratic hammering of her own.

"Oh, I'm willing to wager there's more sugar and cream to you than you let on, Ms. Fortune." To her utter mortification and outrage, she felt one of Nick's hands slide insidiously up her back and nape to her luxuriant mass of sable hair, done up in a stylish French twist.

"You know so much about fashion," he murmured, eyeing her assessingly, pointedly ignoring her indignation and efforts to escape from him. "So why do you always wear your hair like this...so tightly wrapped and severe? I've never seen it down. Still, that's the way it needs to be worn, you know...soft, loose, tangled about your face. As it is, your hair fairly cries out for a man to take the pins from it, so he can see how long it is. Does it fall past your shoulders?" He quirked one eyebrow inquisitively, a mocking half smile still twisting his lips, letting her know he was en-

joying her obvious discomfiture. "You aren't going to tell
me, are you? What a pity. Because my guess is that it does—
and I'd like to know if I'm right. And these glasses." He
indicated the large, square, tortoiseshell frames perched on
her slender, classic nose. "I think you use them to hide behind more than you do to see. I'll bet you don't actually
even need them at all."

Caroline felt the blush that had yet to leave her cheeks
deepen, its heat seeming to spread throughout her entire
quivering body. Damn the man! Why must he be so infuri-
atingly perceptive?

Because everything that Nick suspected was true.

*   *   *   *   *

To read more, don't miss
HIRED HUSBAND
by Rebecca Brandewyne,
Book One in the new
FORTUNE'S CHILDREN series,
beginning this month and available only from
Silhouette Books!

This exciting new cross-line continuity series unites five of your favorite authors as they weave five connected novels about love, marriage—and Daddy's unexpected need for a baby carriage!

Get ready for

THE BABY NOTION by Dixie Browning (SD#1011, 7/96)
Single gal Priscilla Barrington would do anything for a baby—even visit the local sperm bank. Until cowboy Jake Spencer set out to convince her to have a family the natural—and much more exciting—way!

And the romance in New Hope, Texas, continues with:

BABY IN A BASKET
by Helen R. Myers (SR#1169, 8/96)

MARRIED...WITH TWINS!
by Jennifer Mikels (SSE#1054, 9/96)

HOW TO HOOK A HUSBAND (AND A BABY)
by Carolyn Zane (YT#29, 10/96)

DISCOVERED: DADDY
by Marilyn Pappano (IM#746, 11/96)

DADDY KNOWS LAST arrives in July...only from

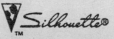

DKL-D

MILLION DOLLAR SWEEPSTAKES

SWP-M96

FORTUNE'S *Children*™

New York Times Bestselling Author
REBECCA
BRANDEWYNE

Launches a new twelve-book series—FORTUNE'S CHILDREN
beginning in July 1996 with Book One

Hired Husband

Caroline Fortune knew her marriage to Nick Valkov was in
name only. She would help save the family business, Nick
would get a green card, and a paper marriage would suit both
of them. Until Caroline could no longer deny the feelings Nick
stirred in her and the practical union turned passionate.

MEET THE FORTUNES—a family whose legacy is greater than
riches. Because where there's a will...there's a wedding!

Look for Book Two, *The Millionaire and the Cowgirl*,
by Lisa Jackson. Available in August 1996 wherever Silhouette
books are sold.

Silhouette®

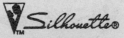

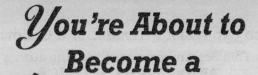